The Hour of Vengeance!

Rage tore out of me, hurtled me out of my trance, found voice in a shout that must still echo somewhere, a madman's roar of sorrow . . . Heedless of the army in my way, I spurred toward Abas the killer. Men, mine and his, scattered before me.

He ran to meet me, waving his dripping sword. I sprang down from my horse, scorning to fight my standing enemy from horseback, scorning to take any advantage. Let him have the run on me! I held the dark sword of Aftalun and waited for him, feeling years of hatred rise to a peak. My time for revenge had come at last.

Also by Nancy Springer

THE WHITE HART
THE SILVER SUN
THE SABLE MOON

and published by Corgi Books

The Black Beast

Nancy Springer

CORGI BOOKS

THE BLACK BEAST

A CORGI BOOK 0 552 12428 1

First publication in Great Britain

PRINTING HISTORY
Corgi edition published 1985

This book is set in 10/11 English Times

Corgi Books are published by Transworld Publishers Ltd.,
Century House, 61–63 Uxbridge Road, Ealing,
London W5 5SA, in Australia by Transworld Publishers
(Aust.) Pty. Ltd., 26 Harley Crescent, Condell Park,
NSW 2200, and in New Zealand by Transworld Publishers
(N.Z.) Ltd., Cnr. Moselle and Waipareira Avenues,
Henderson, Auckland.

Made and printed in Great Britain by
Hunt Barnard Printing Ltd., Aylesbury, Bucks.

VALE

N

Lorc Dahak

EIDDEN

Perin Tyr

Qiturel

Tantalon · Terynon

Lorc Acheron

TIELA

Wall

MELIOR · Balliew

Nisroch

Gerriew

Pol

Varro

Chardn

Ky-Nule · · · · Serriade

VAIRE

Epona

Elsans

Gyotte

Coire Adalis

SELT

Aftalun

Lorc Tutosel

Prologue

I am Daymon Cein, the ancient seer. Now I am only a voice from the beyond, a twittering, formless thing, but once, long ago, when I was a man, I slept under the White Rock of Eala and gained vision where other men might have gained death. It was a foolhardy venture and without real reward, for I soon found fame worthless. But that is an old fool's talk. . . . Later, my daughter Suevi married Abas, the Sacred King in Melior. She bore him a son, Tirell. I watched from afar, with the inner eye, as I watched all whom I loved — all of Vale, in fact. And one chilly autumn night I saw a strange thing.

Little Prince Tirell was only five years old at the time. His nursemaid had checked his bed and seen him safe under the wolfskin coverings. But later he got up and wandered through the corridors between lifeless guards that stood ranked at every turn, remains of kings and queens, generations and generations of them, slain at the high altar of the goddess. The dead kept watch constantly at Melior castle, in erect stone coffins with carved faces, clenched hands, and white, staring eyes. Not many people cared to roam that place alone after dark. But Tirell was fearless, even then, and a fire burned in him that would not let him rest. His bare fingers and toes served him for guidance where there was no light. He was seldom caught, for he was clever and knew every turning of the ancient walls.

On that night he found his way easily, because the moon was bloated and orange as barley. Orange light fell from the high window slots to the cold floors. Tirell shivered along, not knowing what he was looking for any more than the rest of us . . . Then more light appeared, orange torchlight! Tirell approached with interest and caution like a cat's. He knew that

7

everyone but the sentries should have been asleep, but two cloaked figures flitted toward his mother's chamber.

Now for half a year past Suevi the queen, my daughter, had kept to her rooms, seeing almost no one. Of course, Tirell was allowed to come to her. There would be a baby, she told him. He knew as well as I did that the lump under her gowns was a pillow. He sat on her lap and he could tell. But perhaps others were fooled. Tirell kept his peace; what did he know of the royal way of getting babies? And on that autumn night he heard the baby whimpering. One of the cloaked figures carried it tenderly. The other held a torch and knocked softly at the queen's door.

Somebody let them in; Tirell could not see who. As soon as the heavy door swung closed he scampered to the timbers to listen. He could hear his mother's voice. 'He's in good health? Very well, then, here is gold for your silence. There will be more. See the King . . .' Then the door creaked and Tirell slipped away into the shadow of the next sarcophagus. From behind it he peeped and watched the visitors depart. They were Fabron, the King's smith, and his wife; Tirell saw them as plainly as I. The woman was silently weeping and twisting her long red hair.

Tirell went back to his bed and lay puzzling. The next morning his nurse woke him with a face wreathed in smiles. 'Come, my young lord, and see! Your lady mother has something to show you!' The lad pulled on his clothes and silently followed her to the queen's chamber, but he was not much surprised by what he found there. Suevi lay on her couch with her red-black hair pulled back from her pale, passionate face — she was always a hilltop creature, she! Beside her in a velvet basket lay a ruddy, hairless mite. Tirell stared without speaking at the tiny, frowning face.

'Your new brother,' Suevi told him. 'Are you not glad?'

'Yes,' Tirell answered softly, 'glad enough,' and he gave the baby a friendly poke. His new brother was called Frain, and Tirell stood by at the naming ceremony when the priestesses touched the baby with their long knives. Never a word did he say, to his mother or to anyone else, of what he had seen in the night.

8

Book One

Frain

1

I am Frain. I was only fifteen years old when I first heard of
Mylitta, and within a few days the doom of Melior had begun.
All has changed now; Melior is a memory and I am a swan on
the rivers of Ogygia. But I think I am not much wiser.

Tirell was in the habit of wandering in the night, then as
always. We shared a tower chamber, and sometimes when I
did not feel too sleepy I joined him. I liked to hear him talk. It
was better than dreaming.

One night, though, I woke up out of a sound sleep to see
him on his way out of the window. He was hoisting himself up
to the high stone sill by his hands, his feet dangling. I jumped
out of bed, naked as a rabbit, and grabbed him by the knees.

'Are you mad?' I yelled.

'It runs in the family, does it not?' he snapped as he fell. 'Let
me up, you great oaf!' I had sat on top of him.

'Not if you are planning to climb down there,' I told him.
'Have some sense, Tirell! It must be a hundred feet to the
cobbles, and the ivy is old and sparse.'

'So what am I to do?' he shouted passionately. 'Ride out by
the main gates and take the guards to my wooing?'

'By our great lord Aftalun,' I sighed, 'are there not enough
maids within the walls that you must woo one without? I
think —' But he did not wait to hear what I thought. He threw
me off. Tirell was slender, not much heavier than I even
though he was five years older, but when he was truly angry I
believe no one could stand against him. We grappled for a
moment, and then I went flying and hit my head against the
wall.

He could have gone to his wooing then. I heard him pacing

around, but I couldn't move or see. He lit a rush-light, got a soggy cloth, and started dabbing at some blood behind my ear. 'Go to,' I muttered, shoving his hand away, and I managed to sit up.

'If you are all right,' Tirell said quietly, 'I will be off.'

'Then I will be off too, by way of the gates, and you will have me and a troop of guards for company.' I can be angry too, and Tirell knew he was beaten for the time. He cursed and flopped down on the floor where he was.

'I was going to say, before I was interrupted,' I told him after a while, 'that we could get a rope.'

'If I could get a rope in the middle of the night,' Tirell responded sourly, 'I would have tied you up long ago. They're all over at the armoury with the scaling ladders and things.'

'So we'll get one tomorrow, and you can go tomorrow night. Surely the girl will last till then?' I looked at his lean, unhappy face and felt my anger melt, as always. 'She must be a marvel,' I added softly. 'What is her name?'

Tirell sighed and gave in to peace. 'Mylitta is her name,' he answered quietly.

'Do I know her?'

'No, I doubt it. She is not such a marvel. She is just a peasant.'

'Pretty?'

'No, not even very pretty.'

I frowned, perplexed. It was not like him to be so modest about his conquests. 'Thunder, I am not going to try to take her from you!' I protested.

'You couldn't!' Tirell retorted with joy in his voice. 'No one could! She loves me!'

I had never heard him speak so earnestly. Was this my cool mocking brother? At loss for a response, I turned mocking myself. 'Indeed, who could help but love you?' I asked lightly.

He snorted. 'Not like my other maidens, if I may call them that. Bloodsucking whores, every one of them. But Mylitta cares not a bit for throne or torque or wealth or — or any of it. She just — she just loves me.'

My mouth had dropped open. I closed it and swallowed. 'Then she is a marvel,' I replied, meaning it. 'May I meet her?'

'Maybe.' Tirell shook off the mood and got to his feet. 'Go back to bed, young my naked lord.' We sometimes parodied the courtly courtesy between ourselves.

'And you?' I asked.

'I don't know whether I'll sleep, but I'll bide; I give you my word. How is the head?'

'Well enough.' It was thumping like a thousand blacksmiths, if truth be told, but I would never admit that, as Tirell knew quite well.

Tirell slept, as it turned out, and I lay waking. It was not only my aching head that kept me up. I was worrying about Tirell, as I often did. I sensed trouble to come. No happy endings were likely for Tirell or for me as long as King Abas was our father. The altar awaited him, as it awaited Tirell, or me in my turn. Then our ribs and lungs would be ripped out whole, spread and held up to the multitude to reveal the configuration of the blood bird. Princes of the line of Melior were accustomed early to the thought of this unpleasant death. Perhaps that was why many went mad. Abas was one of those.

'Father used to sit me on his knee, when I was small,' Tirell had said to me once, 'and tell me the strangest things — dreams in dragon colours and the thoughts of stones and beasts. . . . And then, likely as not, he would smite me. It is no wonder I cannot sleep.'

'He has never given me anything, either of blows or of dreams!' I had replied, caught between pity and jealousy. The jealousy because our father took no notice of me at all.

'You came later,' Tirell answered, 'when his mood had turned yet darker. Be glad he does not care for you!' But he would not meet my eyes.

I feared for my brother as he probably never feared for himself, reckless and thoughtless as he was. Where could we run to, where could we take the maiden? There was no place in Vale where Abas could not find us. Abas cared for Tirell, in his harsh way, and his vision was frighteningly sharp. Sometimes his sapience seemed almost divine. He would notice Tirell's happiness, and Tirell would pay the price; Abas could not abide happiness, or dogs, or wanderings in the night . . .

I remembered one day when we had been digging in one of our secret places (Tirell was only fourteen then and I was nine, but none of our masters could constrain us — we spent our days much as we liked). We had been digging for clams down near the river. That was daring enough, and forbidden. All children were chided not to dig in the earth, lest they loose the flood that is beneath the land. But even we princes did not dare to wash ourselves in the river after we were done, though it ran only a few steps away. Water was greatly feared in Vale. It was used only with many offerings and greatest reverence. So we went back to the castle to wash in water the slaves had brought with all due and proper ceremony. And as bad luck would have it we met Abas in the courtyard. He seldom took any heed of our comings and goings, seldom came out of his chambers at all; I do not know what had brought him out on that day. He stopped where he was and stiffened with an intake of breath when he saw us.

'Tirell!' He ignored me, concentrating all of his attention on his heir, as usual. I did not realize then how lucky I was. Tirell answered him only with a steady glance.

'You have been in the dirt! You are covered with dirt, black —' Abas had recoiled from his son in loathing. It is hard to describe his horror. I do not think he was concerned with the retribution of the Mother or of any god — he had never showed great reverence for Adalis or Chardri. I did not understand at the time, but I think now that the dirt meant far more than dirt to him — that he was afraid, as he feared the night, that he looked at our grime and saw something far worse.

'Rolling in it, rolling in filth! Wallowing —'

'We were *digging*,' Tirell said with childlike appeal and adolescent dignity. Digging was forbidden, as I have said, but I suppose Tirell preferred that crime to the sort of vague perversity Abas seemed to be spinning. Abas cried out in shock and his horror turned to anger.

'So, digging like beasts, deep, deep, and do you not know what lies beneath?' He moved closer to Tirell, threatening, his long fingers wildly addressing the air. 'Below, dark, black, beneath, within, do you not know? The grip, the dark, the close clutch, the boneless grasp where the water runs — the

14

thing will take you, draw you down, dark, black. You innocent, stay far from digging. . . .' He was quivering all over, his hands palpitating the air nearer and nearer to Tirell's face, and suddenly they shot forward as if they would gouge out his eyes. I winced in terror, myself, but Tirell stood firm, and Abas crowed in an ecstasy of rage. Then he dropped to his knees before his son, his shaking stilled. I think that disconcerted Tirell more than anything that had happened. He kept his face still, but tears made white tracks through the grime.

'My son,' Abas whispered, 'my son, keep far from that darkness.' He reached for him as if to kiss him, but Tirell bolted, and I ran after him. Behind us we heard yells of incoherent rage.

'I hate him,' Tirell panted, still weeping. 'I hate him! He is the dark thing, he himself!'

Who could have borne the burden of that mad love? But Abas saw truly, in his way. That darkness was in Tirell.

He was too much like his father for anyone's comfort. No one was afraid of me, a plain sort of person with freckles and rusty hair, but everyone feared and adored Tirell. When he found Mylitta he was twenty, handsome, extravagant — everyone worshipped him. People would line the dirt streets to see him dashing by in his chariot with his cloak flying and his neck gold-torqued and his lash urging the white steeds to yet greater speed. All the young courtiers imitated his clothing and his walk. Tirell had midnight-black hair and icy blue eyes, and he moved like a leashed leopard; I think people would have turned their heads to look at him even if he had not been prince. His face was flawless, as if it had been carved out of white alabaster. He had the legendary tall good looks and colouring of the Sacred Kings, and he had many admirers. But no friends.

And now he had Mylitta, and what was to become of them? I fell asleep finally at dawn, without a hint of hope; I was used to that.

Tirell had no trouble, some hours later, distracting the armourers while I stole a coil of rope from the supplies and stowed it under my cloak. The cloak was an accursed nuisance now that the springtime weather was warming, but like the

15

torque it was a symbol of rank. And for pranks like this it could be useful.

We took the rope to our bedchamber and hid it under the straw mattress. 'All right,' Tirell said. 'Now what?'

It looked as if he would do whatever I wanted. He was still feeling bad about my hurt head, though he would never admit it. 'I would like a look at this girl Mylitta for whose sake I am risking my skin,' I ventured.

'Not right now, brother mine,' he answered moodily. 'Think of something else.'

'Let us go to see Grandfather, then.' Our mother's father was the wisest and gentlest man in all of Vale. If anyone could help us, I thought, he could. Though, of course, I would not tell Tirell that I was casting about for help.

Grandfather lived way out beyond the Hill of Vision, beyond the White Rock and the huts of the priestesses, over two hours of riding away. Often we had raced the distance, yelling and lashing the steeds, in far less time. But on that day Tirell was in a quiet mood, and we rode gently. He was on a white, as always; it was the sacred colour of the goddess who would someday be his bride. I rode a big, hard-mouthed chestnut. We passed through the cottages and shops huddled beneath the castle walls, then the pastureland and farmland beyond, the fertile valley between the two paps of Adalis. Beyond the farms everything was given over to the priestesses. We cantered up through their grove of sacred trees that ringed the Hill of Vision like a brooch. Once above the trees we stopped, as we always did, to look back the way we had come.

The castle stood on the summit of the other pap of Melior-y-Adalis, the bosom of Adalis. From its walls the land sloped steeply to the enclosing curve of the river Chardri that rounded it on three sides. Melior's towers were built of a rich white stone veined in crimson; in the sunlight they sparkled like blood. The twin bridges over the Chardri, Balliew and Gerriew by name, were built of the same stone. One arched to the north and the other to the south. Without them there would have been no passage to Melior. The Chardri flowed great and steady, even in the drought, fed by springs and by

16

the snowcaps of the mountains to the north.

The Hill of Vision rose no higher than the castle summit that faced it, and the wide curve of the river embraced both. But on the Hill were no dwellings of stone, no grazing sheep — nothing except the huts of the priestesses. On the grassy height stood the great altar, the White Rock of Eala, where the blood of Sacred Kings was shed. It was made of three odd, chalk-white stones, like no other rock in Vale, two supporting the third. This was the very high altar of the goddess. A woman could sleep there without fear. The priestesses of the shrine slept there commonly, and barren women went there for cure. Also, Kings of Melior could sleep there with their brides. In fact, they had to. But if a man slept alone beneath that rock, the morning would find him either inspired, insane, or dead.

Tirell and I rode up and around it. We did not care to go under it, somehow, though it would have cleared the horses easily. The priestesses watched us sullenly. Common folk did not come to that place without an offering, but we came and went as we pleased.

As soon as we passed the altar we faced, almost against our will, the great mountains beyond the Hill. No one ever went to any mountains, but especially not to the huge, dark mountains in the west. At the western foot of the Hill, spanning the reaches of Melior from river curve to river curve and closing the gap in the penannular grove, stood the Wall. It was twice man high and built of rugged brown rock without beauty; it loomed almost as darkly as the mountains. Beyond it lay wilderness. There was no gate.

Our grandfather, the seer Daymon Cein, lived at the very Wall, alone except for a few sheep and some chickens. In his youth he had slept beneath the Rock, and the goddess had given him power. The priestesses half feared him, because of his own greatness and because he was the queen's father. Poor folk would come, make sacrifice on the Hill in order to pass, and hurry on to Daymon. He would receive them gladly and help them however he could. But only the desperate came, for no one liked to venture near the Wall.

Grandfather greeted us with smiles and warm hands, as

17

always. I noticed that he had changed to sandals for spring. His grey beard flowed down over a robe somewhat less than fashionable — less than clean, even. I suppose we princes looked out of place beside him, we in our golden torques and our deep-dyed cloaks and our tall, soft leather boots. But I believe we felt more at home with Daymon than anywhere else except our own tower chamber.

'And how is my daughter today?' Grandfather asked.

'Well enough,' Tirell said, which perhaps was not a lie, though we had not been to see our mother. We often stayed away from her for days at a time, until she sent for us. On this day in particular we had taken care to avoid her, because she might have spied something of the secret named Mylitta with her visionary azure eyes. Her father Daymon was looking at us and saw all this pass through our thoughts, but we did not mind too much. He watched us with detachment, almost with amusement, so that we did not fear his meddling. And yet we felt his love.

'So!' he said, when we had settled beneath a solitary yew tree and exchanged some talk. 'What shall we speak of today?'

'Tell us about Aftalun!' I said quickly, for I wanted to hear about the beginnings. Tirell did not object.

'All right,' said Grandfather, 'but think on it a moment, before I begin.'

I thought of the ancient void. But though Grandfather and Tirell and Mother were visionaries, I was none. Grass and bickering chickens remained, to my sight. Presently, when the tale was manifest to him, Grandfather spoke.

'Before there was Vale, there was only light and water, and no life except the being of the dragon. There was water to the farthest reaches of the void, and in the midst of it the dragon. In him were all colours that the water had not, and he was beautiful in the light. He lay on the water and slept.

'Adalis saw this, the great goddess whom men call by many names, she being Vieyra and Suevi and Morrghu the deadly. And she said to Aftalun, he who wooed her, "If we are to wed, I need a bed on which to lie. Speak to that dragon, that I may also lie on the water."

18

'So Aftalun spoke to the dragon, who awoke with a roar and a spray of golden fire that scorched the dome of the heavens and burned it away and let in the dark. In that darkness Aftalun fought the dragon, wrestling him into the water to put out his flames. And the dragon threw great coils around Aftalun, pressing him and feeling for him with sharp claws, while Aftalun tightened his grip on the dragon's snapping jaws. Water rose up in great plumes and fountains and leaped like a living thing.

'Then the goddess grew afraid for Aftalun, and she became Epona, the great white horse, and struck at the dragon with her silver hooves; but the water clung to her. So she became Rae, the swift red deer, and struck at the dragon with her pointed horns; but still the water pulled at her. So she became Morrghu, the fearsome black raven, and flew and struck at the dragon with her fierce beak; but the leaping water dragged at her wings. Then she became Eala, the great white swan, and swam on the surface of the water and struck at the dragon with her hard heavy bill until his blood spurted forth and splattered her widespread wings.

'Then the dragon turned from Aftalun and made a circle of himself around Eala, with his tail in his white-fanged mouth, and he began to bring forth young. For his being was not like our life, where male and female must meet, but his tail met his mouth and young sprang forth. Tiny dragons scattered forth, flying dragons and swimming dragons and crawling dragons, of every colour and shimmer of brightness, fiery dragons and dragons cold as the ancient waters. But as the dragon spawned, Aftalun climbed upon him and bent his head beneath the water and broke his neck. Then the dragon grew still, and Eala the swan who floated within the circle of his body changed once again to the form of the maiden goddess.

' "Now," she said, lying at ease, "I have my bed." And Aftalun came to her there.

'Then she who is Vieyra and Adalis and Suevi and many more took one more form and became Vale. She lies upon the water and mothers forth life from her body, as the dragon did. It is on her bosom that we dwell. The waters rise from her headlands, from the many springs of Eidden Lei in the north, and the waters traverse her, growing ever greater, until they return once more to the flood that is under the land. Through the Deep of Adalis far to the south they tumble. The waters roar down into the earth beyond sight or fathoming, and the mountains loom above.

'For the dragon still surrounds Vale. His jagged backbone circles our land. To the north folk call it Lorc Dahak, the Dragon Mountains, for it is rumoured that the spawn of the great worm live there yet. And to the south men say Lorc Tutosel, the mountains of the night bird. To the east, where the thunderheads grow, the mountains are called the Perin Tyr, the King's Range. And to the west they are called Lorc Acheron, and what that means folk will not say.' Grandfather paused, and we all looked up at the sharp, dark forms that cut into the sky far above.

'The goddess mothered forth many things in those beginning days,' he went on, 'creatures and plants in all colours of the dragon and the deep. But it was Aftalun who set them in order upon the surface of Vale. He put the sky back in place and constrained the sun to move with the days and seasons. When the goddess brought forth men of male and female kinds, Aftalun became one with us and gave us fire, and grain, and the mastership of cattle and horses, and showed us the workings of forge and loom. He formed us into the five kingdoms of Vale that stand to this day, taking form from the fivefold lotus of Vieyra, with Melior as the jewel at its heart, the throne richest and highest in esteem. Four cantons surround it, spreading like the petals of the flower. To the north lies Eidden, where Oorossy now rules, and to the south Selt, where Sethym holds sway, and to the east Tiela, the holding of Raz, and to the west Vaire, where Fabron is called king.'

'He who was our father's smith?' I interrupted. I always wanted to hear more about this man, and I felt sure that Daymon could tell me some secret if only he would. Smiths were important persons, and theirs was a magical craft of great renown. Sometimes smiths sat at a king's right hand. But that a smith should become a king himself was a marvel.

'Yes, to be sure,' said Daymon, with merely a glance at Tirell. 'Aftalun raised the castle upon the bosom of Adalis

20

with rock white as swan's down, red as blood of dragons. And finally, when all was set in place, the goddess came to him in the form of a bride of mortal kind, as she comes to the Sacred Kings even now. And Aftalun wed her once more, and she bore him a son. And he sat on the throne of Melior and ruled Vale. For years he ruled, and the seasons passed smoothly, until his children were grown and discontent began to gnaw at him.

' "You are still immortal, for you take many forms, and this is only one of them," Aftalun complained to his queen. "But I am only myself, a mortal now, and I must die when my time comes. It is not fair."

' "You do not wish to fly and cry with the north wind?" the goddess teased.

' "Indeed I do not," said Aftalun. "Not as moth or dove, hawk, or even an eagle. Even if those punishing Luoni of yours keep their claws away from me, as they ought, since all my life I have laboured for the well-being of Vale."

' "Be a griffin, and fly with them," she suggested with a hard smile.

' "No," he said quietly, "only a swan will I be, to fly with the flocks of Ascalonia. I have known immortality, and I want it back."

' "You must secure it by your death," she said, and she detailed to him the sacrifice of blood she demanded. Listening to her, he filled up with cold rage, to the brim of reason and far beyond.

' "You are heartless!" he breathed when she had finished.

' "If you do that," she told him coolly, "you will regain your godhead."

'He could not deny the dare in her eyes, even though he knew he doomed his own sons to follow the precedent. "All right, I will!" he cried, and rose to face her with flashing eyes. "But I tell you this, woman: in times to come my sons will bring your daughters to die on that same altar, and not by the knives of your harpies — but by their own fair, white hands."

' "Nonsense," she said frostily. "The goddess weds and remains. It is only men who come and go like mayflies."

' "The wheel turns," said Aftalun with a look locked on

21

rage. Then he went to prepare his doom. With his own great hands he raised the altar upon this Hill of Vision, chiseled the stones from the dragon's teeth, folk say. Now twenty men could not move one of the slabs. How the Sacred Kings have dwindled since those days.'

Tirell and I glanced at each other, smiling, for we knew that Grandfather was baiting us. But he went on without a sign that he had noticed.

'He lay down and let himself be tied to the altar and died under the knives of the priestesses, lay there a night with his blood drying on the stones. Then he stirred, burst his bonds, rose and left the altar in one great leap. He stalked off to the mountains in the east, the King's Range, thus called in his honour. The Luoni made way for him, folk say, and some claim that he lives there yet. He was never seen again, but to this day the tallest mountain, that towers over Coire Adalis, is called Aftalun, the Hero, in his name.'

'A peculiar sort of hero,' Tirell growled, 'who left a bloody altar as his legacy.' True enough, but he had never said so before. Somehow, listening to the story, I found that even the altar seemed beautiful.

'Perhaps he thought you could all bounce off it as he did,' Daymon remarked. 'Kings earned their immortality at a great rate in the early days, if lore tells true. The Sacred King was needed only long enough to lie with the goddess and get her with child; he was slain on his wedding night. But the observance soon eased. The span of kingship was lengthened to a year, and later to seven years, and still later to an even twenty years. Wives follow their husbands to that grim end now, as Aftalun foretold, for custom decrees that they should slay themselves in sorrow. And folk complain that, so gentle have the priestesses become, the souls of the Kings fly away, these days, as mere hawks.'

'I'll be a moth, and gladly,' Tirell snapped. I looked at him worriedly. We had heard the tale many times, and it had never bothered him so.

'For the matter of that,' Daymon told him, 'you're likely to make your own legend, to be laid like a fate on some poor heir of yours many years hence.'

'I plan to make an end of that altar,' he said quietly. Perhaps he expected consternation, but Grandfather only nodded.

'It was raised in hatred and it has been fed with envy. Men say that crops and prosperity depend on the sacrifice of a Sacred King, but better truth would be that the many hope to place their own suffering on the body of one. I agree with you wholly, Grandson. Yet, within the verity of the story, I say: no man has been as great as Aftalun who was god and became god again.' He bent a keen gaze on Tirell. 'Can you understand that?'

Tirell did not answer. I stirred and spoke in his place. 'Grandfather,' I asked abruptly, 'what lies beyond the mountains?'

My old nurse would have said, 'Fear, only fear!' and shut her mouth with a snap. But Grandfather replied mildly, 'Why, the endless water, Frain, if the legends be true.'

'Some folk say differently. Have you ever seen, Grandfather?'

'No. I cannot see beyond the mountains. I know folk claim to have seen dragons to the north, bright shapes flying over the white-crested mountains in early sunlight. And to the south men speak of a great expanse of dry and lifeless sand. To the east, some say, there are storm serpents and thunder giants, a savage race with claws and tails like animals. But fear speaks in all those tales, and truth may not be in them. Men have gone to the mountains from time to time — heroes, on a dare — but none have returned in my lifetime.'

'And to the west?' Tirell prompted, to my surprise.

'There, I think, is fear.' We all looked up at the jagged hulks that loomed over us.

'Though I had a dream, once, that Ogygia lay to the west,' Daymon added. 'And it was no sky realm, but lay on the water, amid vast water, and there were people riding on the surface of the water in vessels called boats.'

Ogygia was another name for Ascalonia, the realm of the gods. But boats! It was a word I did not then know the meaning of. We had no boats in Vale, and no water broader than one could throw a stone across.

'But even that is fearsome,' Grandfather mused. 'Why, I

23

wonder, when a little water is a blessing, does a world of water become a nightmare of terror? Still, it is so.'

'The main fear must lie closer at hand. Who built this wall?' It was Tirell again, he who usually sat silent. Grandfather turned slowly to face him with expressionless eyes.

'I don't know. But you are right. There are fell folk on the other side. I hear them sometimes, living here. Theirs are awesome voices,' He did not shudder, as another man might; he needed no such devices to impress us. We knew he never spoke more than he meant.

'Voices of what? Men?' Tirell demanded, but Daymon shook his head. He had said all that he would.

We ate our noonday meal in silence. It was bread and cheese and such simple stuff as the peasants brought Grandfather in thanks for his help. I liked it better than our fancy fare at home. After we had finished, Grandfather spoke to us, casually enough.

'So, lads, what is your trouble?'

I guess I gaped, but Tirell retorted coolly enough, 'Trouble? I was aware of none.'

'When a man is troubled, always he will turn to examine his roots. Tell me, Tirell —' Grandfather's eyes grew suddenly as sharp as swords. 'Why has your father not yet been killed? His twenty years are gone, and there has been drought in the land these two summers past.'

Tirell barked out a laugh. 'Killed? Because he would take some killing, that is why! He has an army waiting for those who would come to slay him.'

'Even so. But it was not always thus. In past times the Sacred Kings walked tamely to their slaughter. Abas is not one of those. Though he is mad and cruel, he is also clever and bold and proud — it is for that, I think, that my daughter cleaves to him. He is not one to let harm come to himself or his sons.' Grandfather turned his piercing eyes to me. 'You fear too much for Tirell, Frain. There is no need yet to flee beyond the mountains.'

'It can scarcely be said that our father loves us,' I mumbled resentfully.

'Who is to measure the love hidden beneath his hatred?

24

But his pride will serve to preserve you two. Turn elsewhere for love.' The old man rose stiffly to his feet, our signal that the visit was ended. 'Go with all blessing,' he said.

So we went, up the bare grassy Hill and past the altar and the glares of the priestesses and down the slope to the shade of the sacred grove. But I for one was not feeling particularly blessed.

2

'Let us go' — Tirell broke silence — 'and visit Mylitta, since
you wish to see her.' He was quiet, his bearing as quiet as I
had ever seen it, and his face unreadable.

So we turned aside from the track and rode northward into
the grove that ringed the Hill. The trees stretched straight and
tall; it seemed that the sunlight never quite reached the soft
soil beneath them, and there was no young growth. There
was scarcely a noise, even of birds, in the greenish twilight
between those trunks. I kept looking about me nervously.

'She lives where the grove meets the river,' Tirell said, his
voice sounding much too loud in that stillness. 'It is a little
place, a few fields, quite by itself. I have never come at it from
this direction, but —'

I screamed and flung up my hands. A black shape was
hurtling at us from the gloom beneath the trees, a shape of no
creature that I had ever seen. It looked like a horse, but a
grotesque horse with flaring nostrils and pale, flashing eyes.
Black feathered wings rose from its shoulders, and from its
forehead jutted a horn like a black dagger. And the noise!
Thunder drumming and wind whipping in those wings —
Tirell was in the lead, and the thing was on him before he
could do more than stare. His white mare shied and bolted,
throwing him to the ground. He lay there, winded, and the
black beast reared above him, beating those monstrous
wings.

I had stayed on my horse somehow, but it wouldn't obey
me. So I sprang down and ran forward, yelling like an idiot
and waving my fists; I was half mad with fear for Tirell. The
weird horselike thing threw me a glance of utter, withering

scorn and struck me with a wingtip; even that slight blow was enough to send me sprawling. Then it turned and leaped away. It was gone as suddenly as it had come, and the thunder sound of its hooves faded away. Tirell and I sat on the dirt, staring at each other and gulping for breath.

'Are you all right?' he exclaimed.

'You should ask!' I retorted. 'Can you get up?'

We both struggled to our feet and discovered that we were not hurt. I tried to brush the loam off of Tirell's fine blue cloak. 'That was quite a fright you gave the thing, brother,' he remarked. He was often ironical. I ignored him.

'What was it?' I asked. 'Have you seen it before?'

'Only in dreams,' he answered, and I saw then that he hid something with the irony. He had the bleak look that presaged a sleepless night, and he quickly turned away.

It took us quite a while to catch the horses. I was jumping and glancing about the whole time, but we did not see the beast again. Finally we got on our way once more.

'We had better try a little circuit,' Tirell said with just a hint of a smile.

We left the sacred grove briskly and rode down through the cultivated land of the valley. Farmers at their spring planting straightened to give us a courtesy and then stared after us. They learned nothing. The homestead where Mylitta lived, as Tirell had said, was far apart from the rest, halfway down the river slope and beside the sacred trees.

'How did you ever meet her?' I asked curiously.

'Wandering. This is the sort of lonely spot that suits my fancy well. There she is.'

I could scarcely see her at first, in her brown homespun against the freshly tilled brown earth. She was sowing grain. She carried the seed in a girdle at her waist as she stepped barefoot over the warm soil to meet us. Like most women in Vale she was named after one of the many names; 'Mylitta' was a name of the goddess in fair maiden form. But Tirell had spoken truth when he said she was not so very pretty. Her skin was tawny from sun and weather, her mouth wide, and her nose a bit upturned. Yet I watched her as if I had never seen a woman before.

It was her grace, I decided, that drew the eye. Or something less courtly than grace. Her movements were effortless, unstudied, her body strong and thoughtlessly lithe, like the body of a wild creature. She came to Tirell and met his eyes with such love that I felt my jaw sag in astonishment. She took no notice of me at all. Rites of courtesy would be lost on this one. Words like pride, rank, honour would mean nothing to her. The workings of her mind were like the rhythms of days and seasons; she loved Tirell, I believe, because he was young, and manly, and hers. She was a simpleton, but I felt no inclination to laugh at her. I felt awed.

'I was kept from you last night, lass,' Tirell said, 'but surely this night I will come.'

She nodded, accepting his assurance as she accepted sun and rain.

'We have seen a strange beast,' Tirell told her, 'black, like a horse, but with a horn and wings. Do you know anything of it?'

'It lives in the grove and peers from between the trees,' Mylitta answered in a soft, rhythmic voice almost like a chant. 'There is no harm to it, as far as I know.'

'No creature would harm you,' Tirell said, 'but it seemed eager to harm me.'

'I will speak to it,' the girl said.

Tirell nodded and touched her brown hand; he could not have meant more in a hundred gallant posturings. 'Till tonight, then, all peace,' he said softly. We rode away together.

'She is a child of the goddess,' I said when we had topped the slope.

Tirell turned to me with a rare smile. 'I am glad you like her.'

'I do, I like her very much. But liking is the least of it. I mean she is a very daughter of Eala who is Vale. Are her folk anything like her?'

'No, they are ordinary peasants, flattered and frightened of me. Mylitta comes and goes as she will, and pays them little heed.'

'And what will she do about the black beast?'

'I don't know!' Tirell shrugged, half laughing at himself. 'All I know is that the birds sing before her without fear and the butterflies light on her hands.' He gave a sudden whoop and sent his horse leaping forward, leaving me in his dust.

'That's not fair!' I shouted, urging my plunging chestnut after him. We raced along, but the chestnut galloped as if the air were water, and the white kept the lead all the way to Melior. Tirell was laughing, a sweet, ringing laugh from his heart with not a bit of scorn in it; I smiled just hearing him. Tears lay on his cheeks as we pulled up by the castle gates. It was to be a long year before I knew such laughter or such tears from him again.

We came to order and entered the courtyard at a seemly pace. But we had no sooner sent the horses to stable than a servant approached us. 'The King sends for you, Prince Tirell,' he said, bowing low. 'All day he has awaited your return.'

'Mighty Morrghu!' Tirell muttered in dismay. Rarely did the King wish to see him, and it was very ill luck that the notion had taken him on this day, when we had been absent so long. He was likely to be in one of his cold passions from waiting.

'Should I wash, think you?' Tirell asked me distractedly.

'It would take too long. You had better go straight away, before it gets any worse,' I decided. 'I'll come.'

'He did not send for you!' Tirell protested.

'He never does! And he will take no notice, you know that. Come on.'

'But it makes him angry, just the same —'

'Why? Who should have a better right to come before the King than his own son?' I argued perversely. 'I am his son too, am I not?'

Tirell seemed to have no answer. 'Well, come on, then,' he muttered, and we set off toward the audience chamber. I had no good reason for wanting to go along, risking the King's wrath at such a bad time. I just wanted, like a young fool, to see what was afoot.

Servants and courtiers stood clustered by the great carved doors, frightened and fascinated, like birds around a snake.

They scattered before us, and we strode past and entered. I felt my step falter in surprise. Mother was sitting beside the King on her gilded chair that was scarcely less ornate than the throne. Rich hangings set the royal couple off on all sides: Adalis plucking her three apples, the white horse Epona, Eala and the dragon. Vieyra stared down from the wall behind Abas, holding the lotus emblem of Vale. He sat before her on a high throne with bodiless metal heads staring from the arms. More heads, twenty of them, stared from his huge circular brooch, the prequisite of his sacred office and destined death. At its centre was the lotus, the sacred five, and the pin was a long knife that protruded beyond his shoulder. Kings of Melior always wore that reminder.

He turned his glittering eyes on me and spoke. 'Get those vultures away from the door, then stand there.'

I bowed and hastened to do as I was bid. 'Go,' I told the lackeys by the door, and they scattered, for they also had heard Abas's words. I stood on guard, quaking and listening. Some great event had to be in the making, and I fervently hoped it did not concern me.

Tirell stood before the throne. As far as I know, only he of all the court was accorded that privilege; bent knee and bowed head were customary. But Tirell met the icy blue eyes that were so much like his own.

'Where have you been?' Abas asked.

'To see Grandfather.'

'Out nattering with an old man. It is a useless life you lead. You are twenty years old.'

'I would be glad to be of assistance to my sire,' Tirell said smoothly. 'Are there duties for me?'

Abas scarcely seemed to have heard him. His stare had locked on nothingness a trifle above Tirell's head. 'It is time you had a wife,' he went on. 'You will ride to Tiela as soon as possible, to Nisroch. Raz has one daughter left, and she is of marriageable age. Recilla is her name. Obtain her.'

I could not see Tirell's face; perhaps it changed. But his voice as he spoke was level, with scarcely a hint of edge. 'Is it not traditional that the Sacred Kings should wed a maiden with one of the many names, the goddess in mortal maiden form, and that on the night of coronation?'

Abas half rose from his seat in sudden passion. 'Sacred King! Do you wish to be a Sacred King or a King in truth? Go to Raz, I say, and you will die in your bed, not on a bloody altar! I have some power, and he has more. What, youngster, would you spurn it?'

'I spurn no power,' Tirell answered quietly, 'and I die on no altar. But a haughty wife will be a lifetime's misery to me, Sire.'

'What folly is this?' Abas stood at his full height, towering on the dais, and his glare had taken on a fey light. 'I have not told you to cleave to her, only to wed her! Kill her when you can, and save your passion for the whores! Of course you will need a son.' His blue eyes wavered, and it seemed for a moment that they wandered toward me. I wished I could run.

'You look too far ahead, my liege.' Mother spoke up suddenly. 'Indeed, there is no hurry in this matter of Tirell's wedding. Let it wait, I say, if he is doubtful.'

'And I say, Let it not wait.' The King settled to his seat again, but still with a look of stone. 'Raz is ripe for the plucking. Princeling, you are to leave within the week. Go, make your preparations.'

Tirell bowed and left without a word. I longed to follow him, but I judged it wiser to wait until I had been dismissed. I had been noticed at last, and I felt all the danger of it.

'Let him wait, my husband,' our mother Suevi said softly.

'What, now!' Abas glared at her. 'I thought we had agreed that he will need an ally.'

'Yes, and I assumed he would not mind. He is so much like you.' Her gaze would have melted stone, I thought. 'But he has found a love, it seems.'

'You see that?' Abas was startled.

'Yes. Let him wait, my lord, and likely it will pass. I know surely he does not wish to be killed. But if he goes to Tiela now, he will make a sorry wooer.'

'He does not need to woo! He has only to say the word, and Raz will grovel at his feet! No, he must go at once. And he must learn soon that love is no asset to kingship.' Abas rose to leave.

31

Queen Suevi rose with him. 'What, my lord?' she questioned softly. 'Have you forgotten the worthiness of love? We were young once, and lovers.'

I tried not to stare, seeing her anew — her voice was vibrant, her pale, quiet face was fair, her form as fair as a maiden's. Abas went as rigid as a statue, meeting her eyes. He raised his hand — to touch her, I thought — and then his clenched fist lashed out and struck her squarely across the face. The blow knocked her into her queenly chair. Abas turned from her and left, sweeping past me without a glance.

I did not go to Mother, for she was proud, and I knew my face was quivering; I thought it would make her angry. In a moment she also rose and left, with a streak of blood and a dark shadow of bruise on her set face. I waited until her footsteps faded far down the corridor. Then I hurried away to find Tirell.

He was in our bedchamber, pacing furiously, like a caged panther. I decided not to tell him more than I had to.

'Mother tried to get you your way,' I said. 'She knows about Mylitta.'

'What!' Tirell froze in midstride.

'I don't mean that she knows her name. She only said that she could see you had a lover. She had not thought at first that you would mind going to Tiela. You know you have been yearning for years to get away from Melior.'

'Yes, and now I have my chance, hah? I'm not going.'

'Oh, come on, Tirell,' I said tiredly, 'what choice do you have? Mylitta will understand.'

'She should not have to understand! I am a freeman; no law of Vale can make me wed against my will —'

'Except the law that weds you with the goddess in death,' I reminded him. 'Father grasps for power, but Mother seeks only for your life. Go to Tiela, Tirell. Perhaps the maiden is fair.'

He snorted in scorn. 'A daughter of that swarthy Raz? She will be a proper crow. But even if she were as fair as any flower in Vale, I would still cleave to Mylitta.' He had calmed now, and he spoke with a sober conviction that I had never seen in him. I stared at him hard for ten breaths or so, trying to believe.

'All right, brother,' I said at last. 'It is you and Mylitta, then, and I will aid you for all that I am worth.'

He reached over and touched my hand. I remember that.

'But go to Tiela nevertheless,' I continued. 'You are clever. You will find a way out. Make the lady hate you. I will go with you — perhaps she will wed *me*.'

His eyebrows shot up. 'The King our mighty father did not say you were to go!'

'No, but he did not say I could not! I will be gone a week before he misses me.'

'Maybe,' Tirell muttered. 'Go to supper and let me think. Go on, fill your belly. I don't want any.'

I left him, hoping he had the sense not to bolt. For sake of company and diversion I went to the great hall. It was filled with courtiers, and they scarcely let me eat between flatteries and petitions. I stayed, even so, for I knew that Tirell needed time to fret in solitude. I sat and listened to the chanting of the bard.

When the others were yawning I took my leave. I was glad to find Tirell lying on his bed, staring and apparently calm. I handed him some packets of meat and fruit, and he sat up to eat.

'I have not been entirely sulking,' he remarked, straight-faced. 'Before the gates closed I took out a horse, a black, the better to prowl the night. I have hidden him in a copse down by the Balliew. To give me more time with the lass.'

'You will tell her about Tiela, then?'

He gestured irritably. 'I suppose I must! But you at least could spare me more talk of it until the morrow, hah?'

I took the hint and kept silence. After quite a while the bedtime noises of the castle ceased. Tirell had changed into black clothing: black tunic and hose, even a black cloak. Only his torque of hammered gold reflected a gleam of light. 'So she'll know who I am,' he joked sourly, but the truth was that we very seldom removed the things, even to wash or sleep. Torques are devilishly hard to get off. Tirell had once observed that being a prince was just a step above being a slave; their collars were of bronze, and ours were of gold. Tirell was often sarcastic that way.

He paced, impatient to be off. I would have waited a bit longer, in his place, but I couldn't detain him. So we tied the rope to our heavy bedstead and sent it coiling through the high window. I held it, too, while Tirell went up and over, and I held it long after I was certain he was well gone. Finally I pulled it in, stowed it, and wandered restlessly into the corridor. I went to one of those grim little balconies meant for throwing things down on attackers. Melior had never been attacked, but every building in Vale was a stronghold if it was not a hut. I looked lazily over the toothy wall into the courtyard, and I knew at once that trouble was afoot.

3

Men and horses were forming ranks amid a glare of torchlight. The men wore the blood-red livery of the King's personal force, the Boda by name, they who called themselves messengers of doom. I saw the gleam of swords and lancetips, and amidst it all a tall figure and the glint of a torque and the moonlike glow of an enormous brooch. No one less than the King our royal father himself was riding in the mid of night.

I gaped for a moment or two and then I ran downstairs, scuttled across the courtyard in the shadows, and got to the stable. I loosed the first proper horse I could find, one of the royal white mares. I vaulted onto it and clattered out just as the gates were closing after the last of the Boda. I shot through on their heels and veered off into the night, riding hard. The rearward men must have seen me, but they did not pursue me. They were probably afraid to tell the King. He was as likely to skewer them as not.

I rode as directly as I could toward the sacred grove and Mylitta's cottage, but far aside from the main road, for the King and his Boda rode there; the gleam of their torches was visible for miles. I could only assume that this nocturnal sortie concerned Tirell, and I had to give him what warning I could. I raced along the twisted byways and came to Mylitta's house at last with a winded horse, over a hedge and a ditch. I pounded on the cottage door. The man peered out at me stupidly.

'Where are the prince and Mylitta?' I shouted at him. 'Come, tell me, the King is riding!'

He only stared at me. Probably he didn't know. 'If I were

you I'd hide!' I snapped at him, and I kicked my horse toward the grove, hoping . . . But the King was there before me. He must have had a spy, or perhaps it was that damned visionary cleverness of his. I saw the torches flaring ahead and heard Abas shouting. Even at a distance I could not mistake that grating voice.

I eased toward the commotion, mindful of the torchlight on my white horse, not to speak of my white linen shirt! But as I drew near I found that all eyes faced the King and his quarry. Tirell and Mylitta stood side by side, with Boda holding them both. They must have been taken riding, for another man held the black horse by the reins. The King stood shouting and shaking his fist at Tirell. Abas was tall, and in the glare of the torches his shadow seemed huge.

'Thus you obey my commands!' he roared. 'Out at night, over the wall, to rut with a peasant!'

'I would have been back by day,' Tirell replied. His voice was calm, but his face was white and taut with fear. And contempt. *Hide the contempt*, I urged him inwardly.

'Out at night . . . even in the darkest night . . .' Abas was trembling with wrath and a sort of frantic loathing. 'At the mid of night to run from me, to scorn my command . . .'

'No, Majesty, he has told me he must go to Tiela!' Mylitta said in her gentle, musical voice. The King stopped his ranting with a choke to stare at her. She stood straight and graceful, meeting his crazed blue eyes with her wide eyes of brown. It was then that she sealed her fate, I believe, though she did not know it. No one dared to gaze at the King so equably.

I cannot understand how I failed to foresee her mortal danger. Abas's wrath seemed to have stunned my reason. He was hoarse, panting, scarcely coherent, but he kept shouting, and Tirell listened as I did, numbly. 'A dirtcaked peasant . . .' the King gasped. 'Would you scorn a princess for a peasant? Out in the night . . . You are to have no more thought of her. I will see to it. No more joy in the black night. Night . . . no hope . . .' The cadence of mad rage went on with no change for warning. 'Thus will I secure you!' Abas shrieked, and whipped out his long ceremonial sword. I set heels to the white mare at the first flash, but far too late. I saw Mylitta fall while I was yet in midleap. She died without a cry, even as Tirell tore loose from his guards and lunged.

The Boda were all startled and in confusion, some of them trying to restrain Tirell and most of them scrambling away from my charge. They didn't like to risk hurting me, I suppose, without orders, but I didn't care if they tried to kill me. I was desperate to get to Tirell before he came up against Abas and that sword. I shoved through the melee, leaned from my mount, and got an arm around my brother's chest from behind. My eyes met the King's glittering eyes scarcely an arm's length away; he was jerking his sword from Mylitta's body, and his glare froze me in place. My frightened horse tore us away from the guards. Torches were falling and horses were breaking loose in terror and I think Abas shouted again. I held tight to Tirell and to the white mare's neck, and she galloped off into the lightless woods.

Tirell was struggling against me, cursing between sobbing breaths. 'Shut up and hold still!' I gasped. My arm felt as if it would pull off with his weight. The King and his Boda were after us. I could hear their hoofbeats. Then the mare shied. A dark shape loomed ahead of us, a blot, a moving vortex of darkness in that darkest of all nights, shifting and rearing and lifting widespread black wings. It blared a challenge I could not heed. I moaned and shut my eyes as we ran wildly past it. From behind I could hear the cries of the Boda and a long, hoarse scream of complete terror. That was Abas; I was sure of it. And I sensed that he had somehow met the black beast before.

A bit farther on my arm gave way and Tirell fell to the dirt with a thump. I wrestled my panicky horse to a halt. Tirell sat like a stone where I had dropped him.

'Come on!' I begged, tugging at him. 'We'll both be killed!'

'Fine,' he muttered.

'Come on, Tirell!' I was almost weeping, as panicky as the horse, and I tried to lift him. He threw off my grip.

'Calm down,' he said tonelessly. 'They're gone. Listen.'

I stood for a moment, panting. It was true that the wood was quiet.

'But the beast is somewhere about,' I said shakily.

'So much the better.' He got up. 'I'm going back to Mylitta,'

'She's dead,' I whispered.

'I know it.' His voice was dispassionate, and in the darkness of the wood I could not gauge his mood. I stood feeling very small in the night.

'Remember her as she was, brother,' I pleaded. 'She has been — trampled, since.'

'Luoni take our father!' he cursed in a cracking voice, and he strode off. I caught the white mare and went after him, but I had not gone far when I met him mounted on the black, riding hard toward the west. Except for the gleam of his torque he was only a racing shadow beneath the trees; I almost thought it was the black beast. 'What now?' I called to him.

He did not answer, so I sighed and sent the white labouring after him. We galloped out of the sacred grove and up the Hill of Vision, up to where the White Rock of Eala stood gleaming like bleached bones in the starlight. Tirell rode headlong under it. I went around.

'Are you going to Grandfather?' I shouted.

He did not answer. He urged his horse recklessly down the Hill, and I followed more slowly. I was not afraid of losing him any longer, for the Wall blocked his path. Presently I saw a speck of light. Daymon Cein was awake in his hut, it seemed. I rode up to find Tirell standing and studying the Wall. Grandfather came out in an old white nightgown, carrying a rushlight in his hand.

'So, lads,' he said quietly, 'the trouble has come.'

Tirell turned slowly and stared at him, a fey, perilous stare, almost threatening. 'Had you seen that she would be killed?'

'No, lad, I am sorry.' Grandfather's voice was full of pity. 'I saw your love and rejoiced in it, but the King's thoughts and actions are hidden even from himself. Only lately his fell deed has awakened me from my sleep.'

Tirell stared at him a while longer, then shifted his cyan gaze to me. 'Go back,' he said flatly.

'To our gentle father?' I chided. 'He would kill me sooner

than greet me. Thank you, but no. I am going with you.'

'I want no company where I go,' Tirell said. His face was set in a white mask with his eyes burning through it like cold blue flame. I had known his anger many times, anger that passed like storm clouds before a high wind. But I had never seen such a locked and tortured rage in him. I shivered, facing him. It was as if my brother had become a stranger to me, or perhaps someone whom I knew all too well.

'Where are you going?' I asked.

'To Acheron. To my death, if death pleases to take me. I am done with Vale.'

I felt my hair prickle. 'The Wall will not let you pass,' I said, a little too quickly.

'Ah, but it will.' Tirell turned back to Daymon. 'Will it not, Grandfather?'

'It might,' Grandfather replied, almost serenely. 'But it has been prophesied that when this wall is breached the doom of Melior will be at hand.'

'Better yet,' Tirell snapped. 'Do it.'

'Wait a bit. Even in Acheron you will need some provisions.' Daymon went into his hut, and I hurried after him.

'Grandfather,' I whispered, 'what is going on? Are you both mad?'

'Perhaps,' the old man acceded. 'But where is he to go? Back toward Melior? He will be taken before he tops the Hill. At least the Boda will not follow him into Acheron.'

'But Tirell is not fleeing for life!' I cried. 'Did you not hear him welcome death?'

'His rage speaks. But life is not so easily thwarted. Wait and see if he does not live yet a while. May peace come to you, lad. Both of you.' He handed me a packet of cheese and bread and strode back outside with me tagging after. 'Hold the horses,' he added.

I got them by the reins and stood stupidly, waiting — for what, I didn't know. Grandfather wandered over to a spot by his yew tree and slowly extended his arms. He spoke no word that I could hear, but power flowed through him until he seemed as big as the night. His arms quivered, and the stones of the Wall quivered along with him, then rumbled and fell from their places with a noise fit to waken the dragons in the deep. Grandfather lowered his arms by degrees, looking once again stiff and old. Tirell walked over and methodically began to clear a path through the rubble.

Dazed as I was by the events of the night, it did not occur to me that we had put Grandfather in peril. Just as it had never occurred to me to wonder why he lived so much alone, at the Wall. . . .

I joined Tirell, lifting stones until we had cleared a narrow path for the horses. By the time we were finished the sky had turned from black to grey. I could see the shapes of the mountains looking down on us. Grandfather had long since disappeared — into his hut, I supposed. We led the horses through to the far side of the ruined Wall.

But before I could mount, Tirell took my arm with no gentle hand.

'Now,' he said, facing me to the south, 'make your way between the river and the mountains until you come to Vaire. There is plenty of cover, and it is not too far. Fabron will give you aid, if only secretly. I am sure of it.' His voice was hard. I shook off his hand.

'I go with you,' I told him.

'No good will come to you with me, princeling. I am a shadowed thing. Choose your path more wisely.' Tirell's eyes looked like blue jewels, hard and fixed in their sockets.

'If you go to Acheron, I go there too,' I said.

He shrugged coldly and mounted his black. He set off silently and I followed without a word. In a moment we rode into the shadows of strange, twisted trees. But before we had gone far, hoofbeats sounded behind us. I whirled to face the pursuit, but Tirell scarcely moved his head. 'What is it?' he asked indifferently.

'It's the black beast,' I told him.

4

We rode all day without speaking another word. Tirell led, looking like the raven of war in his black cape and on his black steed. I followed on the white mare, and the black beast paced close behind me, restlessly tossing its head. Arrows of fear shot through me all that day; I believed that at any moment I was likely to feel that knifelike horn in my back. But I was too proud even to turn and look at the baleful thing, since Tirell was in such a harsh and desperate mood.

We made our way up the foothills of Lorc Acheron, between ancient, gnarled trees that stooped over us like old, old women puttering at a loom. The ground and tree trunks were covered with shaggy grey moss, and the silence was profound, like the silence after a snowfall. I did not hear even a bird or a rabbit — only the hot breath of that black horned monster behind me. As the day wore on I forgot my fear in tiredness, for I had not slept the night before. The day was grey — all days might be grey in those woods — and I nodded as I rode. By the time the grey turned to black, even Tirell was willing to sleep. We stumbled off our horses, stupid with fatigue, and sank down into the soft, deep moss. I was sound asleep within minutes.

In the dead of night I dreamed that the trees were moving. They crooked their branches and beckoned one another, and their long leaves clustered like greenish hair around their knobby heads. They gathered around Tirell and me, peering.

'Such bold duckies to come to Acheron!' said one in a high, creaky old woman's voice.

'Bold or fools,' said another, sounding puzzled. 'Have men forgotten in Vale what Acheron is?'

'They know well enough, though they will not say it,' the first replied. 'Such bold ducks! Shall we take them now, when they will mind it least?'

'No!' said a voice deeper than the rest. 'Bide a bit and see what the lady says. I sense a mistake here. The littler one is full of life.'

'And there is the beast, too,' another added. 'That is odd.'

'Yes, it should be skulking about Melior. How Abas hates the night, and how he hates the beast!' The trees joined in high, creaking laughter, like the tinkling of twigs in a breeze. 'Hates it and fears it, poor thing! But is this not Abas's son?'

'The black-haired one, yes. It is he that the beast follows. He is a scion of Aftalun.'

'But what of the other, the russet-haired one? They both wear torques.'

'Speak no more of that,' said the deeper voice. 'He is not suitable to our purposes or the beast's. Torque or no torque, we shall not touch him unless the lady gives us leave. Look, even now he stirs. Hush!'

I was straining to sit, to wake and look more fully around me. But the grey moss softly brushed my face, and I remember no more until morning. When I awoke the sun was high, but Tirell was still asleep. The beast lay quietly curled in the moss beside him, with its horned head resting on its hard shining hooves.

I stared at the beast for a while, and it stared back without sign or motion. Its eyes were of a flat, threatening grey, like storm clouds, and a bloodshot white rim showed all around. They did not blink even when I moved to Tirell's side. Warily ignoring the beast, I shook my brother.

'Come on, sluggard,' I called, as cheerily as I could. 'Wake up!'

Tirell roused reluctantly and gazed at me with blank eyes. Then memory struck him, had he groaned under the blow. He covered his face with his hands.

'Come here, brother,' I said softly, holding him. 'Weep it out.' But instantly he spurned the embrace and rose to his feet.

I rose also to face him. 'Have you grieved for her?' I asked, as gently as I could.

'Grieved!' Tirell barked. 'I am a prince, not an old woman,

42

that I should sit in a pool of tears!' He turned angrily away.

'The beast is behind you!' I warned.

'Good!' he retorted harshly. 'Let us ride.'

'Eat first.' I offered him bread and cheese. But he would not eat, so I chewed on my portion as we rode. The land grew steeper and steeper that day, until the horses scarcely could manage the slope. Gradually rock began to show beneath the moss, the trees grew more sparse, until they ceased altogether and we picked our way between soaring rocky cliffs. After a while it seemed to us that the horses could go no farther. We stopped, though we said no word. But the black beast swept past us and took a twisting path up a slope as steep as a precipice. Tirell followed at once, and I more slowly, clenching my teeth. It gave me no comfort that the black creature of ill omen had become our leader.

By day's end we had reached a narrow ledge below crags that seemed to shut out the sky with the sun. The beast trotted along at a speed I did not dare to match. 'What does it care! It has wings!' I muttered to no listener, for Tirell seemed oblivious to talk or fear. I was falling behind the pair of them, the black beast and the black-clad prince, when the ledge suddenly became a narrow passageway between great slabs of rock. In the tiny slit of sky far above I could see stars twinkling, though it was not yet night. Anxiously I cantered after the others, then stared past them. Space showed at the end of the corridor: a clearing or a cliff?

It was a clearing. Even Tirell stopped to stare when we entered. We had found the heart of Acheron.

Soft grey-green grass spread beneath the horses' feet. The lawn sloped gently to a still, oval expanse of water beneath a dim dome of sky and shadowed by mountains all around. It was a lake, but not like the little pools I had known; it was large, clear, and fathomless, like a single eye of the ancient deep. A swan floated on it, a white swan, but I blinked; the reflection was black. In the midst of the mirrorlike water, on a sort of island, stood a curious greenery in the shape of a castle all made of living, rustling foliage. We stared for long moments in the failing light before we could be sure of what we saw.

Slowly we rode along the margin of the lake, staring at that castle like peasants come to court. Presently we found a little bridge of land that connected the island to the shore. So we approached the castle, still staring. It was all made of huge trees and twining vines, gigantic things that must have fed on the very blood of the dragon. Their leaves were of a peculiar silvery green, shimmering like silk, giving off muted flakes of light, even though there was not a breath of breeze in that place. Between the leaves were window slots and parapets and balconies, all as neat as if a builder had planned them. We rode around the living walls to the gap that should have been a gate and entered. We left our horses in the soft, grassy space that served for courtyard and walked into the green great hall.

The structure of the castle soared above us; thick branches that spiraled into steps offered to take us to the very top of it, if we liked. Steps of turf led up to a vast dais. On the dais stood a sort of pavilion, a tent, in cloth of bright, soft gold. And at the doorway of the tent sat a lady. She rose as we walked up to her, and I felt my heart stop at the sight of her; I could not speak. But she looked only at Tirell.

She was slender, fair of skin, and with a face so delicately wrought, so eerily beautiful that it seemed to shine with its own whisper of light, like an echo of moonlight. Long hair of palest gold flowed over her back and shoulders. Her gown was silver that did not shine; it lustered like moonlight, like the other soft things in this place. I hope I did not gape, but I felt as if my legs would not hold me. And I shall never forget the sound of her voice as she spoke; it was soft and cool and clean and lovely, fearsome and yielding at the same time. I could have drowned in her voice.

'I am Shamarra, the lady of this lake,' she said, 'and you are Tirell of Melior. What do you seek here?'

'Death!' Tirell said, and I winced. His voice sounded terribly harsh in this still place. But the maiden's face did not change.

'Death?' she said politely. 'To be sure, there is death to be had here aplenty. Look around you!'

Tirell did not look around; he stared at the shimmering

maiden. She walked up to him. 'There are the trees,' she explained to him, 'very tall, easy to climb and jump from. And then there is the lake. Indeed, the lake is a very font of death. Take some!'

I certainly must have gaped then; she was taunting him! Yet her voice sounded liquid and sweet, and I saw no malice in her look. She faced him scarcely a foot away, meeting his hard, glittering blue eye with hers that were the colour of sparkling water.

'Death!' she mused more quietly. 'You have ridden past death all the way here! What could be easier than to go over a precipice? No, my lord, death is too puny a foe. Have you no worthier adversary?'

Tirell stirred as if coming out of a trance. 'Abas!' he muttered.

'Vengeance,' said the lady softly, her voice like the summons of a distant trumpet call.

'Vengeance on him who slew my lady!' Tirell said hoarsely. 'What have I been thinking of, to let him live after me!' Blindly he turned and started out of the verdant castle, but the lady touched his arm and he stopped where he stood.

'You are a prince,' she exhorted him. 'Plan, bide your time, make sure your stroke. And before you plan, eat and sleep. I will show you where.'

Tirell let out a long breath. 'Even so, Lady,' he mumbled. 'I follow.'

She led us into her pavilion and welcomed us as honoured guests. Within the tent of golden cloth we found every comfort, luxury even, that we could ever desire. Richly patterned cushions covered most of the floor, and a woollen carpet showed beneath. Basins of warm water awaited us, for washing, and fine linen towels. Candles stood burning clearly on tiny carved tables. Braziers glowed, each heating a different delicacy. It should have taken many servants to prepare all that met us, but besides Shamarra I did not see a being in the place.

Tirell sat down in a weary daze, lost to all courtesy as the lady served him fine white bread and amber liquor. She gave me the same, and my hand trembled as I took the cup for fear lest my fingers brush against hers and I lose all composure. I was on fire inside. I could eat only a little. Tirell did the same, then lay back against his cushions and slept. My face burned at his uncouthness.

'He is worn out with sorrow.' I spoke at last to excuse him.

The lady was looking at Tirell, and she scarcely glanced at me when I spoke, though she answered gently enough. 'I know it. Never fear — I am not angry. Have you eaten well?'

'Marvellously well.' I chewed on some strange red-gold fruit, hoping to please her by eating. Presently I spoke again, hesitantly. 'My lady —'

'Yes?'

'You'll think me bold — but is it wise, this baiting of him against Abas?'

She met my eyes then, though briefly, and her glance was not unkind. 'It gives him reason to live,' she said. She turned her gaze back to Tirell's sleeping form. 'Perhaps it will not be too long before better reason comes to him.'

She watched Tirell sleep, as I had sometimes watched him when chance offered; it was a rare sight, had she but known it. When Tirell sleeps, his proud, mettlesome face smooths out into the likeness of a young immortal, fair and free, unfettered by bitterness or scorn. Such an aspect was on him in Shamarra's pavilion, and she sat and gazed at him in long silence, seeming quite unaware or unconcerned that I gazed at her in like wise. I wanted never to stop looking at her, and I don't know when I did. I believe I fell asleep with her image in my eyes.

In the morning I awoke early, before Tirell, feeling as fresh as if I had rested for a week. Eagerly I made my way out of the pavilion and out of the leafy castle to look around me. Though the sun was up, everything still lay in shadow, for high ramparts of rock rose all around the lake and its grassy margin. Shamarra was bathing in the lake, her golden hair floating out behind her. She lifted her arm lazily in greeting and walked toward me, pulling her glistening garment about her. I watched her until courtesy compelled me to shift my eyes. When she neared me I was looking at the willows.

'Did you sleep well?' she asked politely.

46

'Indeed, yes, very well.' My mind floundered foolishly for something to say to her. 'Might I also bathe in the lake?' I blurted. I, who had never bathed in anything except tubs of lifeless water brought from wells by slaves! I have never had much sense where Shamarra was concerned.

'I don't know,' she answered soberly. 'Go and look.'

So I went and knelt by the verge, expecting something strange. The black lotus of Vieyra grew at the very edge, its four-petaled reflection wavering in the lucent water, white. But only my own freckled face stared back at me. A secretive thing water is, all surface and shimmer, hiding mysterious depths for all that it seems as clear as air. I turned to Shamarra, questioning.

'You are an innocent,' she said. 'Nothing in the lake can harm you.'

I grew oddly angry, though there had been no mockery in her voice. 'Then I can bathe,' I said.

'To be sure . . . But there will be a price to pay.' She walked away.

Her warning rang in me. But I felt suddenly absolutely determined to bathe. It was not just obstinacy — though I admit to some obstinacy — it was . . . I sensed, however vaguely, that the lake was a key, a magical means that might make me more like her. I loved her already; I wanted to bathe where she had bathed.

I stripped and stepped in at once. Nothing untoward happened, and nothing marvellous either. I liked the feel of the water on my skin — smooth, tingling, moving over me like a thousand cool fingers. By the time I was done, the sunlight had worked its way down the rocky western mountains that towered just beyond Shamarra's domain. I stood on the grass, dripping and admiring those glowing heights. I gazed until footsteps sounded and Tirell walked up to me.

'All hail, handsome prince!' I greeted him lightly. 'Did you sleep well?'

'Yes,' he said. Then, with his customary cynicism, he added, 'Why? Did she drug the mead?'

'No. In the land of death perhaps all men sleep like the dead.' I spoke thoughtlessly, then stiffened and glanced at my brother. But he merely shrugged.

'It is foolishness, all this talk of dying.' he remarked. 'The lady spoke truth. I could have thrown myself off a cliff almost any step of the way here.'

'I was miserably aware of that,' I said.

'Would you care?' he asked morosely.

'Of course.'

'Why?' His voice was toneless.

I could not tell what he wanted. And a little demon of anger stirred in me; I was annoyed at the dance he had been leading me. If I had known how rare such speech from him was to become, I would have answered him more gently.

'If you go,' I stated, 'then the altar awaits *me*.'

I don't know if he was hurt; my eyes were on the mountaintops. I heard him snort.

'What would you do?'

'Flee beyond those peaks yonder,' I answered promptly. 'Look at them! Aren't they splendid?'

Tirell looked up at the mighty crags and shrugged. 'Our way lies toward Melior,' he said. 'Forthwith.'

I took that as the command that was intended and ambled back to the lakeside to get my things. 'Look into the water,' I called to Tirell, just as a random thought. But he shuddered and vehemently shook his head.

'Thank you, but no! That lake is the strangest thing in this strange place, and I for one will be glad to leave it. You're mad to let it touch you. There is our hostess.'

Shamarra sat on the grassy verge in front of her palace of greenery. Even in the bright sunlight that now reached it, the lakeside seemed dim and grey, and Shamarra's islet dimmest of all. At rest she seemed soft and still as the grass at her bare feet. But as we approached and she stood to greet us she shimmered and shone. The movement changed her.

Tirell bowed to her. 'Lady, I come to take leave of your kindness. My heart burns to be on with the task you have pointed out to me.'

'Vengeance?' Shamarra raised her delicate brows. 'But for that task I think you will need a sword, is it not so?'

Tirell felt that he was being mocked; I saw the muscles of his neck harden. 'I can find a sword, Lady,' he stated.

'Not such a sword as I will give you. Wait but a moment.'

We waited for more than a moment as she walked through the grassy courtyard and disappeared into the leafy keep. We were bound only by courtesy, and Tirell stirred restlessly under the restraint, but he was well rewarded. Shamarra returned with our horses loaded down with food and gear, and even Tirell stared when she handed him a three-foot sword of iron.

Weapons in Vale were usually made of bronze. We had iron, of course, but it was heavenly metal, scarce and almost as precious as gold. Abas hoarded it in his treasure room and drank from fine cups that Fabron the smith had hammered from the stuff, cups little larger than a baby's fist. A sword of iron was a weapon men would shy from in as much awe as fear. It was a plain, dangerous-looking thing with a sombre glint. Shamarra buckled it onto Tirell without comment.

'There is a king's ransom in that,' Tirell remarked softly.

'Use it well,' the lady told him. 'It will cut through any bronze. Guard it from thieves, for there is no other like it. Here is the helm.'

The helm and shield were of iron also. I really lost my breath then. They were both bordered in a knotwork design that made my eyes ache with its intricacy. In the centre of Tirell's shield, half entangled in reaching twigs, stood the pawing form of a winged horse with a single sharp horn.

'The beast has lived long,' Shamarra said.

My weapons and arms were of bronze, fine bronze embellished with scrollwork, to be sure. The lady handed me a little dagger that was made of iron. Tirell was eager to be off. He mounted the black, and Shamarra frowned gravely up at him.

'Why do you not ride the white,' she asked, 'as befits the bridegroom of the goddess?'

Tirell's face hardened and he shook his head. 'As long as sorrow for my slain love lives in my heart,' he vowed, 'I will wear black and ride a black, and let the black beast follow me if it will. Nor will I ever wed any maiden by name of the goddess, however fair.'

'All things carry the seeds of change,' Shamarra said. 'Look yonder.'

She pointed across the lake, past the lone swan that floated white over its twin of black. There on the farther shore stood the black beast looking back at us, its head held high, horn pointing toward the sky. In the still water just below wavered a reflection — an image of white! Fair white were the folded wings and shining flanks, and purest white the horn.

'Remember that,' Shamarra said quietly. 'It may yet be of use to you.'

She stood back, and Tirell started away. I came out of a stupor and scrambled onto my horse. 'Perhaps we shall meet again?' I asked Shamarra — begging, rather.

She laughed, a rippling sound. 'I think we will,' she answered. 'Look for me by watery ways.' I urged the white mare after Tirell, and when I had caught up to him I looked back. The black beast was already pacing at my heels. The lady stood by her lake, watching us go. I waved, and she lifted a hand in answer, but already I knew which of us it was that held her gaze, and my heart was sore.

5

Tirell was the one who found courage to embrace the beast. Though at the time I did not think of it as courage, but as folly, terrifying folly, maybe madness. I had not yet learned that valiant madness braves the dark and comes through it — that is how Abas failed; he was afraid. And I was afraid of the beast and therefore despised it as somehow misshapen, unclean, in spite of the lady's words and the fair image in the water. The real enemy was myself. I was a far worse fool than Tirell, those first few days, and I was of no help to him.

He rode out of Acheron with a hard, straight back, and now and then he laughed a laugh I did not like. Sunk in my own gloom, I felt little inclined to speak to him. The black beast paced behind me, once again content to bring up the rear — to my dismay. Soon I had other cause for dismay. Tirell rode far too fast for safety on the treacherous slopes, and more than once I closed my eyes.

We spent the night on a ledge scarcely wide enough for the horses, and we slept little. Tirell stirred and muttered on his narrow space of stone. Once or twice I asked what ailed him. He gave no reply, so I asked no more. He rode through the next day in a tense, rigid daze, almost as if he were in pain. I learned much later that Abas had been calling him, tormenting him with the inner voice. I did not know that at the time, and I didn't understand — I still don't understand. I am no visionary, and I cannot imagine what those days were like for him.

By nightfall we found easier footing, praise be, and we camped beneath knobby, grey-fringed trees. I distrusted those trees from our earlier meeting, and I resolved to sleep lightly. Still, I was so exhausted and heartsore that I expect I would have been lost in deepest slumber had it not been for the racket Tirell put up. All night long he thrashed and moaned and whispered and whimpered in his sleep. Any other time I would have gone to him, awakened him, soothed him and talked to him until it passed, whatever mood or dark dream it was. But, whether due to the moss or to my own vexation and weariness, I could not or would not move. I lay dozing and listening to him. 'Get away,' he would whimper. 'Let me alone.' Finally, just at first light, he seemed to wrench himself out of it and staggered up. I lay drowsily watching him through a veil of eyelash. He looked wild and all asweat, like a frightened colt. Come here, my brother, I thought in my half sleep. I dreamed that I embraced him. Come here, let me comfort you. But he did not so much as glance my way.

The beast lay not far away, at ease in the grey moss. It lifted its head and looked at Tirell out of cloudy eyes, but it did not move or seem to threaten him; the look was flat. Tirell stood returning that gaze, his head up and his lips drawn back in fear or disgust. I thought surely he would move away. Instead, swaying, step by slow step, he walked toward that fell black thing, as if against his will, as if drawn. I willed myself to jump up and save him from that unseen tug, but still I did not move! Then I saw there was no immediate danger. As he approached it, the black beast inclined its dagger horn, sheathed it in earth, a gesture of peace. All the time it kept fixed on him its white-rimmed gaze. Tirell reached it, sank down beside it, and laid his head wearily against its arched and muscular neck.

'Great Eala!' I blurted out loud, startled fully awake at last.

Tirell paid no attention to me; perhaps he had not heard me. His grimace was gone, and I think he sighed. He sat beside the beast through daybreak into sunrise, stroking its neck and sleek black body, even patting its bony head, scratching around its ears and daggerlike horn. That weapon was raised now, but Tirell seemed to have forgotten fear of it. He stroked the folded wings . . .

His head snapped up. 'Frain!' he called to me in peremptory command. 'Come here!'

I got up and went at once, automatically, like a well-trained servant. But as I neared the beast reluctance slowed me. Tirell beckoned impatiently. He patted the beast again, then took the left wing in both hands and spread it like the wing of a captive bird. His voice came oddly gentle out of his hard white face. 'The creature is crippled,' he said. 'I Look.'

At the curve of the wing was a great knot where the bone had snapped and crookedly healed. It was easy to see, once I had dared to look, that the wing was useless, except perhaps for frightening peasants and fledgling princes.

'He can never fly on that,' said Tirell in tones of pity.

I stared at the beast, jealous that my brother had turned to the animal for comfort when he would not turn to me, angry at myself for feeling that way. 'Come closer,' Tirell urged. 'Touch it.' But I still loathed the beast.

'No, thank you,' I retorted, even more sharply than I had expected. 'You pat the outlandish thing. Stay there all day if you like.'

Tirell's face went stony, and he dropped the wing. 'I don't have all day. Come on.' He rose and went to his horse.

'Why, where do you expect to go?' I cried, still angry. 'Will Grandfather tumble Melior for you as he did the Wall?'

He returned no answer, only glared and started away. He set a hard pace that morning, and I stubbornly drove my white to stay close to his heels. Down and down we travelled, down to the lowest slopes of Acheron. By midday we could glimpse the breached Wall through the thinning stand of trees. And there, still within the sheltering wood, we had to halt. An army confronted us!

Facing the forest with the stones of the ruin at their backs stood archers and men-at-arms and the Boda themselves in their scarlet tunics, all ranked three deep and stiffly alert. Beyond them, within their line, I could see tents and chariots and horses and strutting warriors, all the signs of a good-sized encampment. Tirell and I left our horses, crept to the last cover, and gaped.

'But our kingly father must be afraid!' I exclaimed. 'Is it you he dreads? Or is it these whispering trees?'

Tirell smiled grimly and gave no reply, staring with

narrowed, glittering eyes toward Melior. I continued to survey the soldiers. Some men moved, and beyond them I saw something that bent me like an unexpected buffet.

'Look,' I said. 'Grandfather's hut. It's all destroyed.'

The place was shattered like the Wall. Tirell gave no sign of having heard me. But the beast bounded past us and leaped into the open space beyond the sheltering forest, screaming defiance and hatred at Abas's army. Its voice was hoarse and gibbering and wailing all at once, like that of a man whose tongue is taken away; it was an ugly, hurtful sound. I was frozen by that cry, and for their part the warriors only stood and shuddered. They stared stupidly at widespread beating wings, rearing underbelly, and hooves and daggerlike horn. I think every man of them would have run if it had not been for the restraint of their own ranks pressed around them. Moments passed before they remembered their weapons. One by one they reached for their bows, and arrows started to fly.

I did not move, for Tirell and I were well out of bowshot. But Tirell gasped and ran to his horse. 'Away, quickly!' he shouted at me. 'The beast will follow. Come, before he is killed!'

'Why, we would be well rid of it!' I exclaimed in exasperation. But Tirell had already shot away to the south. I galloped after him, muttering, sure that our noise would bring the whole army onto our heels. Tirell slowed down once we cleared the Wall. We cantered along between the forest of Acheron and the westernmost curve of the river Chardri, which edged ever nearer to us. We glanced behind us constantly, but neither the beast nor the Boda did we see.

By dusk we were riding along the ridge of a high riverbank. We had never thought of crossing the Chardri; no one would have thought of it, not in Vale. Ages past, folk said, when the land was young, Chardri the bard sang to Adalis where she sat on her high throne at Ogygia. She listened to him often, for he sang superlatively well. But soon her favour made him overbold; he spoke to her of love, and she granted him his pleasure as a punishment. Lying on her, he became the river that runs and sings forever from her headlands to her womb.

All the folk in Vale feared him for his godlike anger. Swans dared to light on his back, but no man would willingly touch him. Still, I felt a stirring of some new feeling, an odd sense that he would not hurt me, that I could approach him as an equal. . . . I shook my head at my own temerity. No need to put it to the test. The horses could not have made the bank.

The forest was edging at us from the other side, and presently our way was blocked by our familiar acquaintances, the stooping, twisted trees. We rode into them. But the insidious things seemed to join hands against us. Beneath the shadow of that particular portion of wood was such a tangle as I had never seen. Roots bulged up and branches groped down and fallen boughs crisscrossed the spaces between. Rocks lumped out of the gloomy loam without pattern, like pebbles scattered by a gigantic child. Here and there lay huge fallen trees, each one a barrier. Between stood patches of brambles thicker than hedges. We had gone scarcely a furlong into this muddle when Tirell was forced to stop, cursing under his breath.

'What now?' I asked. 'We are trapped here for the Boda to find. The river confines us on the eastern side, the mountains and this accursed forest —'

'It is nearly dark anyway,' grumbled Tirell, interrupting. 'We may as well stay here.'

'But what if the Boda come?' I persisted. 'They must have heard us crashing off, and they will be after us. We had better try to find a way around.'

'There is no way around,' said Tirell flatly. 'Go get us some water.'

'But where?' He could not be expecting me to find a well in the middle of Acheron forest.

'The river, of course! Go on.' He turned away, dismissing me, as I stared. Had he heard me thinking? All right, I was not really afraid, but I was insulted. Only slaves were sent for river water. I fought my way out of the tangle, seething. There was no talking to him anymore. . . . I slid down the steep bank to the river, careless of my clothing. The more dirt and tatters, the better. They would speak, and I would be silent. I filled a skin bag with water and clawed my way back up, shredding grass and digging my fingers into the dirt. My anger forced me to make the climb; I would not be reduced to calling for help. When I reached the top, I saw a spark of flame in the thicket. Tirell had started a fire. My temper snapped at that.

'Are you insane?' I shouted. 'Must you light the Boda a way to find us?'

'How can the beast find us in this tangle without a light?' Tirell retorted. 'And yes, I am insane!'

I said no more. The stark finality of that last statement chilled me. I sat by the fire, but I felt lonely and cold despite the flames. So he thought more of the accursed beast than of me! I ate the last of our food, not even offering to share, and then I got up and stalked away from the fire, making a show of standing guard. But no pursuers came. Instead, toward morning, the beast came, a darker shadow in the darkness of the forest until it stumbled into the firelight. It was carrying half a dozen broken, feathered shafts, and blood lay in sticky puddles on its black flanks.

'Fetch more water!' Tirell called to me. 'Hurry!'

I went as quickly as I could. All my anger had vanished at the panic in his voice, though I could not understand his concern. Still, to help a hurt thing was worthy of him. . . . I scrambled up the bank, gritting my teeth. When I reached the camp Tirell was pulling out the arrows, one by one, and tightly binding the wounds with strips cut from his royal cloak. The beast stood numbly accepting his care, its head nodding to its knees. In a moment it bent its knees and sank to the ground with a groan. It lay stretched there with closed eyes, unheeding, as Tirell pulled the last arrow from its shoulder and pressed on the place with both hands.

The other wounds, in neck and legs and belly, lay quiet beneath their wrappings, but this one spurted blood. Tirell stemmed it with wads of cloth, but the blood welled up beneath his hands and trickled through his fingers.

'Eala, he'll die!' muttered Tirell frantically.

I stood awkwardly by. It was usual for Tirell to be extravagant over trifles, but I sensed this was no trifle to him. I wanted to help him, but I did not know what to do or what to say to him.

'Come here!' he shouted.

I jumped. 'Me?'

'Who else?' he snapped. 'Put your hands here. Here, here, hurry! If I have no power of healing, perhaps you do.'

I pressed on the wound as I was bid, puzzling. 'Why should I?' I had forgotten my loathing of the beast.

'Come on, just try!' Tirell gestured impatiently. 'Say a charm, such as smiths and tinkers say!'

'I don't know any!'

Tirell grabbed at his head as if it might fly off. 'Just say something!' he cried, but then he looked and came to attention.

'Never mind,' he said quietly. 'The bleeding has stopped.'

I eased the cloth away. It was true; the blood no longer flowed. Probably it had been just ready to stop when I came. The wound lay like an angry red mouth, a tongue of clotted red between its lips.

'Touch the other wounds,' said Tirell.

'What in the world for?'

'Just do it, would you?' he said tiredly. He started binding the shoulder wound. He had to pass the strips of cloth under the neck. The beast scarcely moved for his gentle prodding.

I touched each of the wounds, reluctantly, with my fingertips. Then I got the water and tried to pour some into the beast's mouth. It did not gulp or stir. 'What makes you think I am a healer?' I asked Tirell bitterly.

'You would do better with metal,' a voice said behind us. We both leaped around, grabbing for our swords. But it was no enemy that faced us. 'Grandfather!' I cried, and embraced him.

Daymon Cein stood by the fire, leaning on his staff to peer at us. I wondered how far he had walked to come to us. Perhaps the whole distance from the Wall. 'So,' he said, 'you are going to Vaire.'

'Are we?' I asked.

'To be sure,' growled Tirell. 'What else lies west and south?'

'But why?' I stared at him.

'For help, what else?' He glared up at me from his place by the prone beast. 'Do you think I can take Melior single-handed? But no matter.' He turned back to the wounded monster, stroking its angular head. 'I'll not budge without this beast.'

'There's no budging anyway, in this beastly forest,' I complained.

'And the Boda will be on you in an hour or so, with the dawn,' said Grandfather serenely. 'I'm glad you're keeping a good watch out. I'll sit by your fire. Thank you for the offer.' He let himself creakily down and rubbed his old hands over the small blaze.

'Grandfather, how are you?' I questioned anxiously. I knew by then that Abas was angry at him. 'What will you do, now that they have driven you from your home? Is Mother all right?'

'Leaping panthers, lad, we are fine!' he said emphatically. 'Have a care for yourself! Are you going to sit here and wait for the Boda?'

I shrugged helplessly. Tirell moved grudgingly to join us. 'With deference and apologies to your old bones,' he told Grandfather sourly, 'I dare say it would be well to put out the fire.'

'A bit late for that, don't you think?' Grandfather kept his place, looking cross.

'We could hack our way through this mess of a forest on foot, leaving the horses,' Tirell muttered, as much to himself as to us. 'But I can't leave the beast.'

'I told you, Frain would do better with metal,' Daymon snapped. 'Iron is best. Grasp a knife blade or something, lad, and have a go at it again.'

I gaped at the old man in bewilderment. His grey eyes met mine steadily, and with unreasoning trust I became willing to try. I drew my iron dagger, the one Shamarra had given me, and held the blade lightly between my curled fingers, sheathing it with my own flesh, so that it could hurt no one except myself. I went and knelt beside the beast, the hurt and crippled thing. . . . Something warm moved in me, nudging me, so that I suddenly felt quite certain what to do. I touched each wound, then ran my curled hand over the beast from nose to tail and from flank to flank, feeling the warm force join us like brothers. I stood back and raised the dagger. Power shot through me and out, a white-hot, searing, tearing power that made me cry aloud and left me staggering. I lowered my arm.

The beast got to its feet. It stood shakily at first, with

drooping horn, but then it raised its head and stood firm. In the faint light of fire and early dawn it arched its neck, lifted its wings, stamped and pawed the earth amidst the tangled forest.

'Tirell!' I exclaimed, still shaking. 'Your shield!'

'What!' He crouched and looked about him for an enemy.

'Your shield! Look at your shield, then look before you! This is the place on your shield! It is the same entanglement!'

'Then he has been here before,' Tirell murmured.

He stepped up to the beast and cradled its head in his arms, holding it with his hands below its eyes, so that its dark, pointed horn passed scarcely an inch from his head. I could hardly bear to look. They gazed at each other for a minute or more, and I could feel an understanding grow between them; risk was part of it. Finally Tirell let go his grasp and turned back to us.

'The beast will lead us,' he said.

It started off at once, veering away from the river. Tirell and I scrambled to gather our gear and get our horses. Grandfather rose stiffly to his feet. 'I had better be getting on,' he remarked. 'Farewell, you two.'

'Has the King tried to harm you?' I asked worriedly.

'Harm me!' He snorted. 'I'd like to see him try! Harm me!' He extended a hand, and our little fire winked out as if it had never been. In the dim interstices of the forest I could hear him chuckling. 'Do you want me to put it back again?' he called to Tirell.

But Tirell mounted his horse and rode off without word or notice. I faced my grandfather a moment longer, and suddenly there were tears on my cheeks, childish tears of hurt and despair.

'Grandfather, come with us,' I whispered. 'We need you. He is a very son of Abas. To him I am only the burr that clings to his horse's tail. He is as mad as any Sacred King since the line began.'

'Frain, you know I am too old to ride,' Daymon replied gently. 'Do your best for him, as you always have. He needs you far worse than he knows. Someday you will be able to measure the love beneath his anger. But for now, will you

59

take my word that quite surely love is there?'

I could not speak or touch him, or I would have sobbed. 'Thank you, Grandfather,' I murmured at last, and mounted my white mare and hastened after Tirell.

6

The beast was leading back the way we had come. Tirell followed it willingly. I tore through the brambles to catch them, too tired and confused to realize what we would meet when we came to the edge of the forest.

It was the Boda, of course, with their scarlet tunics and their bronze helms and their curved, slicing swords. They were camped at the river bend, and they sighted us as soon as we cleared the trees. A dozen of them vaulted onto their horses and clattered toward us with a shout.

Tirell sat still on his horse, watching, with sword and shield at the ready. I galloped up beside him and came to a disorderly halt, hurriedly arming myself. The beast was nosing about, looking for a passageway into the intertwining wall of the forest. For a moment it stopped its searching and snorted at the approaching riders. Tirell glared, and it went back to its prodding, snorted again, and disappeared into the forest.

Before we could follow, the Boda were upon us. We set our horses' haunches between the trees and met them. I was exhausted, utterly spent, but I had not yet realized it. Because my heart was thumping and my head felt light, I believed I was a coward. The attackers swam in front of my eyes and nothing seemed real; I had never fought for blood before. My training saved me. My sword moved in the ways it had been taught as I watched it, bemused. The Boda came at us three or four on one, but a long straight sword was enough to hold them off. Their scimitars are ugly things, good for lopping heads off peasants and footmen, but they have no reach.

'Whoreson cowards!' Tirell shouted.

I killed one man while I parried another with my shield.

Then somebody cut me on the head. I swung my sword in a wide arc, and the Boda moved back. They were fighting cautiously, methodically, from which I guessed that they had been told to bring us back alive. But Tirell was raging.

He had never fought well or correctly. He did not have discipline for that. But his reckless rage struck fear even into me, and his long iron sword bit through bronze armour as if it were so much cheese. Three men lay dead to his account—I could see that through the haze before my eyes—and there was blood on many more. But I was failing, swaying on my horse's back, still not understanding why. I tried to swing my sword and found I scarcely had strength to lift it. Then I had to let it drag as I clung to my horse's neck. I would not close my eyes, blur though they might; I was fighting for consciousness. I felt the hands of the Boda dragging at me—.

Then Tirell was there. Tirell was everywhere, charging and lunging and shouting. The Boda scattered before him. He stopped beside me, still swinging that great bloody sword, and the Boda, the six or seven of them that were left, clustered at a little distance, conferring among themselves. I raised my head with an effort, desperately shaking it to clear it, but blood got in my eyes.

'Go on!' Tirell roared, and gave my horse a whack. The black beast was peering out of the forest, waiting for us. The passageway it had found was veiled by a light curtain of spring-green leaves. My mare bolted through, and Tirell followed.

'They'll be after us,' I mumbled, wrestling with my sword.

'Put it away before you hurt yourself,' Tirell said.

I did not put it away. Already I heard hoofbeats. But in a moment a sort of rustle shook the forest, and then trees cracked and fell with a thud across the passageway behind us. The whole forest wall collapsed into ruins, putting up a barrier that no man could penetrate. Grandfather's doing, of course; I silently thanked him. The crash sent our horses lunging forward, and I felt so weak and sick that I barely kept my seat. I had to drop my sword and grab for my horse's mane while I hauled it to a stop. Then I clung there, swaying. Tirell picked up the sword and brought it to me, slipped it into the scabbard himself, without a word. I think he was panting from his exertions, and for my own part I could not speak for faintness. Still, in an odd way, I felt very happy. Tirell had helped me, rescued me from capture. He could no longer pretend complete indifference to me.

'Come on,' he said roughly, and we rode into the forest. The angry shouts of the Boda faded away behind us.

The black beast led us a crooked path that day, around rocks and roots and fallen logs and impassable entanglements. The forest clung to us at every step, its boughs groping for us. The way was so narrow that sometimes we had to get down and lead the horses afoot. When he could not stand our crawling progress, Tirell would draw his sword and slash away at the branches that imprisoned us; the wood seemed to shrink back from the blade. Most of the time I lay on my horse's neck, not caring where we were, nearly in a swoon from the cut on my head and from some malady I could not identify. As the day wore on, I lost all sense of time or direction. When the gloom beneath the trees grew even darker, I thought it was my eyes that had failed me. But Tirell's muted cursing informed me that it was nightfall.

'And what the bloody flood am I to do with you?' he muttered.

I did not understand, but rode along stupidly as we followed the beast through the darkness. I believe I fell asleep on my horse until I felt it come to a stop. 'Hah!' said Tirell. 'A light!'

I sat up groggily and saw a small, steady glow in the distance. Tirell had been leading my horse as well as his own, I discovered. He stood as still as the trees, frowning at the tiny speck far ahead of us. The beast looked around, awaiting his decision.

'You need food and water,' he grumbled at me, 'and we have neither. Confound it.' He gave the reins a jerk, and we went on. Presently the forest gave way to a clearing that seemed to have been punched out of the latticework of trees, a clearing in the shape of a shield. Its upper end was bounded by a towering cliff that looked down on dark water. A sort of pool wandered out of a low cave in its roots and filled an oval

63

basin. Small lights flickered in the water—or was it the white reflections of the black lotus blossoms that clung at the edge? By the pool sat Shamarra, holding a piece of white light that looked like a caught star. It lit her fair face. I straightened on my horse when I saw her, though a moment before I would have said that I could not muster the strength.

'How did you come here?' Tirell asked her curtly.

'Through the watery ways.' Shamarra glanced up at him archly.

I managed to speak; I wanted her to look at me as well. 'Lady, are you queen of this place also?'

'One of me is.' She spoke kindly, as if she thought me a nice, polite child. 'Come here, Frain, and drink my water. You'll find it nourishes you.' She rose from her seat on mossy stones and beckoned us toward the basin.

'Drink that?' I heard Tirell protest. 'It's full of—' But I didn't care what Tirell said. I stumbled down and drank deeply. The water satisfied me as if it were food. I was not surprised, for I was coming to expect all manner of marvels. Tirell drank, grudgingly, then led the horses over. The black beast drank and lay down quietly by the cliff. I flopped down in like wise, without a thought, utterly weary. Tirell sat and faced Shamarra.

'You have lured me here,' he said to her in a low voice. Listening hazily from a place somewhere between sleep and waking, I found it hard to gauge the anger in his voice. Anger seemed fixed and ever present in him those days anyway. It did not matter, I thought drowsily. He had saved me. Tirell my brother the prince was faultless even in anger. . . .

'No, I have only met you here,' Shamarra answered courteously. 'You came of your own device, and very prettily, I must say. Moreover, it is your destiny as a Sacred King, a very heir of Aftalun, to roam in dark and tangled ways. You carry that destiny with you wherever you go.'

'The shield? But it was you who chose it and gave it to me. What is this game you are playing with me, lady? Why come to meet me here, as you will have it?'

'A whim to see you again,' Shamarra said, sounding amused.

'A whim?' Tirell laughed, sounding not amused at all. 'A powerful whim, that takes you under the roots of a mountain along with the swimming dead. . . . That way can be neither short nor easy, whatever you say.'

'It is not a hard journey,' she said lightly, 'to anyone with my powers.'

'Powers? But I know nothing of them. To me you are only what you appear to be, a lass and a liar. Why are you here?'

I jerked out of my drowse at his discourtesy. That he should have called her a liar! But the lady answered him coolly enough. 'I wish to ride with you awhile.'

'Ride with me!' Tirell laughed again, the harsh laugh I did not like. 'Why? And on what?'

'I can ride the beast, if I must,' the lady remarked quietly. 'But I would rather sit behind you, on your horse.'

'You lie again. No one can ride the beast,' Tirell said flatly. 'And there's no room on my horse for you.'

'Tirell!' I struggled to my elbows, full of protest at his rudeness. But even the lady ignored me.

'You do not own the beast,' she told Tirell. 'It serves you freely.'

'Very true. And we do not want your company, or any other.'

'She will ride with me, then!' I shouted, on my feet at last. 'And I ride with you whether you wish it or not!'

Tirell did not bother to rise and face me. 'The youngster fancies you better than I do,' he told Shamarra. I could not bear his insolence to her.

'She is a lady, and therefore a goddess, and she has done you all good and no harm!' I cried. 'How can you so churlishly refuse her?'

'Goddess, lady, wench, or maid, she is but an ash pit to me,' Tirell said. 'You rut with her, if you like.' His face was masklike, unreadable, as foreign to me as a face in a nightmare.

'By Adalis, if you were anyone except my brother,' I whispered, 'I would kill you for that.' I was raging, but as feeble as a child, an infant. My hands felt at the air for support. The night blackened around me.

'Frain, lie down before you fall down.' It was Shamarra's calm voice. 'That healing you did this morning has sapped your strength; you will be weak for a few days yet. Lie down and think no more of anger. We will stay here through tomorrow at least, for the beast also must rest.'

'I will say how long we stay,' Tirell snapped.

'Try to find the way without me,' she challenged him.

'The beast will take us out.'

'Even the beast cannot find a way if the trees will not let you pass. And the trees are mine to command. The beast only solved the riddle they set.'

'Then you admit you lured me here!' Tirell roared. 'To your creeping pool of spook lights—' He sounded like Abas.

Their voices faded away from my hearing after a while. I lay on the ground, unnoticed, with a spinning head, and if I had not been too proud, I think I would have wept. Tirell's locked eyes struck me to the core. Though I had said he was mad, I believe I had not really comprehended his madness until then. His stony despair would not quickly pass.

'So the beast has left Abas to come to you!' Shamarra mused. 'Have you thought, Prince, how ardently he must search for you both? He needs you and hates you, as he needs and hates the beast—but his eye flinches away from Acheron.'

An odd thing happened as I lay choking on tears. The black beast got up from its place, came over, and lay by my side.

I felt somewhat better when I awoke in the morning, and I decided to set things to rights in any way I could. But Tirell sat in sullen indifference beside the black beast, and Shamarra sat in graceful relaxation beside her oval pool, and I could get no talk from either of them. I fed on water—a peculiar pool, that, with no outlet to be seen; it must have been another eye of the flood beneath. Then I groomed the horses, cleaned my sword, and rubbed my shield and my hacked helm. Finally, in a kind of desperate boredom, I began to groom the black beast.

I brushed at its sleek neck and picked the brambles from its mane. My loathing of the creature had entirely disappeared. I don't think I could hate the thing I had healed, or perhaps I could not heal a thing I hated. Now I regarded it as a fellow, a curious sort of horse or perhaps a very queer bird. If it had stepped on me, or tossed its head and hurt me, I don't think I would have found any malice in the act.

I was combing the forelock with my fingers when Tirell spoke. 'Do you think you could heal that wing?'

This was a fairer speech from Tirell than grunts and glares. I gave thought to my answer.

'I know nothing at all about healing, brother,' I said finally, 'except what little I learned yesterday. I would never have guessed it was in me. What made you think I was a healer, Tirell?'

'Anyone with eyes can see it in you!' Tirell replied, a bit crossly. 'There is healing in your every movement and glance. Since you were born, you have been healing me.'

'Then that is why you turn from me now!' I said quietly, with sudden insight. 'Because you wish to bleed yet a while.'

He stiffened and gave no reply. I continued silently with the beast. I ran my hands softly over its sturdy flanks; all the wounds were dry and mending well. I touched the big lump of crooked bone in the wing, held my hand on it tenderly, but no power nudged within me; I only felt tired.

'You and Mother and Grandfather all have gifts of vision,' I said after a while. 'And also our fa—And also the King, and he seems to have power over people as well. . . . But I had never felt power of any kind in me until yesterday, and maybe that was a fluke. Where is there healing in our family?'

Tirell said nothing, but Shamarra's lovely, liquid voice sounded unexpectedly; I felt blessed just to hear her. 'It is true that a gift of healing seems to run in families,' she said. 'Smiths and metalworkers especially tend to have an aptness for healing that makes them highly honoured among common folk and royalty alike.'

Tirell glared fiercely at her, but she continued unabashed. 'However, many folk feel that this propensity is due more to their familiarity with metal than to their parentage. Metal, you know, is a marvellous and magical substance, brother to fire in value and peril. Those who know metal deeply know much that is hidden from the rest.'

'I know nothing at all about metal,' I sighed.

'Indeed, knowledge is the key,' Shamarra remarked silkily. 'Your grandfather the seer Daymon Cein knows many things deeply, and consider: Is not his knowledge power and healing in itself? All of those who sleep under the Stone of Eala carry hidden in them the seeds of healing, for they know the stone that is dragon's tooth and Eala's bone, and metal is the marrow of the bone of earth.'

'I am not one who has slept under the stone.'

'Grandfather is,' said Tirell sharply, 'and our mother carries the seed to us. Haven't you heard her trying to tell you?'

'I don't know—' I hedged.

'That is right,' Shamarra broke in smoothly. 'And until you do know, you will not be able to heal that wing. Knowledge is the key. Truth, if you will.'

I stared at her—stupidly, I am afraid. 'What truth?'

She looked me full in the face for the first time that day and smiled a smile that did not comfort me. 'The truth about yourself,' she said.

I asked nothing more. I had had talk enough. I kept silence till dark.

The next day, with his face still hard and flat as a slab of Eala's rock, Tirell mounted the black and rode away. I sprang onto the white. Shamarra watched us both with a look as blank as Tirell's.

'Come on,' I said, offering to help her up behind me. But she shook her head.

'I'll walk.' Her delicate, pale face reminded me of a sculpture in ice.

'You are too proud!' I urged her earnestly. 'Come, share my mount, though I may be unworthy of the honour.' But she scarcely looked at me, and I knew that she had shut off the sound of my voice from her ears. I was on fire with love and anger and pity all at once. I loved her ardently, as I had loved her from the first—even though, I suppose, I scarcely knew her.

I urged my horse after Tirell, since there was nothing else I could do. He was another whom I loved and who would not accept my help. He rode with heart locked on pain like a dungeon gate. The black beast led him. I followed, and Shamarra walked barefoot, straight and proud, in the rear, a shimmering vision within the gloomy, tangling forest.

We all walked more than rode that day anyway. The beast took us under dark arbors of interlacing boughs, through twisting passages between boulders and bulging roots, around standing boles wider than a chariot and over fallen branches half waist high. The weird trees of Acheron seemed to have gone as wild and extravagant as Tirell. We picked and fought our way slowly along. By nightfall we had found no clearing. We slept uncomfortably in niches between rocks and roots, and hunger began to gnaw at us. We had seen, or at least I had seen, no living creatures besides ourselves all day. Not even birds seemed to live in the giant snare we moved through.

We came out of it, praise be, the next morning, before noon. I blinked in strong springtime light, staring as if I had never seen Vale before, although the scene was common-place enough. To our left the river Chardri curved away toward Vaire. To our right the tall, dark peaks of Acheron marched away toward the southern sky. Meadowland sloped between. Knobby trees still fringed the mountains, but compared to the snarl we had just left they seemed almost friendly, stooping to peer at us. 'Hello, old women!' I cried delightedly.

'Hush,' Tirell growled. 'There may be foes about.' The black beast lifted its head, questing.

'Not the Boda, or at least not those you left,' stated Shamarra. 'Who do you think shut the forest against them?' So perhaps it had not been Grandfather.

The beast snorted and leaped from a stand into a gallop. Rabbits were feeding near the river. Almost before the little creatures could move the beast ran them down, stuck one with its horn and flung it overhead with fierce abandon. It speared yet another before they could scatter to their holes. I sat watching, sickened; but why? I had often seen game taken. A few more coneys lay stunned by black hooves. Tirell rode over and slit their throats. 'Supper,' he said morosely.

I got down to help him, still shuddering. There had been more to this scene than the gathering of food. Blood of the victims trickled over the beast's forehead between its white-rimmed eyes. I wiped it off. Odd, but the monstrous creature was a comrade and an ally. I knew that even then. It rubbed its nose against me, and even in my horror I could not refuse the caress.

We built a fire on the spot, cooked and ate, and left in mid afternoon, carrying the surplus meat with us. Once again I invited Shamarra to ride behind me on my mount.

'I will walk,' she said as before.

'I must ride after my brother,' I told her angrily. 'That is my first duty. But you cause me dishonour, lady, by your stubbornness. It is unseemly for me to ride away and leave you afoot.'

She glanced at me haughtily. 'There is no one to see.'

'There are always eyes to see,' I retorted, though I could not have said what eyes. The lady raised her curving brows at me.

'By Vieyra,' she remarked, 'you are not entirely a fool. So since there is even that much truth in you, I will ride with you—for the time.'

The black beast watched curiously as she took her place. Then we cantered down the slope after Tirell.

7

We travelled thus for several days, with Tirell on the black in the lead, the lady and myself following on the white, and the black beast roaming as it pleased, but seldom far away. Tirell kept to the foothills of Acheron, skirting the borderlands of Vaire. Though the meadowland through which we rode looked lush and fertile, we did not see a dwelling or a human soul. Honeycomb fungi sprang up everywhere in the springtime dampness. We gathered them to eat with our cold meat.

'Why does no one come here?' I asked Shamarra. I attempted every day to converse with her, hoping to improve her opinion of me, though usually she answered with merest courtesy.

'Men fear Acheron,' she replied briefly this time.

'But why, lady?' I persisted. 'You'll think me a fool, but I have been to Acheron—part of it—and I have seen much that is fair, and not too much to fear.'

She was amused, and flattered perhaps, and replied kindly enough. 'You are young,' she said, 'too young to really believe in death, and the Luoni mean nothing to you.'

'Is it my youth that has protected me, lady, or your goodness on my behalf? Surely you are the one that I must thank, that I am not a sleeper amidst grey moss. I heard the trees whispering, that first night.'

Shamarra laughed her laugh that was like rippling water. I think she was perhaps even a trifle impressed! 'One of me you may thank,' she said. 'Only one.'

I could not reply to that, but I was delighted at any speech from her, even riddling speech. 'And Tirell,' I went on, emboldened. 'Is he also one who is too young to fear Acheron?'

'No,' she answered, slowly and seriously. 'Though it is true that he does not fear death, not at this time.'

'He is very brave,' I agreed.

'Courage is the least of it,' Shamarra retorted sourly, and she would talk no more that day.

After perhaps a week of riding I began to notice wisps of smoke on the far horizon of Vaire, and now and then a distant rooftop. I took to skulking around the isolated homesteads at night in search of food, with a bit of spook-fire Shamarra had loaned me for light. Nobody was likely to come near that eerie glow. I carried it in my hand like a bit of fluff; it had no weight, or substance, or even feel to it, and I still don't know where she got it. The stuff gave me just enough light to steal eggs from the hens' nests. I would pull garden greens, also, and once I took a loaf of bread out of a kitchen window. Quite a comedown for a prince of Melior, but I had no choice. Even if we could have traded torques for victuals, we did not dare to be seen by daylight.

We had come far from the true Acheron, nearly into the Lorc Tutosel, what the southern people call the mountains of the night bird. After almost a fortnight of riding, I realized one day that the white mare was going lame. Her gait roughened, and we were forced to get on more slowly. I had always, since the start of this journey, kept close behind Tirell because of an unspoken fear that he would heedlessly leave me—he seemed so cold and uncaring. I had never dared to stop unless he did. But as the white mare ambled on more and more reluctantly, I made a happy discovery: the black beast would circle back to check on us, and Tirell, perforce, had to wait as well. He would never leave the beast.

I fervently hoped that Tirell would not comprehend the problem. He always rode with his back to me, seeming to notice nothing, hear nothing, and see nothing except whatever vision of vengeance floated before his mask of a face and his glittering blue eyes. Perhaps he could even remain oblivious to our slowness. But I should have known better. When we camped that evening he glanced once at the white mare, went to her, and felt her legs. He cradled her big head in his arms for a moment and studied her fine dark eyes as if he were speaking to her. Then he rounded on me.

'She is lame,' he said flatly, 'and sore in her back, too. That is what has come of your hauling that wench along.'

'You would do well to speak better of the lady,' I flared, 'and not risk her wrath! Has it occurred to you that she could destroy you? Is she not a goddess and a form of Adalis?' But Tirell laughed harshly, the chilly laugh that made me flinch.

'She is welcome to my person for destruction!' he laughed. 'Nothing else.' He turned and thrust his hard white face at Shamarra. 'Nothing else,' he repeated. It was as if he had spit on her.

Shamarra stood in all her silken beauty, pale golden hair and shimmering gown, moving only with the breeze and her own breath. She was not stony like Tirell, but just as impervious in her own way. If she had winced, if her eyes had widened as if hurt, I would have struck Tirell, and maybe Morrghu knows what might have happened then. But she looked through him, and in a moment he turned away and went back to the white mare, stroking her back and droning to himself. Presently the droning formed into a singsong tune.

'Hey, nonny nay,
My white horse is grey!
My grey is a black
If you look the right way.
My black is a beast,
My bird's gone astray,
And that's why I say,
Hey, nonny neigh!

Hey, nonny neigh!
My white horse is grey.
We'll all turn to ducks
At the end of a day
And swim in the Chardri,
And that's why I say,
No sense to this play!
Hey, nonny nay.'

73

'Mad!' I muttered.

We ate supper in watchful silence. Afterward, Tirell spoke to me in a tone I could not decipher.

'Tomorrow, you take the black and go on into Vaire. I will stay here.'

'Perhaps I could heal the white,' I mumbled. It was Tirell's stubbornness that had caused the situation, but as always, he somehow made me feel that it was all my fault.

'Whatever you like,' he replied with no emotion at all on his lean, handsome face. 'But I will not go any farther into Vaire, horse or no horse, until I have the protection of its king. I do not wish to be slain by the henchmen of my beloved father before I have had my chance at him. You can go. The Boda won't bother with you.'

I sat up straight in insulted protest. 'They probably have their orders to kill me and bring you back alive!'

'Well, maybe they won't kill you until you have led them to me,' Tirell remarked indifferently. 'Anyway, for every reason you are the one who must continue into Vaire.'

I stared at him, astonished, but mostly at myself. His madness must have spread to me; why was I not aghast—I, the prudent one? The proposal was insane. How could I leave him, how could I even know he would be waiting when I got back? If I got back. Yet, in spite of reason, in spite of prudence, I felt recklessly willing to try the venture, as if death could not touch me. . . . I shook my head in bewilderment at my own daring.

'Very well,' I assented. 'I will go. What exactly is it that I am to do in Vaire?'

Tirell looked back at me with a hint of impatience tugging at the mask of his face. 'Go to the castle at KyNule to see Fabron. Tell him we will need help to take Melior, and have him send retainers. Better yet, have him come here himself.'

I almost sputtered at that. Such arrogance! 'Why,' I asked sharply, 'should he wish to help you at all?'

Tirell replied with a smile I did not expect, a wry, mocking smile. 'Oh, he will wish. You will see.'

I said no more. I spent most of the evening struggling

with the fastenings of my torque, and at length I got the golden thing off. I would be no prince when I rode across the heartland of Vaire.

The next morning I was up with the dawn, folding my blanket to put it on the black steed. Tirell and Shamarra silently prepared to move their camp deeper into the forest. They would keep to the shelter of the trees, in the foothills of southern Acheron, until I returned. I hated to leave them. My mind could not accept this notion of leaving my brother. But mind seemed to have been taken over by some sort of fearless folly, and I could not hold back. I did not even think of asking Shamarra to go with me. We all three assumed she would stay with Tirell. There was no secret as to where her preference lay. It gave me some comfort that Tirell would have her with him, since I believed she had some power to protect him; yet her indifference galled me even worse than my brother's.

Tirell did not wish me good-bye. I went to give him the kiss of leave-taking and he brushed me away as if I were a gnat. Shamarra condescended to follow me to where the black horse stood waiting. 'Food,' she said, and handed me the last of our meager supplies.

'What will you eat?' I asked.

She shrugged. 'There are rabbits and berries about.'

'You'll have no help from Tirell,' I warned her, peering toward where my brother sat among the trees and looked with hard, locked eyes at something only he could see.

She seemed amused at my concern. 'I'll have help enough,' she replied with a hint of a smile. Help of weird trees, perhaps? I did not ask.

'Good,' I said slowly. 'I can go more easily, knowing that you will have a care for him, my lady. But tell me, why do you cleave to him?'

'Would you have me do otherwise?' she parried.

I answered her with honesty that I think neither of us expected. 'I would have you feel my love,' I told her softly. 'I follow my brother, whom I have loved since I was born. But why do you? Surely you owe him nothing, and he scorns you.'

'He is kingly in his grief,' she said angrily. 'He will be Sacred King when he is well.'

'He is mad,' I said.

'There is divine vision and compassion even in his madness!'

'He has shown you no compassion, and little enough to me.'

'Why should he?' she cried passionately. 'You are nothing but a pup next to him!' She turned away, and I rode into Vaire with her words burning like hot iron in my mind.

Book Two

Fabron of Vaire

1

I am Fabron. I was king of the canton of Vaire in Vale when I was alive. I came to my throne by virtue of threats and greed, but I tried to be a good king. I wanted to be well remembered. I rode the rounds of my canton yearly, hearing my people's concerns, and when I was in my castle at Ky-Nule I held court daily. Any of my subjects, rich or poor, could come before me if they wished and dared. I tried to be just, but pettiness angered me, and I think my people respected my anger. Everywhere I went they cheered me. I tried to give them a procession worth shouting for, though I was not a young man or a handsome one. I was short, half hidden by my beard, but I rode tall, and every horse and retainer of my entourage wore ornaments of my own making, most of them gold. For myself I wore a breastplate all in link of iron chain, and a chain belt to my sword, and the staghound, the emblem of Vaire, leaping on my helm. I dressed in sober velvets to set off my artistry. Jewels and brooches show better thus.

But it was not in such array that Frain first saw me. Spring had come and was turning into summer, but I was not holding court or preparing to ride through my domain. Mela, my wife of many years, lay ill with a wasting fever, and I stayed constantly in her chamber, seeing no one. She did not know me. Indeed she had turned dead to me many years before, after we had sold Frain. Not that she was cold or disobedient—she was ever an obedient wife—but something had died inside her. I did not understand; I thought we would have many babies, and what matter was one the less? Abas had need of a child to prove his continuing fertility, to keep his vassals content. He paid me dearly for it, first in gold and later in power when I threatened to expose him. But I paid dearly, too, over the years. Frain was our first child and our last. I had not reckoned, perhaps, on the anger of the goddess who abides in all women.

So Mela lay moaning and did not speak to me or cry out my name, and I could not help her. I felt somehow to blame—I always felt to blame for any ill in her life since I took Frain from her. The door opened. I looked up wearily, expecting another officious servant. But it was Wayte, my captain of guards, with an iron dagger at his throat. Other guards were milling about outside the door like beleaguered sheep. They were armed, of course, and so was Wayte. But they risked his life if they drew a weapon.

It was Frain who held the dagger on Wayte. I knew him at once, for I had made shift to see him a few times during the years, standing behind a buttress and watching him in the courtyard at Melior when he was too young and careless to notice me. He was a sturdy youth now, with auburn hair and high, freckled cheekbones and an earnest, open look about him. He hardly seemed more dangerous than the toothless baby I had given for gold. Yet there he was with his arms locked around Wayte's shoulders and the dagger at his throat. The captain stood almost a head above him.

'I beg pardon, my lord,' he said to me. 'They told me I could not see you, but my business could not wait.' His voice was clean and courteous, like his looks, but there was nothing crawling about it, no anxious entreaty. He is a prince, I thought, and I longed to go to him and embrace him. Instead I kept my place and spoke gruffly through my beard.

'Let that so-called captain of mine go,' I said.

He did not move. 'Your word, my lord, that I will not be harmed.'

I nodded, waving the other guards away. Frain loosened his grip, and Wayte bowed and left without a word, his face angry and white. The fellow was expecting my wrath; he did not know the joy he had brought me.

'Prince Frain,' I asked as collectedly as I could, 'what brings you here?'

He whistled softly. 'I had not expected, my lord, that you

would recognize me! Have you heard of the events in Melior, then?'

'No, I have had no news from Melior. I know your face, that is all. What has happened to bring you here with your fine linen half torn from your back?'

He glanced down at himself ruefully. 'Your guards would never have admitted such a vagabond. Have I your lordship's leave to seat myself?'

'Of course, of course!' I exclaimed hastily, suddenly aware of the poor account I was giving of myself. I was in a lethargy of despair from Mela's illness, roughly dressed, scarcely washed or combed, and now scant in courtesy. I bustled to clear a space on my cluttered couch. 'I beg your pardon. Please sit and tell me what news you will.'

Such a tale he told me. Murder, and a desperate ride into Acheron itself—Acheron, where no sane man will set foot. Then a lake on top of a mountain, forsooth, and a goddess walking barefoot like a peasant wench, and a strange and ominous black beast. I gaped in amazement, but Frain's voice was so careful and modest that I believed every word he told me. At last he explained his errand. 'Tirell hopes—no, expects—that you will help us overthrow Melior. He did not wish to come here himself, for he is certain that Abas has the Boda out in search of him. So he sent me to ask you to come to him.'

'He is mad, you have said,' I remarked dryly.

'Ay, so he is. Though perhaps'—Frain cocked a clear eye at me—'not in that regard.'

'How is he mad, then?'

Frain sighed, thinking, and for the first time I saw real pain in his fine brown eyes; he had kept away from emotion before. 'He has taken his love and grief,' Frain said slowly, 'and turned it all to hard hate and vengeance with a cutting edge. If he could weep it would be the greatest of blessings, I think, but he hardly moves or speaks except for vengeance. There is no human warmth in him these days, not toward any being of human kind. When he eats I think he does not taste the food; he tastes only vengeance. And I cannot say what he sees before his eyes.'

81

'But he fends for himself well enough day to day?' I asked.

'All too well,' he wryly agreed.

'And you, Prince Frain—' How I yearned to call him Frain, my son. But I would not do that. Long silence is not lightly to be broken.

'You need not call me prince,' he put in. 'I have never been "princed" much. Tirell is the prince in Melior.'

'And you, Frain,' I said softly. 'Do you accord with Prince Tirell in this bid for the throne?'

'I have followed him since I was old enough to walk.'

'And now that you are old enough to think,' I returned sharply, 'will you follow a madman?'

'Thinking is the least of it,' Frain replied slowly. 'To be sure, he is brave, and comely, and honorable in his way, and there is vision in him, perhaps even some wisdom. But I believe I would follow him even if he were a wretch. Because of something in me—I don't know what.'

I could not say a word.

'As for the throne,' he continued, 'what else can we do but try to take it? Abas will pursue us until either he or Tirell lies dead.'

'Are you sure?' I asked. 'He is a father. Perhaps he seeks Tirell only to make peace.'

Frain shook his head doubtfully. But before he could reply a long, anguished moan filled the room. Mela had awakened from one of her brief sleeps. I hastily crossed the room to be at her side, taking her dry hand between my own. But she looked through me and past me, as always, seeing nothing to help her. Frain stood beside me, and I caught my breath; her vague grey eyes flickered onto his face. But then she turned away her thin face and tossed her head to and fro in a sort of weak, distracted protest against her own misery. Her red hair lay snarled on the pillow, angry and unkempt. I placed a hand on her brow to still her.

'I could try to heal her,' Frain whispered. The words seemed dragged from him. 'Tirell says there is healing in me.'

'Prince Tirell may speak truth,' I said roughly, trying to hide my sudden hope. 'Though I know more of healing than he is ever likely to learn.'

'I know you were a smith.' Frain turned to me with his steady, questioning gaze, and I could scarcely meet his eyes. 'Can no one, then, heal those who are dearest to them?'

'Maybe not, Frain,' I said quietly, for that was truth. 'But I lost my gift for healing years ago, when I grew too fond of wealth—wealth and power.'

'My baby!' Mela whispered, and her frail hands moved on the bed sheets.

'Try, Frain,' I told him. 'But do not take it too hard if you fail. She is far gone.'

'But what should I do?' he asked.

'What do you think?' I asked in turn.

'There is something to do with metal,' Frain said slowly. 'I used a knife last time. But I hate to touch her with such an ugly thing.'

'A knife can cut away blight from the stem,' I said. 'Clean pain can heal. Use it.'

He did not tell me that he had hardly eaten for days, nor that he had ridden far, in haste, and with little rest. I learned that later, much later, when we were at Melior. He stood by Mela's bed with his back straight and his head bowed, like a hostage for her, and laid a hand on her hot brow. She stirred beneath his touch and whispered again. He curled his fingers around the iron knife blade and moved it over her heart, over her hands and head. He trembled, and I knew what he was feeling, remembered it well. The power moves in you and through you from depths beyond knowing or from some place beyond being—I never understood which. It carries you out of self and you shrink in fear. But I don't think Frain was afraid. He stood with Mela in her own dark place, bent over her, embracing her, struggling to lift her, to free her. His whole body trembled and strained with the effort, though he had not actually moved. Every sinew of his spirit was taut. For the space of countless heartbeats he fought for her, with her, against her—

And for an instant I thought he had succeeded. Her bleary eyes met his and cleared. 'My baby!' she breathed. Then an awful tumult of feeling surged into her eyes, love and rage—and the rage snapped her away from him. I saw it happen.

83

Frain swayed as if he had been struck. His knife clattered to the floor, and he clutched at a bedpost for support. He clung to the heartless wooden thing and sobbed.

I went and put my arms around him. He let go of the bed and cried against my shoulder, cried like the child I had never known. 'Easy, lad,' I murmured, swallowing, patting him clumsily. 'Stop your shaking, now . . .'

He raised his wet face. 'She is trapped in a tangle of rage and despair,' he said wildly, 'roots and strength-sucking vines, anger—I tugged and tugged—'

'I know,' I told him.

'The knife would not cut her free. Knives are like water in that place. I—I was a drifting thing, I didn't know who I was, I couldn't remember my name.' He gulped for breath. 'I—there was something—if I had only known . . .'

If you had known she is your mother, I thought with a pang, it would only have increased your heartache. He had given everything, down to the last dram of his strength; he could scarcely stand. I had never seen such courage. I knew that such had not been my courage, in my day.

Mela lay quite still. 'Is she—dead?' whispered Frain.

I reached out and touched the pulse of her neck. 'No, but she is beyond knowledge or pain, and I am glad of it. She will die soon.' I guided Frain toward the door. 'Come.'

He was still trembling. 'I am sorry . . .'

'I told you she was far gone,' I said more gently than I had ever heard myself speak. 'You did no harm, and more good than you know. Come.' I took him down the corridor, half supporting him. The guards watched us pass in barely concealed astonishment. I led him into my own bed-chamber and laid him down, took off his boots, and covered him and pulled the curtains around him. 'Sleep,' I ordered, and left him there.

My wife died two nights later. I did not see Frain in the interim, though I often thought of him. I ordered the servants to extend to him the fullest hospitality: bath, clothing, food, whatever he needed. I knew he would feel weak and drowsy for a few days, after what he had done for Mela, so I was not really expecting him as I sat with her. In fact, I suppose, he avoided the sickroom, for he was still very young. Death makes grim company. But it came easily enough for Mela. She slipped away without a movement or a word to me. I wept a bit, and then I slept for a good while. By the sun, it was past noon of the next day when I awoke.

I immediately went hunting for Frain. He was not in his chamber—my chamber, really. I prowled about and found him readily enough, though the servants were avoiding me. He and Wayte were at the centre of a crowd of guards and grooms and the like in the courtyard. They were fighting— with wooden swords, I was glad to see.

I wondered if I ought to intervene. Frain could not possibly be at his full strength, not after the effort he had expended for the sake of my dead queen. But Wayte was no fool; he would not let anything tragic happen. I could not believe that he bore the lad any real ill will. And as it turned out, I was right. He and Frain had become well acquainted over the past two days. Wayte had been curious about the youth, and curiosity had already turned to regard. But he had to keep the respect of his men; hence the mock combat in process.

I walked up to the back of the crowd, waiting to see what happened. The lackeys around me gaped and, at my glare, had the good sense to keep silence. Frain was fighting well but not flashily, sweating a bit but holding his own. He was quick with his defence.

'Good!' Wayte exclaimed, teacherlike.

Frain began to warm to the fight. The guards were yelling, goading and cheering Wayte, thinking they would see revenge. But I knew by then that they were more likely to see friendship. Frain began to press his attack, and Wayte's smile broadened with every stroke. He gave Frain a blow to the head that sent him spinning; the lad was down in the dirt and springing up again before I could shout. He was lithe and young, but Wayte, twenty years older, was breathing hard. Frain lunged at him and sent him circling backward around the clearing.

'Time!' Wayte gasped.

They breathed, then fought again. They were well heated

now, battling furiously at close quarters, neither one gaining. But Wayte tired first. His footwork slowed, and he got off balance and fell heavily to one knee. He put up his wooden sword for defence, and Frain struck it so hard that it broke. I sighed in relief; the fight was won. Frain tossed away his own sword.

'Hand to hand now?' he asked Wayte cheerfully.

'Confound it, Frain, that's enough!' I shouted in exasperation. 'Don't you do anything halfway?'

The crowd of watchers gasped and opened before me. Frain bowed to me collectedly enough as I approached him. He was wearing a fine linen tunic that hung almost to his knees and a sort of useless blue capelet. The tunic was soiled with sweat and dirt, and the cape was torn. Blood was dripping down onto it from a welt on his head. 'A pretty prince you look,' I growled.

'He is a marvellous fighter, my lord,' Wayte said, getting to his feet.

'And you are marvellously courteous,' Frain returned. 'Certainly you owe me no great favour. . . . My lord, I have repaid your hospitality by ruining my borrowed finery. I pray you are not angry.'

In fact, I had to smile at his diplomacy. 'Are you two friends?' I asked.

'I think so,' Frain said quietly, and Wayte nodded.

'Then join hands for all to see.'

They gripped hands before the gawking crowd, and then Frain buckled on a bronze sword and came with me. The sword was a fine piece of work, curiously wrought. I glanced at it as we walked silently side by side. 'It is odd for a healer to be a warrior,' I said at last.

He did not reply, but his face moved. I had reminded him of something he wanted to forget. 'I am sorry about Queen Mela, my lord,' he said in a moment. 'I was no healer for her.'

'There are some who cling to their ills,' I replied. I felt calm, almost dreamy, but he had started me crying again even so; I could feel the tears on my face. I let them run. Sorrow turns to poison if it is kept inside.

It was a long way to the tower stronghold I wanted to show

him. We went through the great hall and the audience hall and the council chamber and the passageway beyond to the narrow twisting stair, and so up. Few were allowed to come this way besides myself. I opened the heavily barred and bolted door. Every king has his treasure room, and I felt sure that Frain had seen gold before, but not such gold as mine. He stood thunderstruck. I watched with bittersweet pleasure, knowing that he, himself, was the price I had paid for all that was mine.

'You must be a smith fit for the gods!' he exclaimed.

'Look your fill,' I said.

I knew every piece as he came to it, remembered the labour and the feel of the metal beneath my tools. A brooch in shape of a leaping panther with tiny gemstones for eyes and swirling muscles of combed gold. A mirror with inlaid birds on the back, their tails soaring into patterned curves. A sword with two dragons chasing each other around the hilt and a tiny rabbit crouching on the end. A cauldron with a kingly procession riding around, men and horses and maidens and well-bred hounds. There were far too many to name, but I knew them all. A pitcher with ducks floating across the lid and a hawk stooping on the handle. Belt buckles, drinking cups, scabbards and shields and greaves and helms and clasps. Many bore the lotus device, emblem of Melior and indeed of all the Vale. There were harness rings too splendid for any horse that I had ever seen. There were fine chains and jewelled necklaces that Mela had worn on occasions of state. There were useless things—toys, in fact, for the child we never had. Tiny, snorting steeds pulling a gold chariot with wheels that really turned. Hunters chasing a leaping stag. Metal soldiers. A silver top that never spun quite right.

'It was the dream of my life,' I explained to Frain, 'to make marvellous things, not for some loutish patron but for myself, to hold and cherish. . . . I think you can see I have treasures such as no other king in Vale can boast.'

'Truly you do,' he agreed, touching and turning the objects with careful fingers.

And the greatest treasure lost, I thought. 'Choose a gift for yourself,' I said.

He looked up, startled, questioning. Already he knew how precious those lifeless things were to me.

Sometimes I had made frightening and beautiful creatures such as men seldom see. The dragon, each shimmering scale a single jewel. The flying serpent with head of a ram. The Luoni, the winged women who sit and stare down at travellers from high rocks, knowing they will have their chance at us after we die. The brown man of the Eidden wealds, with his shaggy goat's head. Frain froze with a silver brooch in his hand: a winged unicorn caught in graceful flight, its shining horn raised. I knew it well, the delicate thing.

'Is that for you?' I asked.

'For Tirell, I think.'

'Very well. Then what will you have for yourself? I am sorry I have no torques. I have never made them since I left Melior.'

Frain shook his head dazedly. 'You choose. Something small. I am not used to such splendour.'

Something small, I thought, but very precious for my son who had come to me when I needed him most. There was healing in his every glance and word. 'The serpent is the sign of the healer,' I mused aloud.

'Maybe so,' Frain said, 'but I don't like snakes.'

'No one does. That is why some men worship them. . . . Well, what sign would you like to wear then? What sort of creature are you?'

'A pup,' said Frain bitterly.

I raised my brows. 'Did Wayte call you that?'

'No, no! Wayte has been very kind. It is only that—I do not know what I am. What is the emblem of ignorance?'

'I don't know. But I wish people would remember that the dog is the emblem of honour and fidelity.' I sat down on a trunk. 'Have you heard the legend of the dog-king of Vaire?'

He shook his head, seating himself in willingness to hear. So I told the tale.

'On the night in which Nolan of Vaire was born, his sister, the magical she-dog Vlonda, birthed two pups, and they were called Kedal and Kedur. They lay wit Nolan in his cradle. One was black and one was white, and the baby was red as fire. In seven short years he grew to be a tall man, and the pups grew to be giant hounds, each big enough to fell a stag by itself. They were all constant companions to each other, and the dogs served Nolan as well as if they had been men.

'Now in those beginning days dogs were not yet heard of. That is why Aftalun had bedded and then transformed Vlonda, the warrior maiden: to give this gift to man. Wherever Nolan went with his hounds, people watched in envy and awe. The dogs fought beside him in battle, guarded his sleep, kept his possessions safe from thieves, provided meat for his table, helped him and, in course of time, his children through danger of every kind. They fought with fierce animals, ran through fire, swam through floods, climbed towers and jumped pits in his service, and neither of them ever mouthed a complaint. And Nolan, their master, was the best king Vaire had ever known. No one in the realm lacked anything during his reign.

'Nolan lived for two hundred years. Before he was an old man, every great lord had a dog; wars were fought for the stealing of dogs. But the most faithful followers were put to shame by the faithfulness of the dogs, for it is in the nature of a dog to be constant and in the nature of a man to be willful. That is why each can help the other. But petty men came to envy the dogs, and hate their nobility, and kick them for spite, and use their name as a name of reproach.

'Nolan saw all this with sorrow. He feared that his loyal companions might be subjected to insult after he was gone— for Kedal and Kedur, being born of Aftalun, were immortal. So, in his old age, Nolan turned his canton over to his sons and set out for a final adventure in the mountains to the south. Kedal and Kedur bounded around him like young pups. When the three of them reached the slopes of Lorc Tutosel, he breathed easier, for he judged that they would meet no people there. But at the top of the first pass their way was blocked by a hideous, misshapen old man. "Filthy curs!" he shrieked. "Go dig in garbage, go roll in manure!" Nolan tried to silence the old man, but it was too late. The mocker slipped away, and the dogs had turned to stone.

'Nolan spent the rest of his days in the mountains, living in the open, windy pass between the two stones that once were his faithful servants. And folk will point out to you the peak where Kedal and Kedur still watch over Vaire with tears rolling now and then from their blind, stony eyes. For what Nolan feared has come to pass: every shepherd boy now has a dog, and men have forgotten that dogs are the gift and get of the gods. But no one goes near those mountain ways, for Vlonda remembers. She roamed long in search of her brother and her sons, and folk say she still skulks, brooding, beneath the shadows of Kedal and Kedur.'

'I've never had a dog,' Frain remarked. 'Abas hates them. He will not allow any in Melior court.'

I got up and rummaged about on the shelves, searching. There were plenty of clasps and the like done in staghound form, but I wanted the best. It was presumptuous of me to place the emblem of Vaire on Frain, but I refused to worry; in this way, at least, I would claim him as my son! Finally I found a brooch that satisfied me: a noble dog, done in red gold, leaped within the encircling crown of Adalis. I took off my own dark blue cloak and put it over Frain's soiled tunic, fastened it around his sturdy shoulders with the brooch.

'Wear this,' I said, 'and if anyone calls you pup, smile.' I suppose I was weeping again; he put his arms out to me, hesitantly. I welcomed his embrace. I wept quietly for a while, to get it out of the way, but I was thinking far ahead.

'Stay here a few days,' I told Frain, 'and stand by me at the burial. Then I will go with you to see your brother.'

'You will?' He was startled.

'Yes.' I smiled grimly. 'It seems to me that I also have reason to hate Abas, King in Melior.'

90

2

A fortnight later we reached the southern outskirts of
Acheron with twenty retainers at our backs. I would not have
gone there with any lesser force or for any sake except
Frain's. I looked at him often as he rode. He sat his big,
powerful black horse as if he had been born on it. He wore the
fairest linen I could find him now, and my blue cloak, and he
looked every inch a prince—but warmer, more generous of
heart than any prince of Melior had ever been. Sometimes I
dreamed of seeing him, my son, on that throne, forgetting the
horrible altar. I will not say I thought of killing Tirell—I would
not have slain him by any design—but if any mischance
should occur, I thought, it would be well if I could help Frain
to take his brother's place. I did not know Tirell then or
understand the strange forces that drove him.

As we neared the woods of Acheron Frain gazed ahead
anxiously, but no one appeared to give us welcome. Suddenly a monstrous black creature rushed toward us. The
raven Morrghu, I almost said, but it moved along the ground.
It lifted wide black wings and sounded a kind of stuttering
bray that made me shiver. My men shouted out at the sight of
the thing, and I confess I pulled my horse to a halt. But Frain
trotted forward to meet it, and the nightmare came up to him,
frisking, and rubbed its nose against his leg. He fended off its
horn as if it were a lancetip. Yet he smiled, seeming surprised
and oddly pleased. He caressed the awful creature, rubbing
its head and ears.

'So that is the winged unicorn, Prince Tirell's pet?' I asked,
shaken. 'It is not much like the handsome animal on this
brooch!'

'Yet even this beast can be fair when seen in the silver waters of the high lake at Acheron,' Frain told me.

Then he saw a figure among the trees and spurred forward with the beast after him. Tirell was a tall man, black-haired and with a face like carved white jade, very manly and beautiful of feature but cold. Frain grasped his hand and kissed him as I rode up, giving him the embrace of a brother, but Tirell pushed him aside in annoyance. I felt as if I had been struck, watching.

'King Fabron,' said Tirell, 'welcome. Pray join us at our fire.' Courtesy scant enough, and spoken in a toneless voice. I followed him with no more answer than a nod. But as we came to the fireside I forgot my anger in amazement. Frain was talking to the loveliest woman I had ever seen.

He seemed confused, doubtful before her, not at all like my stalwart son! But as she turned her glance on me I understood why. Her eyes were like sparkling water, all dazzle. I could not see into them. I sensed she was a daughter of Adalis, and I soon had to lower my own gaze.

'Lady, all good ever come to you,' I stammered like a bumpkin, offering my hand in greeting. Only the tips of her fingers touched mine.

We ate, the four of us, in uncomfortable silence. Frain was perhaps more used to that constraint than I, for he made no attempt to break it. The food was delicious, out of place in that wilderness. There were several kinds of fine bread, and meat cooked to buttery tenderness, and strange fruits in sunset colours. I was half afraid to eat, suspecting it was enchanted fare. But for Frain's sake I ate. It was evident that Tirell had not suffered much privation during his absence. I saw resentment and a sort of hopeless weariness form in Frain's eyes. After we had eaten he went wordlessly away to a bed among the trees somewhere.

'So,' said Tirell to me as soon as Frain was well away, 'you have not told him that he is your get.'

I was surprised, but not overly surprised; I knew of the visionary powers inherent in his line. 'What for?' I asked crossly. 'To manifest to him my most greedy and heartless stupidity? I would like him to think well of me for a while yet.'

'He will be no more than a puppy of a man until he knows the truth.' Shamarra's voice flowed like cool water. My reply was colder.

'He has a brother whom he follows with greatest love. Should I tell him that he has no brother?' I turned to Tirell. 'Do you not want his help against Abas?'

'He would help me notwithstanding,' said Tirell with an indifference that turned the compliment into an insult. 'And you, Fabron—will you also help me?'

'Why should I?' I challenged him. 'To replace one mad King with another?'

'You think me mad?' asked Tirell, unconcerned.

'You who spurned Frain's embrace, yes. I think you mad.'

He shrugged. 'Well, for the matter of that, I do not care who sits on the throne as long as Abas is slain. Let Frain have it if he likes. Or take it yourself, since I know Frain will not want it.'

'No!' Shamarra exclaimed.

'I must agree with the lady,' I said stiffly. 'The rightful heir must take the throne. Otherwise, every canton king and powerful noble in Vale will be vying for it.'

'For Melior?' Tirell questioned ironically. 'The bosom of the sweet goddess and site of her high altar? Who would want to be ripped to death on a slab of white stone?'

'He is highly honoured who weds with the goddess in death!' Shamarra cried furiously.

'That is the only way you are ever likely to get me, my bloodthirsty wench,' Tirell told her with honeyed malice. 'It does you no good to pant and whisper in the night.'

She leaped to her feet with flashing eyes. 'Fool!' she shouted, choking. 'Don't you know that I am your sacred destiny? I am goddess, and you will be Sacred King!'

'Destiny be damned,' he said coolly. 'I have told you I will wed no one since—since she is gone.'

'But I am Mylitta!' Shamarra shrieked. 'One of me is. She is in me! All women are in the goddess!'

'Don't say her name with your beak of a mouth!' Tirell sprang to his feet instantly, towering above the fire, and I sat stunned, unable to move. Even in Abas I had never seen such

93

fiery blue rage as shot from Tirell's ice-blue eyes. It smote me like a sword. I thought that he would strike the lady, but indeed I could not move! Then Frain appeared drowsily from between the trees and stepped in front of his brother.

'Out of my way!' thundered Tirell.

'No, brother,' said Frain quietly, as if in calm discussion. 'You will have to knock me down first if you wish to beat a woman.'

Tirell stood for an instant looking like frozen lightning. Then: 'Send her away from here,' he said hoarsely, and strode off into the darkness beneath the trees. Shamarra stood straight and shining, looking after him.

'I will not be dismissed,' she said to Frain. But even as she spoke to him she looked beyond him as if he were not there.

'Do you have the power to fight him?' he questioned her abruptly. 'Who are you? Yours is not any name of the goddess that I know.'

She turned her eyes to him slowly, smiled, and sat by the fire. 'You have grown a bit in Vaire,' she said.

He sat beside her. 'Who are you?' he asked again.

'I am the lake,' she replied.

'The goddess of the lake, you mean?'

'I mean I am the lake, as Adalis is Vale, or Vieyra is Vale should famine arise, or Morrghu in time of war. . . . But I am one with all these forms of the goddess, as they are one with me. I am in Eala and Eala is in me. I am only one of me.'

'Can you shift shapes?' Frain pressed her.

'Perhaps. . . . I have never done so.'

'Then what are your powers?'

She made a sad little face at him. 'Few enough, and certainly not to be named to you! Over Tirell I have not even the power of love. Nevertheless, I will stay with him.'

'How?'

'How can he send me away?' she retorted. 'He has no hounds to chase me.' She rose and walked away. She still held her shining head high, but there was something half defeated in the pace of her steps. Frain looked after her with a sigh.

'Whether she stays or leaves, my lord,' he said to me after a bit, 'do you have a spare horse for her?'

'To be sure,' I said gruffly, and added, 'They are both mad!'

'Can a goddess be mad?' Frain murmured.

'Mad to face Prince Tirell's wrath, yes. And you as well! I thought he would knock you into the fire, and still I couldn't move!'

Frain smiled in rueful understanding. 'Yes, that is the power of the Sacred Kings. The fey glare of addled eyes . . . Yet I cannot believe that Tirell would ever do dishonour even in his wildest rage. But Abas would kill as soon as speak whhen his mood is fit. Him I would not face.' He looked bleak. I thought suddenly of a small and frightened boy.

'You grew up with this?' I groaned with emotion I had not meant to show. He looked at me in puzzlement, at the guilt written plainly on my face. How I longed to beg his forgiveness. But he must have taken my despair for doubt.

'Tirell was not always frozen in rage,' he told me softly. 'Time was when we would steal away together to the forbidden places near the river, hunt eggs and snails and sail sticks in the puddles. When we played marbles, he would win all mine and then give them back. He built things for me, toys that Mother never thought of, like a catapult or a bow. I was always littler, tagging along, but no one dared to trouble me when he was around. He would swagger and lie to the schoolmasters to save me a blow when my lessons weren't done.' He stared into the fire, remembering.

'Was that often?' I asked, smiling.

'Often enough,' Frain admitted. 'But after Tirell was about fourteen or fifteen none of our masters dared to constrain us. We were wild things. We rode where we would, and fought each other sometimes and were sorry afterwards, though neither of us would admit it. . . . He always roamed in the night, and sometimes he cried. But he does not cry these days. Good my lord, it is not Tirell that you see, but a shell and a stranger—no more. Think on that.'

'I will try to remember,' I said.

I had to brace myself to talk to Tirell the next morning. But I did so, and got him off alone, and we agreed that, if he should take the throne, he would name Frain as my heir. That settled, we made plans. I told him that he could win the support of Sethym, my neighbour, king of Selt. Sethym was fervent in his adherence to the ancient rituals of Vale, eager to replace the aging King Abas with younger, more vital blood for the goddess. Also I hoped that Oorossy, ruler of Eidden, the northern canton, might aid us. I knew him to be a kindly man who hated Abas for his cruelty. But of Raz I could say nothing. He kept to his vast domain and vouchsafed no word, or at least none to me.

I think Tirell would have liked to have stayed near the mountains. Their loneliness felt safe to him, though they filled me with dread I could not explain, especially these mountains of Acheron—why should a man be afraid of nothingness, of twisted trees where no birds sing? Anyway, Tirell was obliged to leave his retreat. Summer was well started, and he had to prepare his bid while the weather favoured.

So we made ready to ride to Ky-Nule, whence he would travel on to Gyotte in Selt. There was some juggling of horses. Frain took his place beside his brother on a big, bright chestnut, and Shamarra rode up on a white mare. I have never seen such a woman. She could not have been hammered out of silver or gold; she would have to have been carved from ice, or from water itself for delicate, fluid grace. Yet there was metal in her, hard metal in the way she confronted Tirell. He looked through her and turned to Frain with a cold stare.

'I told you to bid her begone.'

'How?' Frain retorted. 'She is a goddess and goes where she will. Do you have power to bind the wind or stop rivers from flowing?'

'I have muscle to bind her to one of her precious trees,' Tirell snapped. 'I suppose your courtesy would not allow of that. But did you have to give her your own horse?'

'Mine?' Frain asked coolly. 'The white? Since when am I marked for the goddess? Let her ride her own sacred steed.'

Tirell seemed mollified, and we were able to get off without much more ado. Tirell and Frain took the lead, side by side, torques gleaming and cloaks thrown back from their shoulders in the summer heat. All my men admired Tirell; I could see that from the first. His stature and his boldness inspired awe without demanding it. He would make a King that men would die for. I rode just behind him, beside my lieutenant, and I passed my time in watching my son. How I longed for him, in my grief, and how I hated Tirell. Frain should have been riding with me.

For his own part, he watched Shamarra when he could. She did not keep ranks, but ranged all around the troop, ahead or to one side, with the black beast gamboling after her. She rode effortlessly, as if she were of one body with her horse, aside, with her pearly gown trailing down. . . . No one could laugh at Frain for gazing at her. We all kept glancing at her like enchanted things. All except Tirell.

When we had journeyed about a week, Tirell turned around to speak to me—the first time, I think, that he had done so. 'Boda,' he stated tersely. 'Are you willing to fight?'

'Where?' exclaimed Frain and I simultaneously.

'Beyond the rise, I think. Their red shirts swim before my eyes. About a dozen. There is still time to turn aside.' I could see that he, himself, had no wish to turn aside. He was trembling, a tremor scarcely visible, with rage he could not entirely contain, and his face twitched. The beast snorted, and he spoke to it sharply.

I could scarcely believe that he had given me warning and choice. 'If I fight the King's retainers,' I said slowly, 'it will be an act of war, and my throne the forfeit.'

'Then, since you will be of small use without a throne and an army,' Tirell growled, 'I suppose we had better turn aside to that grove yonder.' He gave the signal, and we rode into the copse that hugged the rise. There were twenty-three men of us, the lady, and the beast.

We waited a while, Tirell still quaking with his subterranean rage—rage that went as deep as grief, Frain said, rage that was grief transfigured. Perhaps it was his own blood-red rage that swam before his eyes. I was just about to think he had misled us when the troop of Boda rode over the brow of the rise. There were fourteen of them, in scarlet tunics hung with long fur fringes—in the old days it would have been human hair—and bronze greaves below, and helms winged like the raven of war. The land was dry already, even in early summer; it looked as if we were in for drought again. But a troop of riders such as ours cannot help but leave a track even on the dryest ground. I watched anxiously, hoping the Boda would overlook it. But when they came to the place where we had turned aside, their captain stopped and studied our traces. He gave a command, and they pivoted toward the coppice.

'Frain and I will slip out the other side,' Tirell muttered to me. 'You tell them what tale you will—you suspected robbers, or some such. Perhaps we will see you again before we leave Vaire.'

'No!' I blurted, suddenly panicky at the thought of being separated from my son. 'I will protect you. Let it come to fighting if it must, and let none of them live to tell of it!'

'Wait,' whispered Frain. 'It's Guron.'

'What?'

'He taught me archery and a bit of leathercraft. . . . Let me see if I can talk to him.'

He rode forward. I gasped and reached to stop him, but too late. Frain rode out in the open, his hand raised in greeting.

I have remarked before now on Frain's courage. But besides and beyond that he had an air of artless self-assurance that had astonished me before then. The lad had good common sense; he had showed me that in conversation many times. And he saw as clearly as anyone I knew—but, Mother of us all! that he would ride out alone before a troop of armed enemies! How could I call him foolhardy? His daring provided its own shield. The troop stopped abruptly, spears levelled, but no one hurt him. They must have been as flabbergasted as I.

'Guron,' Frain called out, almost gaily, 'whatever are you doing in the Boda now?'

'Half the castle is in the Boda and out looking for you,' returned the older man grimly. He gave his followers the signal to stand and rode forward to where Frain awaited him. I started to sweat for fear of treachery, but I saw his face, a furrowed, thoughtful face, and breathed easier. He held no weapon. He would have given his hand for Frain to clasp, I think, if it were not for all those watching eyes.

'How is Grandfather?' Frain asked softly.

'Wandering,' Guron replied, 'like so many of us these days. He is to be shunned for betraying his trust in regard to the Wall. Abas's orders. But I expect some folk will dare to help him, for he is well loved.' Guron spoke rapidly and very low, but he stood so close to the trees that I could hear every word.

'And Mother?' Frain asked, swallowing. Your mother died a few weeks ago, I thought with a pang. But Guron's answer was scarcely kinder.

'Imprisoned,' he replied. 'She must have pleaded for you both too strongly. But no one except the King wishes her harm. The guards give her food on the sly.'

Frain flinched at the thought of that proud queen in such need of charity. 'And us?' he asked. 'What are your orders concerning Tirell and myself?'

'Capture. I may injure you if necessary, but you are not to be killed.' Guron could not quite meet Frain's steady gaze.

'The King desires that royal privilege himself?'

'I can't tell, lad,' said the man unhappily. 'It's true that he's been wild as the very wind since you went, furious and still as stone by turns. But he looks for Tirell. . . .' Guron looked down in confusion, trying to explain. 'He sits without eating, sometimes for days, chanting to himself—Tir-ell! Tir-ell! Sometimes he screams, something frightens him, but he keeps trying. He sensed something to the southwest and sent us here, several troops.'

At my side, Tirell stiffened and muttered to himself.

'More are all over Vale,' Guron continued. 'Lad, I feel . . . It is not all hatred that seeks Tirell so.'

'I saw his face,' Frain said flatly. 'He would kill us both in a minute.'

Guron lowered his eyes and did not reply.

'There are twenty-some men hidden at my back,' Frain added after a pause. 'Are you willing to be put to rout by them, Guron? Certainly I do not wish this to come to fight.'

'Let them show their numbers to my red-clad minions yonder and I will be glad to flee. I must attempt to capture you, but I will say farewell first, and all good come to you. Now I will reach for my weapon, thus.' Guron grabbed at his dagger, but Frain started back with convincing quickness, and I shouted a command. Spears bristled out of the coppice where we hid. Guron wheeled and galloped back to his troop.

'There is no need for him to see *whose* retainers are hidden here,' Frain said by my side.

'He is an ass if he does not know,' Tirell remarked sourly.

'He knows—but perhaps he will find a way not to know. Did you hear what he said about—'

'I heard.' Tirell turned away.

The Boda kept their distance, watching the wood. As long as Guron had an excuse to think we were still in it he could do that. So we crept out the other side of it, using it as our shield, and hastened away. I deployed scouts rear-ward, for I reasoned that sooner or later Guron would have to make a show of pursuing us. We did not stop that night, but rode on through the darkness, changed our direction several times, and rode hard all the next day. In three more days we reached Ky-Nule with no further sign of the Boda.

3

It had been planned, or at least I had let it be planned, that Frain and Tirell would continue their journey without me. What excuse could I have, I, a canton king, for roaming about with two renegade princes? I could send some men with them, certainly, first relieving them of the staghound badges that identified them as mine. I could even send Wayte. There were few men whom I trusted more. Surely, at this critical time, it was my duty to keep close to my throne, watching narrowly over my canton and raising the army that would march to aid Tirell when his time came.

'Red shirts lodged here while you were gone, my lord,' Wayte told me when he made his report. 'Three troops of them are camped now by the bridge of Epona, and more by the Varro bridge. Fifty men in all.'

I sighed, stood up, circled my chair and sat down again.

'My lord, it is no secret that they seek the princes, and it is no secret that you ride with them,' Wayte said quietly. 'The countryside is filled with talk of it.'

'The princes prepare to snatch the throne from their mad father's grip,' I stated. 'Will you aid them, Wayte?'

His sober face looked as surprised as I had ever seen it. 'I am your man, my lord. It is for you to tell me what I am to do.'

'But I will not be here, Wayte.' I settled back farther in my chair, bracing myself. 'I will continue to ride with the princes. You must rule here in my stead, raise an army and march to Melior when the time comes, and withstand Abas if he attacks meanwhile.'

Wayte opened his mouth several times before he spoke. 'Prince Tirell is a madman, folk say,' he remarked at last, mildly.

101

'And now I am another?' I heard the hint. 'Perhaps, Wayte. It is foolhardy.'

'Yes,' he agreed far too readily. 'But of course you will go in disguise.'

'No, Wayte. I am going to be honest, this once.'

'The princes, then, hidden among your retinue—'

'I doubt it. They are not the sort to hide.' I shot a smile at him. 'If you could have seen them ride—Wayte, they'll have half the countryside flocking to follow them. Tirell senses danger and doesn't care, and Frain seems convinced no harm can befall him, and he has half convinced me.'

'They are insane to go so boldly,' Wayte said.

'We are all insane. Melior is a tiny plot of land ruled by a king who does nothing except wed and die, and yet we pin all our hopes on it. Well, Wayte?'

'What?' He surveyed me doubtfully.

'Will you give your word? It is well that you obey my behests, but it will be better yet if you obey your own heart. So I ask you, will you do your utmost for Frain's sake?'

He looked utterly bewildered, but then he smiled. 'For Frain's sake and yours. Yes, I will do my best.'

'Here, then.' I handed him the great key to the treasure chamber. 'Use what you need to hire mercenaries and buy supplies. Melt down the gold if you have to.'

He could not believe he was hearing me properly. 'My lord?' he mumbled.

'Spend what you need to, wear what you like,' I told him irritably, and dismissed him. He went off dazed, poor fellow. I knew he would not make himself a crown of the gold, but I hoped he was not dreaming of ruling Vaire after I was gone. He knew I had need of an heir. . . . But I had made him no promise.

Frain was surprised to hear that I would ride with him to Selt, and puzzled, and pleased. Tirell was neither surprised nor pleased, I felt sure, though he said nothing to me at all.

We left with upward of thirty retainers. Any more would have been cowardly. Our way lay toward the bridge of Epona that crossed the Elsans, a smaller river that ran into the Chardri. I hoped that most of the Boda would be at the Varro bridge, the one that crossed into Tiela from Vaire. In no way could the Boda know that we were going to Selt first, since we had decided that among ourselves.

The journey from Ky-Nule to the Epona took several days. I sent scouts ahead when we came near the bridge, and my heart sank at their report. Four troops held the Epona.

'Guron must have joined them,' Frain said.

'They will try to take us soon, if they have any sense,' growled Tirell. 'They have their scouts, too, and they know we are here. Already the others will be hurrying down from the Varro to cut us off from behind.'

'Then let us hurry on up to cross by the Varro,' I suggested, only half joking.

Tirell eyed me sourly. 'Is the Elsans shallow farther south, my lord Fabron?' Frain asked. 'We could walk across.'

And Tirell was supposed to be the madman! I gaped at my son; there was that blithe daring of his again! I had never heard of a freeman setting foot in a river. The streams cut through Vale like so many knife strokes, passable only by the few bridges that curved high above them. Lives had been spent in the making of those bridges. Lives had to be spent even for the digging of a well, in sacrifice to the goddess and the flood beneath. There was a power in water. Even the shallowest stream could grow fingers that would pull a man down into oblivion. No one would name those boneless hands.

'You've been daft ever since you let that sneaking lake touch you,' Tirell growled at Frain.

'The Elsans runs deep and swift,' I stammered. 'There is a legend—'

'Yes, yes, every river has a legend,' Frain interrupted impatiently. 'What of it? You have ridden through Acheron, Tirell.'

'To my dismay.'

'Why? You have found us powerful allies. How can we come to harm when the lady is with us?'

'No!' Tirell flared. 'I need no help from any slut. We will take these Boda now, before they have had time to prepare for us.'

'They have had *weeks* to prepare for us,' Frain protested.

103

Still, we really had no choice, or at least I thought we did not. We formed line of battle at the top of the rise. As you might know, they were expecting us. Some stood ranked on the bridge itself and some mounted before it. I counted more than fifty men.

'If those on the bridge stay there,' Tirell told the troops, 'we shall not have to fight them all at once. Use the force of your charge to unhorse as many as you can. Ready!'

Indeed they were ready, not because of his words but because of the blue fire in his eyes. He was taut with leashed fury at the sight of those red tunics below; yet his every move was like a cat's for grace and control. My men sat straight on their horses, looking as soldierly as I had ever seen them. Then Tirell shouted—roared—and we all thundered down toward the river.

Tirell and Frain broke through almost to the bridge. I believe they could have fought their way over and been gone if they had cared to leave the rest of us. But they set themselves to back and side in the midst of the press and fought foes at every hand. Frain fought splendidly. I was not born to the sword, myself—my people joke that I use it like a hammer—but I know a swordsman when I see one. Tirell was no swordsman, but more like a reaper at harvest. He had a great iron blade that bit into everything for a lance's length around him. Boda screamed to escape him.

The battle is all bits and pieces in my memory; they always are. We seemed to do well at first, but then it became harder. I remember Frain bearing a man down, then turning his sword and stunning the fellow with the hilt—it was Guron. Tirell shouted constantly, cursing Abas and all his adherents. Once he bellowed, 'Fabron!' and lunged to my side; someone was coming at me from behind. The Boda had outflanked my end of the field and had us surrounded. Tirel and Frain positioned themselves by me, fighting off foes all around, and Tirell cracked out a curse that made me shudder, swore by the blood bird, his own dying soul. . . . Then the man I was facing screamed and fled. I almost did the same. The black beast had joined the battle.

Not many of the Boda cared to withstand the force of jet-black, pawing hooves, a stabbing horn and vast, beating, thunderous wings. But even more than its power, I think, the sheer strangeness of the beast unnerved them. Another strange thing was happening as well: from time to time the river Elsans would reach out with a soft, uncanny grip and pull a man in. Six Boda were swept down the swift current, screaming, and the others fought desperately to get away from the brink. My men cheered and pressed them back.

'The bridge!' Tirell roared.

He leaped his horse onto the stones of the arch. Frain and I flanked his sides; there was no room for more than three abreast. The dozen or so men who held the bridge shrank back. They had been watching their comrades bleed for some little time by then, and that is enough to give anyone second thoughts. In the first rank stood an officer. He faced us pluckily and went over the stone railing with Tirell's first blow. Two more went more painfully, and then the rest broke and ran, all nine of them, into Selt.

Behind us, the battle was over. Shamarra joined us, picking her way down the hill on her white mare. 'Well fought, Prince!' she called to Tirell, her eyes sparkling.

'Were you meddling with the river?' Tirell demanded.

'I have some small power over water,' she answered coyly.

He snorted and turned away without a word. I set to gathering my men, and in a few moments I could have wept. Only a dozen were left, and some of those were too badly wounded to ride. Tirell stood checking his black horse and the black beast, running his hands over their limbs. Frain was sitting his horse rather stupidly, looking at Shamarra. But he shook himself out of his trance and came to me before I had to call him.

'Are you all right?' he asked me.

'Well enough.' I had taken a few cuts, but those of us who had been under the special protection of Tirell's iron sword had gotten off lightly. Three of my men lay groaning. 'Frain,' I asked, 'can you help those fellows?'

He knelt, took his iron dagger, and passed his hands across them. No human healer can return the hurt instantly to health, but everyone who watched could see how their pain lessened, their bleeding stopped, their hope and strength increased. My men glanced at each other in wonder. Two of them stood with hacked and useless arms. Frain touched them also, then turned to his brother. 'Are you all right?' he called softly.

'I am,' came the curt reply, 'and the beast also. We had better be riding.'

I left one man who was well with the five who were hurt, to catch horses for them and help them back to Ky-Nule. The other six prepared to come with us.

'This is a paltry force, my prince,' I mourned.

'No help for it,' Tirell said brusquely. 'It would be well, perhaps, to slit the throats of these Boda. Some of them may yet live to trouble us.'

'No!' said Frain sharply before anyone could move. He and his brother matched stares for a moment, and then Tirell turned away, expressionless.

'Very well,' he said. 'Let us ride.'

We clattered across the blood-splattered stones of the bridge and into Selt. Shamarra went readily, not seeming to mind the gore, close behind the princes. The beast snorted at the bridge and then lunged across.

We rode for the rest of that day and well into the night, constantly mindful of the nine Boda who were roaming somewhere about; we wondered if they would join with more. We knew we must make our way to Sethym's court city of Gyotte as quickly and secretly as we could. I kept a watchful eye on Frain, for healing saps the innermost strength. He rode stubbornly, his eyes vague and glazed with weariness. By moonrise he was ready to fall from his horse. Though I did not like to speak before the men, I called to Tirell.

'Have a care for Prince Frain, my lord. He is spent. We had better stop and let him rest.'

'Healing is wearier work than battle,' came Shamarra's clear voice across the night. 'It is all giving, no taking of prizes.'

Tirell did not reply to either of us. He merely got down from his own horse and got up behind Frain on his, taking the reins from his brother's limp hands. I led the black, and we went on.

'There's one vow broken!' Shamarra cried happily, with her

rippling laugh. 'I thought you were never to mount any horse except a black!'

'I may break more vows before I am done,' Tirell retorted grimly. 'But in the night all horses are black, lady, and every queen a whore. Remember that.'

We rode in silence. In the frosty light of a half moon I could see Frain's head nod back to rest against his brother's neck.

In the morning Tirell went back to his black. For the next few days we all rode in a close group, for I did not have enough men to scout for us, and we breathed in fear of the Boda. Shamarra and the black beast no longer gamboled off to one side. I could see that Frain was tormented by the lady's closeness. I worried about him, for he had not had enough rest to restore his strength, and I wondered if he could defend himself. But when he took leave of the van and dropped back to the rear of our little cavalcade I could not deny him, even if it had been my place to do so. He rode beside the black beast, and my men felt easier for his presence; the creature made them shudder.

Gyotte is a hilltop fortress with two great painted eyes staring from its gates, ever watchful for approaching enemies. After three long days of riding we had it in sight, stare and all. The sun dipped low as we toiled up the stony road to the gates.

The Boda came at us from behind, out of the shadow of trees and the glare of the opposing hill. We all swung around with startled shouts at the sound of their clattering charge. But they closed with us almost before we could draw weapons. The force of their attack was lessened by the slope, praise be, but Frain bore the brunt of it. He put up his sword and fought—if I had not seen him fight so splendidly a few days before, I would have said he fought well. The black beast interceded for him fiercely, and Tirell surged to his side, cursing and pushing my men out of his way. We were hard beset. It was a full troop of Boda, nearly a score, and they had us on three sides. Only the height of the cobbled road helped us withstand them. Tirell raged and foamed and fought like—like a very madman. But even so he had the sense to see that we must not be surrounded. The lady Shamarra had galloped the small distance to Gyotte and was pounding on the gates. We followed her, carefully retreating, fighting all the way, and set our backs to the wall with the lady in our midst. I fought with sweat and blood running into my eyes, and I could hear Tirell all the time, roaring and snarling like a great cat. I could not look for Frain. After a hazy time I began to realize that I might never see him again, and a squeezing fear turned my stomach against me. I felt old and doomed, and the Boda seemed as many as ever.

I did not understand when Tirell shouted the retreat. I had nowhere to retreat to, backed up against the wall of Gyotte. But then his long iron sword cleared away the foes that faced me and his hard hand propelled me toward the gates. The gates! Sethym had opened Gyotte to us, and a swarm of his retainers poured out; he wanted to make sure no Boda lived to bring Abas's vengeance down on him.

I found Frain within the courtyard, resting his head on his horse's mane, deathly pale and making the red steed's neck redder than it had any right to be. Shamarra stood beside him, and then she turned to me with real sorrow on her face; I am sure of it. Tirell had me by the elbow. The gates clanged behind him. We were safe. But I stood watching Frain bleed onto his horse, and I suppose I must have fainted.

4

I awoke in a kind of sickchamber, much later. Frain was sitting beside me with his auburn hair curling over a bandage and his face still too pale for comfort beneath. Tears came to my eyes as I reached out to him.

'By Aftalun, lad, I feared you were dead!'

'It was close for all of us.' He took my hand absently. 'Some did not live. Your men, I mean. They all died of wounds, within or without the walls. I could not help them.' He tried to speak collectedly, but pain tightened his face, and I loved him for it. Some kings spend soldiers like coin, but we had eaten and ridden with mine; they were comrades to us.

'We only lived who were under the protection of Tirell's long sword,' I murmured.

With a slam of the door, Tirell strode in as if he had heard his name. One hand was bandaged, but otherwise he looked whole and as irascible as ever. 'Get in bed!' he barked at Frain. 'Blood of Eala, brother, he'll mend without your help.'

'No fear,' Frain replied. 'I don't have strength to lift a finger on his behalf.' He stayed where he was.

'See that you don't!' Tirell scoffed stormily. He turned to me. 'My lord Fabron, if you are feeling well enough, would you please tell me: what manner of fool is this Sethym?'

I had to smile. Sethym was rather a fool. He was a good neighbour for all that, though we skirmished from time to time just to keep our men mettlesome and ourselves respectful.

'A ceremonious fool,' I said. 'He lives for ritual. He cloisters his men before a battle, and he will not eat anything red—he says that is the food of the gods. He claims that a fate is laid on him that he may not eat the meat of a rabbit, lest he die. The

109

sight of a white rabbit or a white bird would kill him. He scarcely ever goes out, for fear of seeing rabbits or omens. He devoutly worships the goddess, and he pays mighty tribute to the Sacred Kings.'

'I thought so,' Tirell growled. 'He and Shamarra are two of a kind. He has a sort of den here, a temple of the goddess, barred to men on pain of death. Maidens on the rugs, fancywork on the walls. She is housed there, looking down her long beak like a proper bird of prey. Sethym loves me because I am wearing a torque.' Tirell paced the room in quiet fury as he talked. 'He would be delighted to see Abas slain, but he wants him to go to the altar. I had not thought to give that satisfaction to the priestesses.'

'Have you thought,' Frain asked in a low voice, 'that it may not be well to be a parricide? I cherish no fondness for the priestesses, but I believe their hands are better suited to such blood than yours.'

Tirell snorted. 'You have taken a blow on the head,' he retorted, not too harshly. 'Get to bed, will you, so we will be able to ride within a few days! This Sethym makes my flesh crawl with his ghoulish hospitality. I believe he's already envisioning me as altar meat in my turn!' He left the room as ungently as he had entered, slamming the door behind him. Frain winced, because his head hurt, I suppose, and sighed.

'Sethym is not a bad king, for all that,' I said cautiously. 'His many fears force him into worthy deeds that he hopes will earn him the smile of the goddess. And he makes a fine war leader. His men follow him with awe. They think he is touched by the wing of Morrghu because he is so—strange.'

'A fitting comrade for Tirell,' Frain muttered, lying gingerly down on his bed, which stood not far from mine. 'Yet madmen can't agree, it seems. How could he liken Shamarra to a bird of prey?'

I gave no answer, since he expected none. I suppose I have not said in so many words that Frain was in love with the lady. He had not told me so, but I had eyes to see, and he often looked at her with his heart in his face. At meal-times he would sit by her and try to pass a few courteous words, though her eyes flashed in reply. I would have hated her for

110

her coldness to him if she were not in herself such a marvel. With Tirell she seemed quite different, her eyes deep pools of meaning, though her head rode as high as ever. But, so strange is the world, he would hardly speak to her except in cold, insulting tones, or even look at her if he could avoid it, and she scorned Frain in like wise. Swans and serpents! I wished she could have at least more gently refused him. I knew she was not for him, manly and fair though he was; she was ancient in spite of her lineless face, and he was all ardent youth. But I could not tell him that. I had lived long enough to know the fate of the meddler.

We lay and drowsed through the day, talking now and then. Servants tended us and fed us well. When our room darkened we drowsed more deeply. But sometime when everything had gone black as a pit and silent as the stalking of owls I realized that Frain was gone.

Probably he felt restless after a day in bed, like myself, I reasoned, and he had gone to find some fresh air, or perhaps to find his brother, for Tirell often wandered in the night. I tried to go back to sleep. But obstinate distress nagged at me, and after a while I got up and set out to look for him.

I had visited the castle of Gyotte before, but I had never become accustomed to its many eyes. Every surface of the place was covered with charms of protection, many of them demon faces with startling eyes made out of clamshell from the Chardri—expensive stuff gathered at a high price of lost slaves. Doors and corners and all the furnishings were bordered with monotonous designs. Red tassels clung to the corners of all the hangings, and on every door gleamed a spiral with a bit of mirror at the centre to send an enemy's curse back at him. The glimpse of my own reflected eyes was enough to make me jump, amid all the other ones. At every doorway, even serving ways, stood guardian pairs of carved beasts: dogs, griffins, swans, stags, man-headed horses, many more. Their blank white eyes watched me pass. Carved, glaring cats stood in frozen leaps above the archways, and from everywhere the many forms of the goddess stared down. All the corridors were lit day and night by the flickering, dusky glow of many little lamps with shields of rosy glass, each with its own red tassel hanging down. They filled the place with a heavy scent. Sethym must have spent a fortune on oil and perfume.

I walked the silent hallways, flinching. I cower in Gyotte even when I am invited; I would hate to have to invade it! I met no one except a few surly guards of human variety and the many lifeless ones. Trying to think where Frain or Tirell might go, I left the keep for the courtyard. The night was raw. I saw a few guards moving on the wall, but no one else. I made the circuit of the place, feeling foolish, and I was just about to return to my room when I heard soft voices. I stepped into an archway, instantly embarrassed by my own presence. Frain and Shamarra were talking somewhere close by.

'No men are allowed here,' said her cool voice, 'but you may pass, I suppose. Do you like it?'

'Your bower by the lake does you better honour than these hacked walls,' he answered curtly. 'Have you seen Tirell, my lady?'

She laughed the low laugh of wintertime water under ice. 'You know Prince Tirell does not come to me, and certainly I do not seek out his lodgings! No, I do not know where he is.' Her voice took on a wry tone. 'What is it that you want of me, really, Frain?'

'A touch of your hand,' he said quietly, 'or, failing that, a smile. But mostly I wanted to look on your face and see that you were well.'

'Look your fill,' she said in a tone I could not read. 'But see these so-called maidens here, pretending to sleep and peeping at you through half-lidded eyes, smiling behind their soft hands? They have you undressed already in their minds. Any one of them would give you a touch and more to make a man of you.'

'They will have to forego the pleasure for the time,' he said bitterly. 'Have you no thought for love, Lady?'

'In my house we love by different rules. Here comes someone to show you how.'

One of the maidens was rising from her place. I had found the door by then, a heavy metal door hidden down a passageway with stairs, and I was looking in through the bars. The

112

maiden was just a dusky, dark-haired movement in the ruddy lamplight, her eyes pools of deep shadow. She walked boldly and gracefully up to Frain and placed both her hands on his neck just above the torque. Her soft clothing fell back from her breasts.

'There is a touch for you, Frain,' Shamarra said blithely.

'You mock me,' Frain replied without moving.

'Take her!' Shamarra urged delightedly. 'She likes you. Or would you rather hurl her away?'

Frain did neither. He spoke to the girl, not even loudly. 'Go.'

She stepped away from him and stood at a little distance, staring. He was a prince, as I have said; he knew how to command. But she was puzzled, I suppose. She gazed at him, bare-breasted, for the space of a few breaths, and then the night was broken by a shriek. A wiry, gesticulating figure bounded out from behind the altar draperies, and all the girls scrambled to attention at the sight of him.

'Churl!' he screamed. 'No man is allowed in this most holy retreat of the goddess!'

'I am no man, but a pup,' Frain shot back. I had never heard such bitter anger in his voice.

'He is a warrior, a healer, and a most esteemed prince,' stated Shamarra perversely to Sethym. 'But do you not count yourself man, my lord, that you are here?'

'I felt certain you would afford me welcome,' he answered sullenly. Sethym was a peculiar fellow; he shaved his head as well as his beard, and he moved in jerks. He saw Frain's torque and glanced about the room jealously, trying to swallow his wrath.

'You hold the keys to the doors,' Shamarra said, 'but Prince Frain needed my hand at the locks to let him in. Your maidens dreamed of him and stirred in their sleep. Who is welcome here, lord?'

Sethym snapped his mouth shut and fingered his sword hilt. Gulping, I decided I had better also enter the strange, red-hung bower. I pushed open the heavy door and bumbled in, drawing the stares of the excited maidens. 'Why, hallo, Sethym!' I exclaimed with all the heartiness I could muster.

113

'Hallo, Fabron, old fellow!' He was glad of the diversion. 'I was going to visit you tomorrow, after you'd had a chance to mend a bit. What are you doing out in the night?'

'It's weary work, all this lying in bed,' I said, shrugging. 'And after riding with these princes, I have become accustomed to strange hours.'

'Though I think I have never seen you in a stranger place,' came an ironic voice. Tirell stumped in, swinging his bandaged hand. 'Well, well, here we are all together,' he remarked with heavy mockery. 'Together in the underground garden of Gyotte.'

Shamarra shrugged and went back to her couch, lying down with tantalizing indifference. The other maidens stood in a frightened cluster.

'I suppose we could go to my audience chamber,' Sethym muttered, embarrassed.

'At this time of night?' Tirell laughed. 'No, indeed. These two sufferers need their rest! Lord Fabron is swaying where he stands! Frain, can you help him back to that room of yours?'

We went without a word. I must admit that Tirell was right. I was still very weak, and in pain. Frain saw me into my bed without speaking and then flopped on his own. I must have slept then; I remember nothing until dawn. When I looked over he was still there, staring at the ceiling with a jaw like iron. I did not try to speak to him.

Tirell slammed in a bit later. He did not look tired, although he had probably been up all night; he never looked tired. He went directly to Frain and stood staring down at him like the carved panthers on the vaults above. 'What ails you?' he asked, evenly enough.

Frain stirred restively and parried the question with another. 'When can we be gone from here?'

'When you two are strong enough to ride! Which you will not become by roaming the night! And when I have obtained Sethym's promise of arms and aid! Speak him fair, brother. Has he done you any wrong that you are so knee-deep in wrath?'

'No,' Frain retorted grimly, 'no wrong. He has taken nothing that is mine.'

'Including your head,' Tirell remarked pointedly, 'which

114

you forfeited by entering his little bower of flesh.'

Frain made no reply.

'For this matter of Shamarra,' Tirell continued, although no one had mentioned Shamarra, 'I do not think Sethym will be so bold as to go to her again. He seemed very weary when he left her, and not from pleasure, either. I think he will sleep tonight.'

'And if he does not?' Frain cried, half lifting himself from his sickbed. 'Sethym has muscle in his fool's body, and he has the keys.'

Tirell smiled mirthlessly. 'By blood, I'd pit that hellion Shamarra against a troop of such as him any day or night. But for the matter of that, I'll skulk about. She will be guarded. I give you my word. Now will you keep to your chamber tonight and rest?'

'You couldn't drag me away,' Frain replied bitterly.

Tirell left without another word, banging the door behind him. Frain lay back on his bed. His mind and heart were as sore as his body, I judged, and we spoke little that day. I slept lightly that night, but I might have known he would not stir from his bed; he had given his word. Tirell came early the next morning, for all the world like a soldier on watch, to make his curt report. And I felt very strange, because I had been incensed that he showed no love for my son, and now I was jealous that in his own angry way he showed love of the truest kind.

Within a week we were rested and halfway healed and making ready to leave. Sethym gave us a troop of retainers and plenty of advice.

'The bridge of Serriade is held against you, my scouts say,' he informed us. 'About fifty or sixty Boda are camped there. But my men of the motherhood will win you through, never fear! They are sons of earth, every one. I see to it that they know no women and eat only meat and raw roots. . . . The Boda lost the blessing of the goddess, I believe, when they ceased to bathe their initiates in real human blood. These days they are cowards—they use juice of bulls instead. But even in their depravity, how can they turn their swords

115

against sons of the Sacred King! Surely the goddess will punish them in a glorious battle on the plans of Melior.'

'Melior has no plains,' Tirell rejoined with barest shreds of patience. 'And if we are ever to reach it at all, we had better hope that Raz will permit us to cross his domain in force. Assuming that we win through to Nisroch, do you think he will give us welcome?'

Sethym rolled his protuberant eyes. 'I scarcely know! You might mention my name. One of his daughters was my second wife, you know. A nice girl, but I had to slay her. I have had bad luck with women. Five I have taken to my bosom, and not an heir yet—'

'About Raz,' I reminded him hastily. Shamarra looked ready to attack.

'Well, as for Raz, I have not seen him for years. You know I seldom go out, my life is so girded about with portents and forebodings. I have many enemies, many who wish me ill, and they bring witchcraft against me—'

'What do your advisers say?' Tirell interrupted stonily.

'Hah? Oh, they say little; they are of no use. But as for Raz, when I knew him we were friendly, of course, but it seemed to me that he was arrogant, lacking in respect for the goddess and in allegiance for Melior. He struck me as a vain man, always encrusted in jewels.' Sethym ogled us, then sank his voice to a sepulchral whisper. 'And these days, men tell, he has gone from bad to worse. Folk say he couples with serpents!' Sethym paused, evidently expecting shock and consternation. But we were all jaded by days of his excesses and merely favoured him with our mild surprise.

'He even worships the enemies of Eala!' Sethym protested more loudly. 'He has raised altars in honour of serpents and ram-headed serpents and dragons with horns. And he keeps serpents in his bailey, and he feeds the ugly things with human flesh. Can you imagine! All men know that human blood belongs to the goddess. It is heresy to offer it to crawling vipers—'

'As long as he does not feed them his guests,' Tirell put in morosely, 'we might yet come to terms. Sethym, my thanks for your help and hospitality. It is time we were going.'

But leave-taking is never as simple as that, of course, and it was another hour before we were actually on our way. Sethym's final courtesies expanded almost beyond endurance. I blessed whatever powers prevail that his fear of the multitudinous rabbit kept him from riding out with us.

We got through the gates at last with two troops of men, spare horses, and, of course, the black beast and the lady Shamarra. The beast had been housed in an enclosure within the walls, and no one had dared to come near it. Tirell had been obliged to care for it himself. What with that, and standing guard for Shamarra, and checking on Frain, and having to be civil to Sethym, it is small wonder that Tirell was eager to leave Gyotte.

We headed north, toward the Chardri and the bridge of Serriade that would take us across into Tiela. Once more Shamarra and her white mare and the beast frolicked at their whim, and once more Frain watched, as the other men watched—who could help it? But there was a different quality to Frain's gaze those days. I do not think his devotion to her had lessened, and his anger had long since abated, for he was not one to hold onto wrath. But he seemed older, with a guarded, waiting air that was new. I doubt if Tirell noticed. Sometimes I wondered if he saw Frain, or Shamarra, or even the road before us very clearly.

It is useless to speak much of that journey, for it lasted only three days. On the morning of the fourth day we awoke to find ourselves consigned to our own familiar company. Sethym's men had deserted us during the night. They had taken nothing that was not theirs; they had simply made shift to quietly depart. I could not blame them too severely. The Serriade was manned with twice their force, if report ran true.

'That's what comes of meat and roots and no women,' Tirell grumbled. 'Well, let us turn around.'

'Back to Gyotte?' I inquired with sinking heart.

'Aftalun, no! I don't want to see Sethym again for as many moons as I can possibly avoid him. But we cannot cross the Chardri, it seems, so we shall have to go around it, beyond the Coire Adalis. We must take to the mountains.' His eyes sparkled as if he had said we must take to the skies. And indeed, to my way of thinking, the one was as outlandish as the other.

'Can you be serious?' I squeaked.

'Surely,' Tirell remarked in mild rebuke. 'I'll warrant you the Boda will not follow us there.'

5

I had to admit that the Boda were our greatest fear for the time. We mounted in haste to be away before they found us. We left the main road and took to the countryside, riding as quickly and furtively as we could. None of us was in condition to fight even a few Boda. So once more we fled, riding late into the night and the night after and the night after that. More than once Tirell led us on a queer sort of dogleg without saying why. I could only conclude that he was seeing red shirts swim before his visionary eyes, as before.

We skirted Gyotte to the east, hoping our enemies would be searching for us more toward Melior, and rode on through parching heat. That summer's drought was the worst yet. I scanned the distant Perin Tyr constantly for a sign of rain, but not a wisp of cloud appeared on that horizon. The sky was always blue, a bright, hard blue one learned to curse. The land seemed made of ashes and old bones. The dust always found its way to our mouths and eyes, even when we rode abreast. By the time we finally reached the mountains I was too weary to be very much afraid of them anymore, especially since we found pools of water hidden in the hollows of their flanks.

The Lorc Tutosel were not much like the hulks of Acheron I had first approached with Frain. But they were just as deadly in their way—death and danger are in all the mountains that encircle Vale, but such lovely peril in those southern mountains! Slender trees sprang up all around their feet, swaying like dancing maidens in lacy, fluttering clothing of green and gold jewelled here and there by bright, bold-throated birds. There were no birds in Acheron, but I was not much comforted by the ones I heard in Lorc Tutosel. I wondered which of them might be the night bird of the song.

The night bird sings
Of asphodel;
The day bird wakes
And flaps his wings
And cannot fly
And lifts the cry
O Tutosel, Ai Tutosel!

The night bird sings
Of Vieyra's spell,
Of Aftalun's
Sweet hydromel
And dark chimes of
The wild bluebell
In reaches of high Tutosel.

The dawn bird wakes
And lifts his wings
And cannot fly
And sadly sings
O Philomel,
O mortal's knell,
O Tutosel, Ai Tutosel!

All very mysterious and rather melancholy. The ringing of a bluebell signifies death. I took some surreptitious and superstitious comfort in the fact that it was not the season for those flowers. I sensed even then that the Lorc Tutosel were as seductive and treacherous as that strange bird of their name. Still, we rode gently on their cool, tree-shaded slopes; we slept soundly in their heather—and even though they cozened me to my death, years later, I look back on them with longing and delight.

We made our way eastward toward the Coire Adalis, the Deep of Adalis, where the river Chardri plunged back to the flood beneath. The mountains grew wilder and steeper by the day, and we edged upward on their slopes, for we hoped to pass well above the horrible chasm at the foot of Aftalun, tallest peak in all the encircling ranges of Vale. Frain looked daily for Aftalun, and he longed to climb to the very top of Lorc Tutosel to see what lay beyond. But we never came near those awesome heights. We travelled just above the tree line, scrambling along crazily tilted slopes of shale between thickets and patches of heather, leading the horses most of the time. Cliffs soared above us, and sometimes a nasty drop yawned below as well. Tirell nearly came to grief on such terrain.

We were all walking separately because we were nearly out of food and each of us was on the lookout for game. Frain was down among the trees, hunting rabbits or whatever came his way, and I had an arrow at the ready for grouse. Where Shamarra was, perhaps Eala knows. She wandered off every day and returned to us at night with nothing to show for it, calm and aloof, seemingly quite careless of our company. Even the black beast was friendlier. It slept curled close to Tirell each night, except when Tirell was wakeful and skulking about, when it would nestle next to Frain. It never came to me for comfort, or to the lady.

But on this day, as I was saying, a grouse went up with a sudden clap of wings, as they always do, and I shot my arrow and missed. I watched the bird go, muttering. Just as it reached a cliff far above me I saw it falter in the air, and a stone rattled down. The bird flopped and fluttered at the edge of the cliff, and Tirell ran toward it with reckless speed, stooping for another stone. He must have been very hungry, or else lusting for the kill. As he reached his prey he slipped and sped neatly over the edge of the cliff, sending the shale flying, shouting hoarsely. He caught hold of the treacherous rock with both hands, and there he hung.

I don't know how long it took me to get to him. It seemed forever, and I know I climbed as I had never climbed before. I was gasping for breath and streaming sweat when I reached him at last, and his straining face looked white as death. He had not cried out after that first scream.

I got him by one wrist and hauled him up until he could lie on his gut with his long legs flailing the air. He rolled and wriggled his way to safety, and we both lay panting.

'Where is that accursed bird?' he wheezed.

It was gone, of course, and I never found my arrow either. I gave no reply. I was too old to find my wind so quickly.

After a little while Tirell sat up and looked at me with no expression at all on his pale, handsome face. I lay back and met his stare, still puffing, hoping for thanks but not really expecting as much—not from him.

'So, Fabron,' he said slowly, 'you no longer entirely hate me.'

I had almost forgotten by then how I had hated him at first, when my wife was newly dead and my son newly found and dreams of revenge and glory floated like a mist at the back of my mind. His perception startled me, since I had not judged that he knew, he who seemed to go through his days in his own haze of dreams. Shock and guilt stabbed me, but I did not bother to turn away from his gaze. Let him see.

'No, I no longer hate you,' I replied equably. 'Though Eala alone knows why not. You are cold and bitter enough to turn spring back to winter, Tirell.' He had not titled me, and I returned him no title.

He grunted in reply, got to his feet, and reached down to help me to mine. I took his hand gladly. It was not thanks, but it was a gesture of friendship such as I had never known from him, and well worth the sore back I suffered for days afterward. We took a while to catch our horses and then went on our way. But we had no supper that night. Frain had lost arrows too.

'Such cunning hunters,' Shamarra remarked cattily.

We went hungry the next day also. But the third day, when still nothing had seen fit to blunder into our clutches, she met us at dusk and gave us marvellous fruits to eat. Each was as round as a sun, ruddy as a westward sun, firm and filling as bread but juicy and sweet.

'Red fruits! The food of the gods!' Frain exclaimed, only half joking. He ate greedily, and I did the same, ecstatically gulping as many as I could hold. But I noticed that Tirell ate only a few, and those grudgingly. I wondered what ailed him.

For the next several days when we bagged no birds or

122

rabbits we had fruit, which was better anyway, to my way of thinking. Even the horses and the beast had some, for we were finding no water on these high slopes. Within a few days we left the trees and even the thickets far below us. We could look out over them to where the Chardri made a great silver flow and a green corridor across the sere land, where slaves worked hard pouring water from the river on the crops. No freeman would set foot in the river for fear of death, but slaves could be driven. . . . We sighted Aftalun at last, a great peak, and we could see where the Chardri roared into a gaping blackness below sheer cliffs.

'Aftalun has two faces,' Frain said, studying the mountain.

It did indeed. A rugged line divided two vast stony surfaces, one in light and one in shadow. The peak resembled the jutting edge of a blunt and massive axe.

'They both frown,' Tirell complained. 'We can see water, even hear water, and yet we can get none.'

We listened. It was true; we could hear the distant thunder of the deep.

'It is a strange world,' said Tirell. 'Well, let us go on.'

It was rough going. We walked along ledges or slopes scarcely level enough for footing, leading the horses, and often we had to twist and turn and retrace our steps to find a way forward. After a few days of this, Shamarra had no more fruit to give us. We were all plagued by hunger and thirst. But the worst trial, I think, was not the thirst or even the fear of falling, but the Luoni. Like great, dirty-coloured birds they clung to the rocks with their wrinkled claws, turning toward us the heads of emaciated women. Long, drab hair streamed down around their stubby wings. Wherever we went they sat above our path and watched us with their rolling, sunken eyes. They did not threaten us; they did not even cry out or speak. They only watched us, but I have never felt so tormented. Once I came upon one clinging to a rock scarcely a spear's length away, staring at me sideways out of her craterous face. I stared back defiantly because I was afraid, and I longed to kill the foul thing, but her human head prevented me.

We spent the nights on slopes and ledges, scarcely sleeping

for fear of falling and for unreasoning fear of the Luoni. Even Tirell did not stir during those nights. Finally we came to the edge of the shadowed face of Aftalun, where the roar of Coire Adalis sounded directly below us and the Chardri ran at us like a glistening road out of the west—and we could not go on.

We cast about for a whole day trying to find a way. Aftalun would not let us pass. Sunset came, its bloody rays streaming down the Chardri, and we stood confronting a blank, curving wall of rock, standing on a ledge scarcely wide enough for the horses. Frain and I stared hopelessly at each other. We had found ourselves on that same ledge half a dozen times before in the course of the day, to no avail. Those accursed Luoni watched us silently from above.

'It's a cave,' Tirell said suddenly from behind me—we had got out of order on the jumbling slopes. 'Go on in.'

For the first time I seriously doubted his ability to lead us. 'It's only the shadow of the rock in this harsh light, Tirell,' I explained patiently. 'The sun strikes across it slantwise—'

'Exactly,' he roared, 'and it won't last another minute. Get on in, I say!'

I opened my mouth to protest again, but Frain simply walked into the shadow and disappeared, leading his horse. I must have blinked ten times before I followed him. He stood waiting for me just within, and he spoke to me as I entered to encourage me. The cave seemed bigger on the inside than the outside. I stood comfortably beside him, and I heard Shamarra stop beside me.

'Go on!' Tirell grumbled from the rear.

'Likely it will drop us into the deep in a step or two,' I whispered. I was trembling with the strangeness of the place. Utter darkness surrounded us, even though there should have been sunlight just behind. I did not dare to turn and look. 'Make a light, Shamarra,' I begged.

'I can't,' she said flatly, with no trace of self-pity in her voice. I don't think any of us realized how exhausted she was.

'Let me pass,' said Tirell scornfully, and I felt his hard hand move me out of his way. We all walked along, following each other's sounds. The floor did not seem to slope.

'We'll go off the edge in a minute,' I pleaded. 'Can't we stop here, light a fire, and maybe sleep? There seems to be room enough.'

Tirell barked out a laugh. 'In this hole? I'd as soon sleep on the ledge!' He pressed on. But soon, to my astonishment, I realized that I could see in a dim way. We were all walking through a kind of featureless grey expanse. After a while it occurred to me that there was nothing to prevent us from riding—no walls, no roof—so I got on my horse. Frain and Shamarra did likewise. Tirell continued to stalk afoot.

I saw more clearly every moment. By some marvel we were not inside a mountain at all. Or if we were, the mountain was as big as the world inside. We rode across a broad countryside lit with a muted, pearly glow that seemed to come from everywhere and nowhere, showing no roof, no dome of sky, no encircling mountain wall—I felt as if I could float away into the misty light. Still, I grew less afraid of going off an edge into the deep; falling seemed likely to be of no consequence in this country. The land looked soft and gentle, like down pillows on a tufted bed. The trees and grass seemed fluffy as fur. I saw comfortable-looking thatched houses and people and cattle and everything necessary for prosperity, but all hazy to my eyes, like a dream. I do not remember sounds, or any colours at all.

I do remember the castle. I remember watching it grow nearer during what must have been hours, even days, of riding. I was no longer troubled by hunger or thirst, and I cannot recall any weariness. I never tired of looking at the castle. It entranced me with its shimmering intricacy; it shifted like a structure of leaves in the directionless light, puzzling my smith's eye. I sensed pattern, but I could only trace change as I drew nearer. The place was immense and the colour of moonlight.

From within the castle seemed as boundless as the countryside. Servants met us, blanketed our animals and took them to stable, welcomed us with every courtesy. They led us to a great hall, to a feast. Guests thronged around the tables, decked in jewels and robes and making merry. I remember a starry sparkle of gems and a lulling hum of talk. But I must have been more tired than I realized; the people seemed to ripple together before my eyes, all the colourless colour of water. In his fair linen. Frain floated swan-like in their midst; Shamarra's hair and gown formed a waterfall of silver and sunny gold. Tirell's black figure stood like a lance, shocking my bleary eyes. A pool of silence grew around him. He stood and stared at the dais, and I followed his stare, saw a king rise to give us welcome.

He stood twice the height of any man I had ever seen, massive, his great, muscular arms folded across his broad bellows of a chest. He verily seemed to shine in that muted place, golden, like a sun. I felt half afraid of him until I saw his face crinkle with smiling cheerfulness, his eyes that were merry and wise and very old although his body was that of an arrogant youth.

'Welcome!' he cried. 'Come, seat yourselves and drink and feast. All that we have is yours.'

'Filthy old cripple!' Tirell shouted back. 'I bow before no living man!'

I gaped, and Frain turned as if he had been struck. The reply made no sense! But the giant on the dais seemed in no wise affronted.

'Why, I am no living man,' he declared. 'Lady Shamarra, Prince Tirell, Prince Frain, Fabron king of Vaire, you are very welcome. I am Aftalun, first god, then first man, then first to taste of death, and I rule death here. I am king of the dead, and here we hold our revels. All that we have is yours. Drink and eat!'

'Drink and eat!' Tirell roared. 'I would as soon eat the red mushroom of madness! Aren't you the ass who built that bloody altar?'

I tensed unhappily, feeling sure it would come to fight now. But Aftalun only mildly turned his eyes.

'Why, yes,' he replied. 'But then I was a man, intent on strife and glory. Now I am a god again, and I say rest, drink, and eat.'

Someone handed me a cup of mead, and I gulped it down. It was the sweetest I had ever tasted. I took no further notice of Tirell's sulkiness. I sat at a table and devoured fine wheat bread and crisp, hot pork and poultry and sweet red-gold fruits such as Shamarra had given us. Frain sat beside me, smiling.

'Eat more slowly,' he cautioned. 'You'll get a bellyache.'

I turned to reply and nearly choked. Just beyond him sat a courtly, winsome woman—Mela! Smiling, coifed, and crowned with a graceful circlet, she did not look much like the queen Frain had seen. Indeed, he seemed not to recognize her as she passed him dishes in solicitous and motherly style. I struggled out of my seat, knocking the bench awry, and blundered over to her.

'Mela!' I cried, tears trickling. She glanced up at me in amazed sympathy.

'Why, good sir, whatever is the matter? You must be exhausted. Here, let me help you.' She rose and got me by the shoulders, guided me back to my seat. A good thing, for I was tottering and I couldn't say a word. 'You'll feel much better soon,' Mela assured me. 'Here, have some more of the hydromel. It must be hard, so hard, to have come here through the darkened ways.'

I took a huge swig of mead to please her. 'You don't remember,' I sputtered through it.

'Remember?' Her clear eyes, so much like Frain's, frosted over with thought. 'The flight with aching wings and burning lungs, that I remember. And the dive—I was too frightened to dive, but I had to. After that, nothing but liquid light and ease. . . . Your way has been far harsher. What is your name, good sir, and how do you come to know mine?'

'Fabron,' I told her. 'I—you—never mind.' She was all that she had ever been: generous, beautiful . . . And more—she was at peace. Though words unspoken filled me with an urgent ache, I would not disturb that peace, not for anything. Not even to show son to mother. Mela deserved such peace after what I had done to her. I turned to warn Frain to keep silence in case he had heard me call her—

I don't think he had heard a word. He sat staring at the dais. Tirell was up there, seated between Shamarra and another maiden, glowering fiercely. Shamarra ate coolly and daintily in the place of honour by Aftalun's side. Tirell seemed not to have touched his food. All looked much as usual in regard to

127

those two, so I wondered what had riveted Frain's gaze so.

'Mylitta!' he gasped. 'Right by Tirell—and he doesn't know her!'

The other maiden was a plain, pert lass with all the warmth of summer in her smile. She sat serenely observing the assembly with occasionally a humorous glance at the sullen figure beside her. She offered him viands as courtesy dictated, and he answered her with snarls that abashed her not at all.

I swallowed. 'She doesn't know *him*,' I said to Frain.

'I suppose not. We're truly in the realm of the dead,' Frain murmured. 'I know Aftalun said so, but I didn't understand. . . . Fabron, Tirell must never know, never, that he sat by her side and glared. It would break his heart for good. Promise me.'

'Of course,' I told him. 'Have some more of this excellent mead.'

I felt suddenly quite content. I sat and conversed pleasantly with my dead wife. How nice that she could not remember what a bastard I had been! She listened to me with friendly interest, and I talked and ate until warm weariness overcame me. After a while someone showed me to a chamber and I slept. Frain to the contrary, I suffered no bellyache. I never felt any ache of any kind in that place, not after that first feast.

We stayed for days, I suppose, though there were no days and nights, only sleeping and waking. There were many amusements to take up the waking time, and of course meals, as many as one liked, and luxurious bathing. But I spent much of my stay in Aftalun's realm with my wife. We became good friends. We would walk about together. She showed me the sights of the castle that never seemed to end, and we listened to music in every courtyard. I loved her with all a youth's passion, but I did not woo her. My flesh was quiet those days.

When not with Mela I was to be found with Frain. Aftalun did not neglect his guests. He spoke with us when he could, and I found him to be a marvellously amiable fellow in spite of his immense strength.

'I thought Acheron was the land of the dead,' said Frain as we sat with him one day. The same question had occurred to me: How could there be more than one deathly realm?

'Is that what men say in Vale?' Aftalun asked, smiling.

'No one says it, but everyone believes it.'

'Well, they are right. It is. The goddess rules Acheron, and I am the king of the dead here to the east. But it is all one ring of mountains, really, and it is all one place to those who travel the watery ways.'

'I don't understand,' said Frain.

'Think of the sun, how he sets in the west and rises in the east each morning in renewed life. And think of the bosom of the goddess and her womb: She who takes also gives.'

'The flood beneath,' Frain muttered. 'You sit at the gate the Chardri makes, and Shamarra sits at the lake. . . . But we did not come here by any watery way. Are we dead?'

The question above all questions that I had not dared to ask. Frain had nearly ceased to astonish me with his courage. But perhaps he surprised Aftalun. The giant cocked an amused eye at him.

'Do you remember dying?'

'No,' answered Frain ruefully, 'but I was plentifully miserable. Perhaps I did not notice.'

'We have eaten your food,' I put in softly, 'which all the legends say has power to keep us here.'

Aftalun shook his head. 'If you wish to go, and if you can summon the strength, no one will prevent you. It is true, the path is dark and steep. But I will show it to you myself.'

'And if we wish to stay?' Frain asked.

'Why, then you are my welcome guests!' Aftalun spread wide his great hands. 'But I should warn you, Frain, destinies do not change even here. The lady likes you no better than she did in Vale.'

It was true that Shamarra kept as distant from Frain as ever. I pitied him, but I did not entirely grasp my own problem until a few days later. Frain and I were lounging on couches after dinner, listening to the lutists, when Tirell came and stood over us. 'If you two are rested,' he said with only the faintest trace of mockery in his voice, 'it is time we were going.'

Frain got up slowly, with a sigh, and stood beside his brother. I could tell he left regretfully and only because Tirell

129

wished it. But I could not move. I lay as if dead. Half of my soul had already rooted in this place of peace and comfort.

'Aren't you coming, Fabron?' Frain asked.

Tirell stood silently with knowledge gleaming ironically in his eyes. Tell him he is your son, that gleam said, and perhaps he will stay with you. Perhaps not. But the thought awakened all the old pangs of guilt and shame in me, and anger at Abas, and love for Frain—above all, that love. I wrenched myself to my feet, feeling as if I had been torn. In pain too deep for words or weeping I followed the others to Aftalun's audience chamber.

Shamarra sat with the giant king, playing at dice with him. Tirell nodded coldly at them both. 'We have come to take our leave,' he said.

Aftalun gestured vague assent. 'That is my sword you carry, you know,' he remarked. 'And my shield. The beast is ancient, you see, and madness was not always a curse. Use your weapons well.'

'Lady?' Frain questioned with a note of alarm rising in his voice. Shamarra had not moved from her place.

'I am staying for a while with this King here,' she said. 'A Sacred King,' she added, staring directly at Tirell. 'He has husbanded me since the time before time.'

Tirell burst out in a laugh of the most genuine amusement I had yet heard from him. But laughter rang badly against his brother's sorrow, and there was no cause for it that I could discern. We all stared at him. 'The more power to you both!' he guffawed.

No one smiled. 'Insofar as she is goddess I have loved her,' Aftalun added, 'and I have hated her for the same reason. . . . Well, Frain, you cannot always be expecting her to make lights and fruit for you. It wears her out. You should know that, lad.'

Frain stared speechlessly and turned to the door. He wished only to be gone quickly. Why were we going, he and I, each of us leaving a heart's love to follow a callous madman? Because the ladies needed us not at all. Even Tirell needed us more.

Tirell lingered, still snickering. 'I cannot believe you are the one who built that bloody altar!' he exclaimed.

'What, Prince, because I was more than man, should I therefore have been less than a fool?' Aftalun grimaced. 'Go in peace. Do you need me to show you the way?'

'Snakefeathers, no!' Tirell left with a roar of new mirth. I could not follow. Aftalun's eyes were on me.

'So you are really going,' he marvelled softly. 'I expected it of the other two, but not of you. They are younger, and they do not know or understand the ache you suffer. . . . You are a very brave man, Fabron.'

'Lord,' I whispered, 'pray tender my parting regards to Mela.'

'I will,' he said wryly, 'but she won't know what to do with them.'

'Why does she not remember?'

He shrugged. 'She might remember when she has healed. Some do. Go with all blessing, king of Vaire.'

Dismissed, I stumbled after the other two. When we had mounted I laid my head on the horse's neck and knew nothing more. I cannot tell what way we went. When I awoke we were far down Aftalun's shadowed face, riding northward along the Perin Tyr, bound toward Nisroch in Tiela—and the black beast was following us.

Book Three

Tirell of Melior

1

I am Tirell.

I will not speak of Mylitta. Even now, ages and changes later, it is difficult for me to think of her. I remember how I loved her, but more often I remember how she died—was killed—and the black beast came to take her place.

I was afraid of the beast at first. But I was defenceless, naked to every gust that tried to shake me, weak and helpless until I took it as my shield. People think it is a gift to be a visionary, but it is more of a curse. It made me terribly vulnerable. Abas groped for me even in Acheron, where I had thought his mind would not venture.

'Tirell,' he whispered to me in my exhausted sleep, 'my son, come back! You will perish in the darkness. Tirell, Tirell, my son!'

He had not called me so since I could remember. I should not have answered at all, but I wanted my bitter triumph. 'You're far too late,' I told him, and he seized me with a bloody, invisible grip.

'The beast!' he wailed. 'Tirell, get away from the beast! Darkness of Acheron, darkness of Aftalun, darkness of the deep, Tirell, beware the beast, black get of Vieyra, black brother of the demon birds, black devil of the deep, Tirell! Slay the thing—it hunts you! Come back and we will slay it together, coward that I am. . . .'

'Get away,' I muttered, waking.

'I will kill whatever threatens you, my son!' he pledged. I cursed him and wrenched myself away, put up a wall of will to defend myself, but the effort left me drained. Waking was not much better than my haunted sleep. In the gloomy dawn

135

the beast lay near me, a living nightmare, and in my mind Abas shouted with fear. I was like him; I hated to be like him. I was afraid of the beast too—Eala, yes! But I loved it as my own precious madness. It was part of me. It had been with the line of Melior as long as the altar, I sensed. I felt its call—not unlike the tug Abas was trying to put on me, but I trusted the beast more. It at least would not try to talk. I went to it and embraced it, feeling Abas shriek within my mind. I learned later that I was not the only one he kept awake those days. He set the whole castle on edge with his rantings and noise.

'Let me alone,' I whispered into the beast's mane, hugging it close for protection. Abas gasped and snapped away, gone—for the time. He could not long abide the beast.

'I will find you,' he told me hours later as I rode. 'That thing cannot keep me away. I can feel you. I will find you and bring you back and slay the monster. . . .' He gurgled to a stop as I sent with my mind an arrow to his heart.

'You've done quite enough killing already!' I hissed. Then I beheaded him, held that picture in my mind for him to see. I had found not only a shield but a weapon in my madness. Let Abas pester! I answered him with thoughts of vengeance, hardened myself into a knot of hatred so that whenever he surprised me he would find no cause for hope, never! I wanted him to fear his doom. That is the better part of vengeance. I wedded myself to anger. I wince to think of it now, but then I fed on anger as the beast fed on bitter twigs.

'Vengeance!' Shamarra had said to me in a voice that echoed down the runnels of my hatred.

She offered me bitter food from the day I first ventured to her mountain hut. Raw rowanberries, forsooth! And hazelnuts, and a sort of seedcake fit only for birds. I had to eat the stuff or starve. Even then I felt small liking for her or her tittering old women of trees or her brooding, waiting death's face of a lake. To be sure, I felt her power—especially at first, when I was weak—and it caused me to like her the less. I could not see why she followed me. I thought it was only to torment me, but I realize now that she could not have known how she tormented me. Men say she was uncommonly beautiful, so perhaps she did not understand how her cold, carved face distressed me. Whenever I saw her thin lips I thought of Mylitta's that were full and soft and warm, her warm brown eyes, the heady comfort of her breasts—I have said I would not speak of her. But Shamarra was a mockery of her womanly form and grace, a pale, thin-nosed parody of my lost love, and I hated her for it.

I could not hate Frain, though all the demons of air know I tried. He followed me as faithfully as the beast, but he wanted me to speak to him, touch him, and I could not. Love is poor food for rage and revenge! I pushed it far from my mind, but the stubborn stuff remained somehow, and the beast found me out about it. We were of one mind, the beast and I. It would nuzzle Frain and curl up next to him in the night. It liked Shamarra as a playmate, though I myself would not even look at her, and the time also came when the beast showed love for Daymon Cein and even Fabron by the end of my travels—while I could barely look at them without a snarl. Well, those were dark days.

There is no need to relate all the twistings and turnings of my journey. All of Vale has heard the tale of those times, and truth to tell I remember them strangely. Frain and Fabron speak of Aftalun as a sort of shining giant in a vast, splendid palace, but I remember a crippled, withered old fool sitting on the floor of a cold cave and croaking, 'Bow, you churl! I am the king of all that I survey!' Those horrid Luoni sat with him, and we all ate more rowanberries—how I loathed them by that time! But Frain and Fabron loved the place, and Shamarra chose to stay there for the time, and who is to say which of us saw truly?

I will say one thing for Aftalun's cave: Abas could not find me there. But I heard him questing as soon as I emerged. 'Tirell!' he cried. 'Tir-ell! You cannot flee me forever!'

'Flee, O meat of sweet revenge?' I retorted in arrogant high spirits. 'This is a pleasure outing!' I could not help feeling better since we had left Shamarra. But Fabron was as morose as a whipped hound.

'Where did summer go?' he grumbled.

The season seemed to have gotten the jump on us. We must have stayed longer in that miserable cave than I thought. Leaves were already turning on the mountain trees, and not just from drought, either. There was a chill in the air. I had hoped to have my bid ready within the summer, but there seemed no chance of that. Still, once away from Shamarra I behaved more pleasantly than I had in a long time—until the Boda found us.

My own folly was to blame for letting Abas focus on us. He had his ways of communicating with his doomsters in the field—trained birds, for one—and he was not long in setting them on our track. Fabron saw them coming across the plains of Tiela; I was not paying attention.

'Ruddy bloody bastards yonder,' he announced in gloomy tones.

We took to high ground. But they had spotted us, and we spent grueling days—weeks—trying to shake them. They trailed us along the gently rolling terrain at the base of the mountains while we struggled along the steep upper slopes. We were never able to gain much on them, in spite of days much too long, even nights sometimes, spent travelling. Still, we managed to loop around them to the northward and get out on the Perin Spur, a ragged line of peaks extending toward Nisroch. Then we made a run for it with the Boda on our heels.

We made Nisroch barely an hour ahead of them. That accursed place! Raz's city be damned. May I never again feel such helpless, venom-spitting, hair-bristling fury as I did before those high, unyielding gates. The castle stands all alone on a muddy plain along the river Pol. Raz must have seen us coming in the distance and ordered all his people inside, for not a human face awaited us and not a sound of welcome. We could get no answer at the gates except the long, soft hiss of a huge snake that poked its head over the pikes to peer at us. A sweet reception! But I was not so easily to be frightened away. I pounded on the timbers with my sword hilt and shouted for admittance until I was hoarse. By the ancient Five, I had not come all the way from Acheron just to be ignored!

Not a soul stirred in answer to all my curses. And soon we were obliged to flee back to the Perin Spur with the Boda on our heels. The cowards, they would not follow us there. And Raz, king of Tiela, had been too cowardly to let us in while they threatened! At least Frain, with his customary and maddening generosity, gave him that excuse.

'If he knew they were there,' I argued.

'He has the reputation of being clever, so I expect he knew.'

I snorted. 'He is a coward all the same. Sethym let us in with the Boda at his very door.'

'You have said yourself, Sethym is a mad fool,' Frain retorted. 'Because he aids us, do you therefore expect Raz to?'

I was beginning to dislike the argument. People had to help us, for any reason and no reason. 'Is Fabron a mad fool to aid us then?' I snapped.

Sitting by Frain's side, Fabron rolled his eyes. In fact, his actions were rash, and he knew it, and he knew I knew why.

'I used to be as clever as Raz,' he remarked, 'but I am not any longer.'

'Adalis be praised,' I said sourly.

So we had not gained even a glimpse of Raz or a word with him after all our strivings to reach his domain. And, by any name of the goddess, I would not pound on his gates again, not though we were out of provisions, beset by winter, and had no place to shelter. We would just have to go on toward Eidden. So we travelled northward for weeks, clear out of the Perin Tyr and into the Lorc Dahak, keeping to the flanks of the mountains and ignoring the Boda in the valleys below, foraging for food and looking for a likely cave to take refuge in when the snow fell. Which is how we came to find Grandfather.

There were plenty of caves, but most of them were too shallow or too small. So when we spied a truly gloomy-looking hole one freezing day we all three turned aside to investigate it. The entrance was high enough for horses. We walked in to a good depth, to a point where it became too black for us to see.

'Light a torch, somebody,' Fabron said peevishly. He was afraid of the dark, though I would not say so to his face.

Lighting a torch is a weary business, but there really seemed to be no alternative. So we were all busy with rags and oil and flint and steel when we heard a sound that made us spring to attention—a long, low, sighing sound, not too far away.

'Snake!' Fabron whispered in frank terror. 'Let's get out of here!' He had been jumpy about snakes ever since Nisroch.

'No!' I shouted. I hate taking direction from anyone, but I believe I have never been so utterly unreasonable as then. I strode blindly deeper into the cave. A sudden, inexplicable tug had taken hold on me, not from Abas, but—who, or what? Frain and Fabron scrambled after me, forced to leave the horses, hissing at me to stop. I paid no attention. I couldn't. The call was strong, close at hand, urgent.

'Come on,' I mumbled at Frain. 'No time to lose.'

I realized in vague surprise that I could see where I was going. A dim light glowed from somewhere ahead. In a few more strides I rounded a turn of the cave and came in sight of a dragon.

I stopped, the ache and the call still strong on me, but I couldn't answer. I couldn't help myself. I was stunned, held thrall, by the unblinking gaze of the dragon's yellow eyes. Nothing could have shielded me from those eyes. A question shot from them, an ancient, ancient riddle that sent me floundering into floodwaters of confusion, snatching at splinters of self, fragments scattered by the many facets of those mirroring eyes. White reflections and black, black . . . How would I live? What horse would bear me? I thrashed in a directionless deep—

'Tirell,' a tight voice called me, not even loudly, but the summons snapped through me. Frain needed me.

It does not sound like much, but it is probably the hardest thing I have ever done; somehow I embraced my scattered selfhood, found form, and shifted my hypnotized gaze. Frain was kneeling by a kind of lumpy bundle on the cave floor at the very feet of the dragon. I had just sense enough to realize that the huge, shimmering creature had not harmed him—not yet. Towering above him, it continued to puff slow, steady breaths of gently luminous warmth. The whole cave felt warm as a womb. It was the dragon's breathing we had heard.

I could not draw my sword for fear of enraging it. I moved

cautiously to my brother's side, glanced down, and swayed in shock. What looked like a crumpled cloak blown to the floor was Daymon Cein, withered as a winter leaf.

'Is he alive?' I exclaimed.

'I can't tell,' Frain whispered numbly. 'He is warm, but the dragon warms him.'

I lifted a frail hand. It lay limply in mine. 'Frain, help him!' I cried. I could not imagine what he was waiting for.

'Watch the dragon for me.'

He drew his dagger, and then I understood. The race of Dahak cannot easily withstand the touch or even the sight of iron, and Frain had to use iron for healing. If the dragon attacked—but instead it narrowed its topaz eyes in discomfort and scraped its great claws along the cave floor, drawing back a bit. It held its ground a few paces away, still warming us with its quiet, even breathing. Why should it concern itself with us at all? I sensed quite surely that the beast was dangerous, very dangerous, perhaps as dangerous as I. And at the same time I grew quite certain that it would not destroy us. It regarded mankind with a fatelike indifference. Why, then, did it come to our aid?

I heard a moan and looked down to see Frain shaking with strain and beaded with sweat. 'Vieyra,' he panted, 'old hag, let go!'

I knew then that it was no use; Grandfather was gone. Once that mighty crone places her chalky grip on a man she never loosens it. But Frain would not give up. He would not. He knelt there with one hand on Grandfather's forehead, the other on the old man's bony chest, and though he did not move I could see that he expended every dram of his strength and will for the sake of Daymon Cein. He struggled until I could have shrieked just from watching him. I don't know how long I stood watching, waiting for a moment of defeat that never came. Finally, without any giving in at all, Frain simply toppled, unconscious, taut and drenched with sweat. I caught him before he hit the hard stone, wrapped him in my cloak, and laid him down. What inexplicably good fate had sent this marvel to Melior to be my brother?

There had been no sense of victory, but a movement

caught my eye. Grandfather lay breathing deeply, easily, and he stirred in his sleep.

I turned away. I had to turn away from joy. I had forgotten about the dragon even in that short time, regarding it as only a useful piece of furniture that made light and heat. But it woofed at me sternly, a warning rumble, and I stopped, almost laughing. I had forgotten about Frain's dagger, still clutched in his hand. I sheathed it and started to smooth the stiffened fingers that had held it, but I found I could not bear to touch my brother so tenderly. What a coward I was then! I dropped Frain's hand and stumped off to find Fabron.

Poor Fabron! He had fled the cave sometime; I am not sure when. I found him with the horses just outside the entrance. He stood weeping into the mane of his roan. 'What ails you?' I grumped. 'Everything is all right.'

He wouldn't answer me.

'Get in there,' I told him. 'Frain is going to need you, and I must find us something to eát.'

'Frain needs you far worse than he will ever need me,' he retorted in a muffled voice.

'That's not my fault,' I shot back. Truth, but I was sorry as soon as I saw him wince. We tethered the horses, and he went in without another word, dragon or no dragon. I realized later what an ordeal that must have been for him. I roamed the mountain for hours, glad to be by myself, but I am afraid I made a sorry hunt of it. I returned near dark with nothing to offer except a few wrinkled crab apples. But near the cave entrance I found a fire, and roasting over it the carcass of a stag.

'Glory be to Eala, you're back!' Fabron exclaimed when I found him. 'I've been running back and forth all afternoon tending the meat and trying to keep an eye on these two.' The invalids in question were still sleeping. Fabron disappeared within an instant, off to look after his dinner. He had not been able to build the fire any closer without filling the cave up with smoke. I flopped down, and the black beast came and lay by my side. While I had been off wandering, it—he—had stayed by Frain. Odd—the creature had no gender that I could see, but in those days I thought of it as male. An extension of myself. I know now that it was far more, but then my mind was taken up by other things. In particular, that night, by my empty belly.

'Did you shoot the stag?' I asked Fabron when he returned.

'No, a dragon brought it.' He looked sheepish. 'A blue one with wings. A smallish one, but still quite big enough to scare me—ah—witless. I thought I was done for. I drew my sword, but the thing just dumped the deer at my feet and left. They don't look friendly. Why are they feeding us?'

I didn't know and I didn't care. We ate until we bulged, and we tried to get some broth into the others without any luck; they were both too deeply asleep. Fabron and I watched by turns that night in case Frain or Daymon needed us. Neither of us feared our resident dragon anymore. I even offered it a haunch of the meat, but it just laid its great head down on its claws and blinked at me. I slept deeply when it was my turn to sleep, deliciously warmed by its breath. There was no stench; why will people say that dragons stink? Ours was a comedy, shining monster with scales the colour of wisteria except where they faded to a pearly hue on its breast. Peculiar colours for so large a beast; they seemed more appropriate for a bird. I had not noticed its wings then, tucked up against the very roof of the cave, or realized that it was a flying creature. All the flying dragons were the colours of sky and sunset.

When I awoke in the morning, Grandfather was sitting up and staring at me keenly.

'You look poorly, lad,' he greeted me. 'What has happened?'

I sputtered. 'I am much the same as ever,' I finally managed to say. 'What has happened to you, that we found you folded up like a broken wing?'

'Why, I crawled in here to die, as an old thing will.' He made that statement sound perfectly unremarkable. 'So I cannot understand why I am sitting here talking to you now.'

I did not answer, only stood up and crossed to where Frain lay, noted his breathing, felt briefly at his face. He half roused from his slumber and turned away from my touch with a groan. 'I have failed again,' he murmured.

'Frain!' Daymon breathed, suddenly agitated. 'What have you done!'

143

'Frain, wake up,' I said, shaking him. He sat up dazedly, came face to face with Grandfather, and sobbed. The old man clutched him, and I was obliged to support the pair of them; one was as unsteady as the other.

'Frain,' the old seer demanded, 'what have you given, what have you bargained away?' He looked more stricken than I had ever seen him. Tears trickled down his sagging cheeks and into his beard.

'Nothing!' Frain said. 'Vieyra does not bargain.'

'I thought not,' Daymon exclaimed. 'So why am I alive?'

'I don't know.' Frain lay back on his bed, swallowing at his tears, grinning. I stood up and stared at him with veiled concern and something of awe. Grandfather sighed and gave in to joy.

'Frain, Frain,' he chanted in happy exasperation, 'have you never been told that no mortal healer can cure old age?'

I turned to go out. But halfway up the passage I met Fabron coming down with a kettle of stew. 'Get on back,' he told me with wicked satisfaction. 'It's snowing. Snowing hard.'

So I had to stay, hearing their talk, seeing their smiles, feeling their love for each other and their love for me—and I could not smile or speak. There was Abas yet to be attended to, and I hated him the more because he had made me what I was. He was in me, haunting me. He would have utterly ruled my heart and soul if it were not for the beast and Frain.

'The dragon was warming you,' Frain explained to Grandfather after they had eaten.

'Then I must be intended to toddle along for a while yet,' Daymon mused. 'Well, it is very strange that so much trouble should be taken for a stray like me.'

'If you are a stray, it is by Abas's fault,' I said angrily.

'No, lad, it is by my own doing.' Grandfather looked at me with watery old eyes; when had his eyes changed? 'I broke my trust when I breached the Wall.'

'But you did that to save me!'

'I know it, lad. What quaint creatures we mortals are! But all my powers seem to have left me since. The doom of Melior must have touched me in its advent.'

'Melior is still standing,' I scoffed. I was frightened, scarcely able to comprehend that he, the seer who had guided me as a child, had changed. Even though I was changing myself. . . . Frain seemed frightened as well.

'Grandfather,' he said sharply, 'what do you mean?'

'Just what I said, lad. I am nothing more now than a silly old man who happens to be related to you. You should have saved your strength.' He smiled, but he was not entirely joking. I had never heard him say anything so harsh.

'He loves you,' Fabron remarked reasonably. I could not speak of love. I got up to pace.

'I don't need you to topple Melior for me,' I barked at Grandfather. And that was the closest I could come to telling him that his worthiness to me did not depend on his lost powers. But in my hidden depths I felt ardently glad to have him with me again, and frightened of that gladness as only a madman can be.

2

We stayed in the cave for several days, until our meat was gone and Frain and Daymon were reasonably strong. The dragon left us after the first day, but another one slithered in to take its place—a really purple one this time. They changed off regularly all through our stay. One was columbine pink, one vermilion, one saffron, and they all were so big that they scraped their way through the strait passage that loomed like a catacomb to us. The horses would not come near them, but the black beast accepted them much as I had. It was usually to be found nestled next to Daymon or Frain.

Long before the first week of our confinement was up I took to pacing the cave in vexation, striding up the long corridor several times a day to watch the snow piling ever higher outside. It looked as if we were going to have to winter in our cave—and why not, with a bunch of aloof but benevolent dragons feeding and warming us at no expense of our own? Still, I chafed and fretted, longing to be on my way toward Eidden to seek. Oorossy's aid against Abas. Inaction galled me, the more so because it left me time for thoughts I would rather avoid.

'A person would have to be mad to trek toward Eidden in that snow!' I fumed at our group one evening. They stopped their chatter and looked at me with mouths agape, as if I had indeed said something quite ridiculous. Only the dragon seemed to understand.

Take the inner ways, it said. Its voice sounded right inside my head. Certainly its mouth had not moved, but I knew it was the dragon just the same. I stiffened to attention staring at it.

Take the inner ways through the mountain roots. We will

146

lead you and feed you, king that will be, it said. I walked straight up to it and gazed hard into its amber eyes.

'Why?' I demanded.

By way of reply the creature gave me the riddle again. I found my way out of it more quickly this time, albeit painfully. 'I am what I am,' I said.

That is why.

'Because I can answer, you mean?' I scowled in exasperation. 'And you could have talked to me all this time, and kept silence?'

Surely it was plain to see that you wanted no talk, scion of Aftalun.

True enough. But my companions seemed to be hearing only one side of the conversation; they were staring at me in consternation. 'What is going on?' asked Fabron.

'The dragon says we are to follow it through the mountains. There must be more passages like this one.'

'Riddleruns, the people call them in these northern parts,' Grandfather said. 'They go on forever, as twisted and tangled as those knotwork woods where I left you.' He shook himself mildly, shaking off folly. 'Or at least they go as far as northern Acheron.'

'I only need to get as far as Eidden,' I muttered.

It was a hard decision to make. We had to leave the horses, steeds we had clung to even on the most absurd terrain, clinging to remnants of rank. But Grandfather was too old to ride, even if we had found a mount for him, and how were we to feed the animals through the winter? They would not come near the dragons anyway. So we ended up turning the horses loose, sending them off with a whack and trusting that they would find shelter, for they were valuable animals. I hoped the Boda would be puzzled by the strays.

The black beast did not leave, of course. 'What about this one?' I asked the dragon of the moment.

Does it eat meat?

I shook my head doubtfully. The beast ate many odd things, twigs and thistles and all sorts of fuzzy moss and prickly things in addition to grass. But I could not imagine it eating meat.

147

We'll feed it, said the dragon, reading the required items from the images in my mind.

So we spent the next two months, maybe more, winding our way through the incredible riddleruns of the Lorc Dahak. Our progress was slow, because the passages wandered up and down and in any direction and because Grandfather walked, as he did everything, sedately. We all had to walk, lugging our gear, following a dragon's waddling hind end and flanking an impressive length of tail. But I did not complain too much about our crawling pace. At least we were not sitting still, and I had the dragons to thank for that.

We did not learn much about them, not even names, if they had names. They were even less talkative than I. Inscrutable, unpredictable, they were at once a threat holding itself at bay and a vital, useful ally. We trusted them out of necessity, and at the same time we knew we were insane, living in a madman's world, to do so.

They were uncouth. They would do odd things without warning—flop down and go to sleep, or scuttle off to relieve themselves, leaving us stranded in the most profound of darkness. But they cared well for us in their offhand way. They brought us meat, even cooked it for us, scorched it rather, with blasts of their hot breath. They intuited that we also desired other food and brought us sundry offerings: bundles of hay for the beast, tree branches (not much use, unless they happened to have fruit on them), cabbages, a wicker basket of eggs, and once a freshly baked loaf of bread, delicately presented between two saberlike ivory claws. Grandfather frowned at all this.

'People will be more likely to shoot at us than welcome us in Eidden,' he said.

So I asked the dragons to please be discreet. But they could tell my heart was not in it; I had no desire to starve! They restrained themselves to the degree that they did not bring us domestic animals, only wild game. But I had to be careful not to think of chicken. One night—or, at any rate, on one occasion when we were sleeping; we all lost any sense of time—I dreamed about cheese. The next day a whole wheel of it appeared, skewered on a dragon's spiny wingtip.

'They're fattening us for the slaughter,' Fabron declared nervously.

'Why would they bother?' I grumbled. 'There are villagers enough about.'

'They're so remote,' said Frain. 'Why do they bother with us at all?'

We all wondered that. I had only the answer the riddle had given me, that I was what I was. And the same applied to Grandfather, I surmised, since they were nursemaiding him when we arrived. He had been a seer, and I was of the royal blood ... But, talking with the dragons from time to time, cautiously, I found that they cherished no great reverence for kings, seers, Sacred Kings, or Aftalun himself. More and more I came to believe that they tolerated me because I was, like them, a cramped, convoluted, and hidden thing, a wanderer of the inner darkness. With my black beast I was their brother in some sense, those dragons.

'If they mean us no harm,' said Frain morosely, 'it is on your account, or Grandfather's. They'd chomp me in a moment.'

He was right. Grandfather was a wanderer too, a stray, as he had said.

We never found out much about what had happened to Grandfather—where he had been, how he had become ready to die. He refused to pity himself or burden us with any guilt on his account. 'Blood of Aftalun!' he would grumble when Frain questioned him. 'It's no more than I expected, lad.' There were no marks on him; I can at least say that. I could not bring myself to ask him any of the questions that lay nearest my heart.

And as for the rest, he could tell me nothing. Not why Raz had so willfully refused me entry, or how Abas spent his days, the number of his troops, the nature of his preparations. . . . He did tell me that Abas was thought to have invaded Vaire. That was the rumour in the countryside. He could not say whether my mother, his daughter, was alive or dead. Not that I asked. But he told me he could not say.

We plodded on. It must have been about midwinter when we reached the large, central dragonworks where hundreds of the creatures lived in a great chamber hollowed out of Lorc Dahak. Not all of them were flying dragons. Some were crimson delvers that seldom ventured out of the mountain roots. They treated us not ungently, but their courtesy held a quality even more forbidding than that of the others, as inexorable as the mountains themselves. Flyers and diggers alike, they lived lazily, amusing themselves from time to time by melting a rock with their breath to see what was inside. If they found something pretty, they were likely to plaster it onto themselves somewhere. That and an occasional twilight foray into the outer air in search of venison seemed to be their only pursuits.

I decided I would not ask them for aid in my impending war. How could I ask such impersonal creatures for aid in a merely human affair? I might as well have hailed the wind. Still, they must have heard my thought. Or perhaps Daymon asked them. But I did not know that at the time.

We spent a while, perhaps a few days, in the dragonworks. Then we journeyed on toward Eidden. I am ashamed now that it took me so long to realize how hard all the darkness was on Fabron. I rather liked it, but he only bore it, and it wore him down. He started whimpering and thrashing in his sleep, and he lost his appetite. Frain started worrying about Fabron, which caused him to droop as well. Grandfather fretted about both of them, and none of the lot of them would bring their trouble to me. I marched along bullheadedly for a few days, letting them all be noble. But finally I couldn't stand it anymore. I spoke to our dragon of the day.

'Is it still snowing outside?'

Not snowing any longer, but no thaw yet, either. Still toothy cold.

'Well—' I frowned. I knew that if I took the others up to have a look around there would be no getting them back down. But maybe part of me was yearning for fresh air and open spaces too, by that time. 'Lead us toward the outside,' I said at last.

It took a week or thereabouts to get out. When we finally saw a glimmer of light that was not dragon glow, each one of us caught breath and hurried toward it. Our guardian dragon left us without a word, slipping out of the mountain and taking wing into—what? We faced a black void aimlessly splattered with white. A patternless jumble of black and white loomed below. We all stared, wondering what had become of the world during our absence; then we all started to laugh. We had emerged into night, a frosty, moonlit and starlit night, and we looked down on snowy, wooded slopes.

'Do you feel better, Fabron?' I asked. He glanced at me in surprise, for he had never complained.

'I hope the Boda have been thrown off our track by our little—er—sortie,' he replied.

'And I hope spring is near,' Frain added worriedly. 'Look at the snow! We are going to miss our creepy-crawly friends.'

'If not warm of heart, they were at least warm around the mouth,' I quipped. 'Should we go back inside?'

'I can stand the cold,' snapped Grandfather, and that seemed to settle it. We were done with the riddleruns.

3

The thaw began within a few days. The many streams of Eidden, the freshets that fed the Chardri, bulged with springtime floodwater. They flowed so deep and swift, even the smallest of them, that often we had to trudge miles through the hilly land before we were able to bridge them. Some days we scarcely seemed to get any nearer at all to Qiturel, Oorossy's holding, a spot far south near the forks of the Chardri. I judged that, afoot and at an old man's pace, it was likely to be midsummer before we reached it. And so it proved—the more so because we were caught in an unseasonal storm.

It came up as suddenly as a serpent out of a well. Or rather it came down, flying and hissing down from the north, sweeping down the flanks of the Lorc Dahak, biting cold. It struck before we had time to do more than look at the grey sky. In a moment Vale had turned featureless white, a white that might as well have been the blackest gloom of night. We stood in it, instantly lost and shivering, with no shelter to hope for except groves of small trees. We had kept near the mountains for fear of the Boda. No one lived so near.

'We have to keep moving,' Frain said, 'or we'll freeze. Perhaps it'll blow itself out.'

We stumbled along, keeping close together, over ground already covered with white fluff. It would not be long before it soaked through our boots and froze our feet. Grandfather didn't even have boots, only cloth wrappings. I wished I could carry him, but I knew better than to try that yet.

'We're likely to go in circles,' Fabron puffed. 'Perhaps if we can find a stream, follow it down to some homestead . . .' We all knew there were no homesteads for miles. And we all knew there was no time. It had been late afternoon when the sky blotted over. I would not say it, but already it seemed to me that the whiteness was turning grey. An early dusk was coming on.

The black beast snorted and surged ahead of me. I understood that summons. 'Follow the beast,' I ordered, 'and keep ahold of each other.' We joined hands and stumbled along on feet that were gradually going numb. I was just as glad we had not found a stream. I had no fondness for water that moved—creeping stuff! Ever since I had met Shamarra I had been seeing strange things in water, the more fearsome because only half visible. I preferred the cleaner blindness of night or the snow.

Night came all too soon. When dusk deepened to the extent that we could no longer see the black beast amid the white snow—a grey beast now, frosted with rime—I grasped it by the mane and we struggled along in the dark. Frain grunted and let go of my hand, forcing me to stop in near panic; I could have lost him in an eyeblink. Grandfather had fallen. Frain stooped over him, and I could hear the old man complaining, 'No, lad, I don't want any more of your strength. I've taken enough.'

'Get him onto the beast,' I said.

'That creature is not meant to be ridden,' Grandfather snapped. As if I didn't know that! But I considered that in this contingency . . . What a cantankerous old man. I swept him up in my arms, slung him over one shoulder. The beast let out that awful bray of his, urging us forward.

We struggled along. Frain clung to my belt and I clung to the beast. I could hear Fabron wheezing somewhere in the rear. We slogged onward, gradually wearing down, like the toys I used to make Frain out of bowstring. . . . He leaned more heavily on me, and I leaned more heavily on the beast. I don't believe the beast was tired, but if it were not for him I am sure the rest of us would have toppled in a moment, like a row of stick soldiers. I remember almost nothing until the wind suddenly stopped. Then I snapped my head up, startled into alertness. We had come into some sort of shelter. I could smell animals and hear their faint stirrings all around me. I could faintly see a milky blur that was the entry through which we had come. Then it darkened, and I heard a footstep. Someone had come in behind us.

The figure carried a faint light like a spook—no, the glow was of too warm a hue for that. It was a lantern shielded against the wind. In a moment the man slid the panel—no man, not in any ordinary sense! I staggered back a step. Wise, black-barred golden eyes met mine. A goat's head with curling horns rose above a muscular torso clad in rough woven wool. It was the brown man of Eidden Lei.

'My lord,' I murmured, gaping at him, feeling as if I might faint. He reached out to steady me. I tingled all over at the touch of that hand; it was warm and covered with fur. I trembled with awe. His strangeness was deity, and I felt it as I had never felt godhead before. I had not felt such awe of Aftalun or Shamarra.

He lifted Daymon from my shoulder. 'Your flock needs care,' he said.

Frain and Fabron had slumped to the floor of the building—it was a big stone barn with a thatched roof, full of all sorts of beasts. I got my two charges each by one arm, hauled them up one on either side, and followed the brown man, supporting them the short distance to his home—cot? It was a sort of domed beehive of stone, cleverly constructed, with a warm hearth at the centre and a hole at the apex for smoke. We set Frain and Fabron and Daymon Cein on the dirt floor. There was no furniture to speak of, and chickens wandered about, cross at having been disturbed. The fire had already been banked for the night. I stirred it and piled on sticks while the brown man brought us something to drink in wooden noggins. One sip set us all to sputtering and livened us up considerably. Fabron looked around at a raven roosting on a corbel halfway up the wall, at a fox cub peering at him over a bushy tail, at the chickens, which had settled into a dusty hollow by the door. Then he took note of our host and looked aghast. But Frain faced the brown man in his quiet, accepting way and said what I had not yet been able to.

'Our thanks to you, Lord. We owe you our lives.'

'It is my function to shelter strays,' the brown man said. It was hard to read expression in that unsmiling animal face or in the voice, guttural and earthy, not quite human. But I think his was not a statement of deprecation or even of pride. I think it was of essence, to comfort us.

He took the wet wrappings off of Daymon's legs and feet and rubbed the cold flesh with his hands, which were furred and stubby, like paws, with strong black nails. I had experienced the power of that touch and it was with more trust than surprise that I saw Grandfather's colour return. Sluggishly I forced myself to tend Frain in like wise. He seemed very weak. He had been lending his strength to Grandfather, I realized, probably all through that long trek. Fabron got his own wet boots off. The brown man filled our cups again and pointed me toward some covered wooden bins along the wall.

'I have various kinds of grain, and there is honey. Can you humans eat those things?'

I was to be cook, it seemed, for Frain had fallen asleep with Fabron still fussing over him. So I made some crude oat cakes stuck together with honey—mouse cakes, my nurse used to call them—and toasted them over the fire. Fabron sat and munched his stoically. Grandfather ate a little, but I could see that we were going to have to grind grain for bread. In the morning.

'Why is Frain so weak?' the brown man asked. 'He is too young to be so spent.'

Of course he knew who we were; we wore torques. But I suspect he would have known regardless.

'He has been healing me for hours,' Grandfather replied. 'He should have saved his strength. I am a useless old thing.' He spoke very bitterly. I suppose Frain's generosity distressed him. The brown man looked at him in mild surprise.

'Every creature has value apart from its worthiness,' he said. 'That is why I am here. And it is a truth you know well, Daymon Cein.'

'I no longer know *anything*,' Daymon retorted truculently.

'Even the ants know their own truths!'

The fox cub came and sniffed at me. 'A wild stray?' Fabron remarked to turn the talk.

'To be sure. Like Tirell.' I wondered if the brown man could be joking. There was no humour to be seen on that bearded goat's face.

'But wild things wander by nature. How can they stray?'

'They depart from their truths much as men do. The fox cub is the offspring of an incestuous relationship. Not his fault, but he is outcast, his mother dead. The raven has broken rookery law. You saw the deer in the other building—the stag has failed to uphold leadership and has been expelled from the herd. His doe came with him.'

'And how have I strayed?' I asked, addressing him for the first time. I tried not to sound sharp, but I dare say I did because I was secretly trembling. He paid no attention to my tone.

'It is not in truth for the son to hate the father,' he said.

'Nor is it in truth for the father to slay—' I stopped, dry of mouth and visibly shaking. He was terribly strange, but something in him called me, and that call frightened me. It tugged like the strange force that had drawn me to Grandfather where he lay dying in the riddleruns.

'Indeed, it is abomination, what he has done,' the brown man agreed about Abas. 'But how can hate help you?' Then he looked at me and let the question go unanswered. 'Tirell, we will not be able to speak justly while you are afraid. What about me troubles you so?'

'You are half beast,' I said with trembling voice.

'To be sure. Like you.'

I stared at him, caught on an edge between anger and awe, unable to speak.

'Because the beast is half bird, do you therefore fear it?'

I moved my unwilling mouth. 'I feared it at first,' I whispered.

'You are very brave, then. Befriending it was both wise and brave. Abas, who hates the beast, has never been able to drive it from him, but the time will come when you who love it will freely let it go. . . . Why does Abas hate the beast, Tirell?'

I turned away my head. 'The beast has been with my family since the beginning days,' I said at last. 'The shield tells me that.'

'And has no one ever told you more?' he wondered. He

settled down further into the firelight, looking at me out of flickering golden eyes. And he told me the tale of the beast.

'In the beginning the beast was only a dream of Aftalun's, and thereby a prophecy. In his dream he saw it amidst the tangling trees of Acheron, a place he had never been. He took its image as his shield device for the sake of its fearsome look and its mighty wings. He had a sword made to go with his shield, and the work was done by Ulv, the smith of the gods in Ogygia.

' "That is a sword of double edge," warned Aftalun's bride. "And the shield is heavy. It may yet become an insupportable burden." She was the goddess, and he loved her for what she was and hated her for her hold on him. So he heard her words with laughter and awe.

'After twenty years he built his altar and died on it and left it for the east, went up in swan form with chains of gold and silver trailing from his neck, men say, though some say he strode off in his own body and form. He had three grown sons: Aymar, Aidan, and Tyr. The time had come for one of them to take the goddess and die, as the newly formed order would have it. Aymar was the eldest, but he had no desire to be slain. Nor did Aidan, who would have been sacrificed the following year if his brother failed to give the goddess a son. So the two of them plotted between themselves to send Tyr, the youngest, to the altar in their stead.

'This was done by means of the ceremony of the choosing of the goddess. Tyr loved a maiden of one of the many names—Evi was her name. He had secretly pledged himself to her, and they planned to run away and wed. But on the day when all the maidens of many names were required to appear at the Hill of Vision for the choosing, the priestesses touched Evi, even though she had darkened her face with soot. Aymar and Aidan had bribed them with gold.

'So Tyr had the choice of letting his brother have his beloved and being forsworn, Luoni bait, or of taking her himself and being slain. Once he fully comprehended the trap that had been set for him he rose to the challenge as Aftalun had, with bitter daring. He was crowned Sacred King, sat on the dais and feasted, took the maiden for a night of tender love, and walked to the altar the next morning shrouded in black rage, suffused with rage. He let himself be tied down, let the blood bird be taken without a cry—and then, in a death spasm, he broke his bonds and rose, toppled toward Aymar. He turned into the black beast. Some folk say that his soul went up as the beast, and some say that his whole body and being changed in a clap of thunder. But it amounts to the same thing. The beast has a name, Tirell, and it is Tyr.'

'We are truly of one flesh,' I muttered. 'He is my ancestor—'

'He is in you, as you have long known.'

I shifted my position with a sigh, feeling less afraid of the brown man now. 'What then?' I asked. Frain lay sleeping, Grandfather sat back with half-hooded eyes, Fabron listened with open fascination.

'Tyr charged at his brothers, intent on killing them, bugling, baleful, fire-eyed. They escaped him for the time in the crowd. Aymar took Evi as his shield, a coward's act. The two brothers got to their horses and fled back to the castle, taking the woman with them.

'The beast stationed itself before the gates of Melior, never moving, never even trying its wings, and no one dared to come near it. Aymar and Aidan were trapped within their walls. After a month of this Aymar went quite mad and hanged himself in his tower room. A few months later Aidan reached the last stages of desperation. He armoured himself and went out to face the thing he feared. He stood bravely, struck at the beast and broke its wing, but he was slain. The beast went away toward the west, and men forgot it as quickly as they could.

'After the proper length of time Tyr's son was born to Evi. Torvell was his name. The boy grew to the age of twenty years, when he was required to go to the goddess and the altar in his turn. He took his bride in obedience to the priestesses, and as he was being led to the Hill of Vision his father came to him, thus giving him the only gift he could—the black madness that takes all pain away. Torvell went up as an eagle. . . . And such has been the grim gift of Tyr to many of his

158

descendants, even in these latter days, when the demands of the goddess have gentled.'

The tale was done. I took a few breaths and then turned to Grandfather. 'Why did you never tell me?' I demanded.

'I never knew. The history of the beast is one that men have taken care to forget, like that of Acheron.' Grandfather blinked at the brown man in a sort of professional appraisal. 'You must be very old.'

'Does he—does the beast remember?' I whispered.

'I think not in any clear sense—though it embodies much of what is human. It has sheltered here often over the years—and by knowing it, Tirell, I have known you.' The brown man bent his golden gaze on me. 'But if I fight for you, it will be in large measure for Tyr.'

I got up and bolted toward the door. I could not stand the touch of those wise eyes. But Fabron got ahold of me. 'Tirell, no!' he cried. 'It is black night and blinding snow out there—you'll be lost for very sure.'

'I am only going over to the barn to see the beast,' I mumbled.

But the beast nosed his way in through the blanket as if he had heard me call. So I had no excuse to leave. I settled in the most shadowy corner of the hut, holding fast to the beast as if the creature were my talisman, hiding my face against his crest. I was more afraid then ever, for I had felt that tug again, and I had sensed the name of it. It was called love, and it was the same force that Abas was using to try to lure me back to Melior.

It was still snowing in the morning. I spent the day grinding grain into flour between two rocks, working so furiously that the powder smoked and toasted on the stone. The hard labour eased my feelings somewhat. Fabron watched me and whistled. 'Such fervour!' he exclaimed, not expecting an answer. 'Well, better thee than me, Tirell.'

He helped me with the cooking. We had milk and eggs. We used some of each to make my flour into a kind of paste that we wrapped around sticks and held over the fire. The lumps came out black on the outside and gummy on the inside. Still, Frain ate the stuff ravenously, and Grandfather put down a fair amount. His disposition seemed to have bettered since Frain's strength had improved. We offered our so-called bread to our host, but the brown man did not bother with it. He crunched raw grain between his strong yellow teeth.

It snowed for three days. The brown man would go out to care for his animals in his bare, shaggy, black-nailed feet, leaving wrenchingly human footprints in the snow. He would bring us water in a jug. He seemed to find his way through the white dither of snow by instinct, like an animal, trudging off into the directionless storm and returning before we had much chance to worry. Perhaps he could scent the water. It came from a stream; I could tell that as soon as I looked at it. Those deathly swimming things were in it, with spook lights in their shrunken hands. They looked straight at me in the close quarters of the hut, and I recoiled in shock.

'What queer creatures you mortals are,' the brown man sighed. 'Frightened of fresh water, frightened of mountains and whispering trees, frightened of night and shadows . . .' His gaze shifted to Fabron. 'Frightened of truth. . . .'

'Don't you see them in there?' I demanded.

'Of course. They are what gives the water strength, and so you. Death is the seed of life. Everything you eat is dead, Tirell.'

'I don't see a thing,' Frain said, puzzled.

I wouldn't drink the stream water. I melted snow in a pan for myself; there are no dead things in such lifeless water. But the jug haunted me—that, and the brown man's kindness. Long before the storm abated I took to pacing the beehive house in unrest, nearly frantic to be gone. Finally, as suddenly as it had begun, the snow stopped and began just as quickly to melt. It was spring, after all. Green buds showed above the white ground.

I boiled eggs for our journey and made more of my awful bread. As I cooked the brown man tried to talk to me.

'You are not so very different from me,' he said. 'Part beast, as we have said, and also part immortal, being a descendant of Aftalun.'

'He did not frighten me,' I muttered.

160

'He and Shamarra are of Ogygian kind, sky gods. But I am of earth, as was the maiden you loved.'

'Don't speak of her!' Spasms of pain rippled through me; I had to clench myself like a fist to keep from blubbering. 'Abas will be sorry he did not slay me as well,' I said finally, angry because of the pain and the fear.

'He has no desire to slay you. Every day he seeks you earnestly.'

I barked out a laugh. 'He would kill me cheerfully enough if he had me in his reach! He would kill his own mother if the mood took him. Anyone who knows him knows that. Ask Frain what Abas is capable of doing.'

'Frain sees the most clearly of you all, in his youthful way,' the brown man agreed, speaking very softly, for Frain stood just outside the door. 'But in this one regard he falls short of truth. He believes himself to be Abas's son, but he has known no fatherhood from him. Therefore he thinks you stand in the same peril as himself.'

Angered the more because the brown man seemed to know all our secrets, I could not answer. 'Why are you so enmired in rage and hatred, Prince?' he asked me. 'You will make fit food for the Luoni.'

'Sisters of yours?' I inquired acidly.

'In their way, as Mylitta was in hers. Yes.'

The name pierced me like a fiery lance. I sprang up and lunged at him, straight through the flames, scattering cooking gear and cursing. I can't tell what I might have done to him—though, he being what he was, I believe I could not have hurt him much. But Frain hurried in and came between us. My rage always seemed to reach him somehow.

'If only she had not been killed,' the brown man mused as if I had not moved, 'all would have been well for you, Tirell. Now I can't see what is to become of you, and neither can Daymon Cein.'

Frain reached out toward me. I was all in tumult; I suppose if I had let him touch me I might have wept, and perhaps that would have saved me from much sorrow later. But I turned away from him as if he were made of white-hot iron and ran outside, into the wilderness. I did not rejoin the others until they had gone a day's journey toward Qiturel.

161

4

I was fit only for the company of catamounts from that time on until Melior. Perhaps I did not always act it—I hope I did not—but I felt it, fear driving me wild inside, the brown man's remembered touch and Grandfather's old head bobbing along at my shoulder—if only he would walk faster!—and Fabron and Frain—all I had wanted were followers, and I had found friends, confound it. Love distressed me; clashing with my rage, it kept up a constant foam and splatter in my mind. And there was Abas still calling—damn Abas!—and I knew I did not dare to answer. We were afoot, helpless; his Boda could have caught us like insects in a moment if they had known where we were. So I could vent none of my spleen on Abas. I wanted only to be finished with my hatred, have my business done, settled—but Grandfather crept along.

And there were all the streams in the way. Eidden is full of them. Eidden Lei—Eidden Hills, the name means. They are covered with pine forest, and the streams run down between. Some of them stretch all the way back to the mountains.

'We are *never* going to get to Qiturel,' Frain complained, 'if we must pussyfoot up and down every trickle until we find a bridge. Ford them, for mercy's sake!' He was impatient, as tired of the journey as I was.

'You've grown bold in your old age, lad,' Grandfather remarked frostily, staring at him, and he subsided. But he repeated the argument at every rivulet we met.

I would not go near the streams, in spite of all Frain's urgings. I could see the swimming things in them, waiting to touch me with their cold fingers. I would not even drink the stream water Frain dipped for me. I would find myself a well or go thirsty. But one day, when we came to a particularly broad but shallow stream and started up it toward the mountains again, Frain lost his temper.

'Mother of Aftalun!' he shouted fiercely, and splashed in until he was wet to the boottops. He stood with water running about his ankles, hands on hips and glaring at us. 'Am I being eaten alive?' He lifted each foot fastidiously. 'Pulled down? Carried away?' I still remember the sweet daring of him, standing there, but at the time I was speechless with wrath and fear.

'Come on!' he challenged us. 'Tirell, you pugnacious coward—'

I found my voice. 'Frain, I'll thrash you for that!' I roared.

'Come and get me,' he said, grinning, and threw a handful of water at me.

I went in after him, of course, blind as a charging bull, and found myself on the other side before I knew it. He had led me there, the rogue. I stood on the bank, shocked and panting, and he went back for Grandfather.

'Do you want me to carry you?'

'Great goddess, no!' Grandfather glared at him and picked his way across, leaning on his staff and with Frain's hand at his elbow, however he attempted to shake it off. Fabron followed the pair of them, sweating a little and staring straight ahead. The beast nickered angrily and plunged across. And there we all were.

'Now,' said Frain smugly, 'can we be getting on?'

So after that we waded across the shallow streams. But the time saved did not improve my temper—Eala, no! I felt everything rising to a peak in me, felt myself drawing nearer and nearer to what frightened me, or being drawn, being driven, and fear and rage walked with me. I had come through darkness, spoken with dragons, walked in water—I would not have been able to touch it a few months before. But every step caused me fresh terror.

The journey wore on. The brassy sun beat down every day. There was no escaping the promise of drought, even there in shady Eidden, the brown man's country, where the silver mists rose in the morning and the rolling ranks of hills broke through—I loved them. Bah! Love! Something was trying to heal me. It was healing Grandfather.

'It's coming back, Tirell! It's starting to come back!' he whispered to me excitedly one morning a few weeks after we had left the brown man.

'What is coming?' I growled, though I already knew.

'The sureness, the sight!'

I thought as much. I had seen it growing in him days before he spoke. The rest of him had not changed much, but his eyes had gotten younger. 'Why, what do you see?' I asked.

He grimaced. 'Only those dearest to me. I can feel Frain's presence there beyond the alders.' Frain went off by himself more and more those days. I shrugged. I had known where Frain was too, if only because the black beast with its animal senses knew.

'And,' Grandfather added, 'the presence of your mother in Melior.'

So she was yet alive. More love to harrow my heart.

Our pace hastened a bit. Grandfather's step was growing stronger, and it continued to strengthen all the way to Qiturel. We arrived at last in the heat of early summer and were admitted by a suspicious gatekeeper. He would not let us in the keep, but he went off to get Oorossy, shaking his head. We must have looked like beggars. Well, in a way we were.

To my surprise I saw an old acquaintance nearby—my faithful black steed! The horse was tied outside the stable, as if he had been making trouble. I went over and stroked him, and he eyed me sourly. There were no manners in that horse, but he would carry a rider till he dropped.

'Yours, Prince Tirell?' asked Oorossy, coming out to greet us.

'He used to be. How strange that he has come to you!' Not strange, really. The steed was big and powerful, a war horse, so he would naturally be sold to a lord's stable. I wondered what had become of the other two. We never found out.

'No, he's yours,' Oorossy declared, adding a curse or two. 'The big, hammer-headed, foul-tempered, graceless plug! Take him and welcome! Fabron, Prince Frain, you're welcome.' He clapped Fabron heartily on the shoulder. 'Choose mounts for yourselves. It is not seemly for royalty to go afoot. Daymon Cein, I am at your service. What may I get you?'

'A drink of water,' Grandfather snapped.

He took us inside to have wine instead. I found, to my dismay, that I liked Oorossy. He made a proper shrewd, rough and roaring canton king. He fed us well and couched us well and found us fresh clothes in the morning. After breakfast we held council and I told the tale of our wanderings. We had virtually disappeared for the past six months, and not even Abas seemed to know where we were. Oorossy said that all of Vale was in ferment with wondering what had become of me. The time was good for challenging Abas. His forces were divided between three places: Vaire, where he laid siege to Ky-Nule, and the Wall, and Melior. The people were murmuring, foreseeing yet another season of drought. Only the lack of an heir to the altar prevented insurrection.

'I will be sacrificed to no goddess,' I told Oorossy as courteously as I was able.

'Why, neither would I,' he agreed instantly, with great good humour. 'But there is no need to tell everyone that right away.'

'Wayte will march toward Melior as soon as the siege is lifted,' Fabron said eagerly. 'And Sethym will march as soon as he receives word.'

'Sethym! That big sissy!' Oorossy lamented. 'Is there no other help we can depend on?' He leaned back in his chair and fixed an appraising gaze on me. 'What a pity you didn't see Raz.'

Oorossy had sense. He was no slave to honour, he frankly hated Abas, and he did not mind fighting either, but he questioned my chances of winning such a battle—my sanity, even, for undertaking it. Well, he had to be persuaded to throw in his lot with us in spite of sense or reason.

'I am not going back to Nisroch,' I stated.

'Why, no need!' Oorossy replied, straight-faced. 'Raz and a few hundred picked men are marauding through my bottomlands right now—'

'What!' I shouted, and everyone else jerked to attention.

'—and a few days' journey will take you to him,' said Oorossy.

'But—how—' It was Fabron, floundering.

'He does it every summer,' Oorossy added mildly. 'He always leads the raids himself, makes a jaunt of it. They loot the little towns, terrorize a few countryfolk—'

'And you sit here?' Fabron demanded.

'Why, yes. I don't want to turn his little sorties into a war. He could take Eidden in a few weeks' time with perhaps half his force. I often wonder why he has not.'

'Have you never met him at all?' asked Frain.

'A few times. He offered me one of his daughters once, and I had to go to Nisroch to make a courteous refusal, since I already had a wife at the time, which he knew well enough. . . . He seemed proud. He has a right to be proud. He must dream of power, sitting on a canton as big as the rest of Vale and rich to boot. But he keeps to himself. I'm still not sure whether he's selling daughters or giving them away. Folk say he offers them to his snakes, but the snakes won't have them.'

Grandfather stirred reproachfully at this bit of gossip. 'He schemes and dreams,' he stated. 'Someday he will act.'

'And then Adalis help us,' said Oorossy cheerfully. He was gazing at me again with a hint of a dare in his eyes, and I knew I had to meet it.

'You will aid me if I can make an ally of Raz,' I said.

'To the top of my bent.'

'All right, then.' I rose. 'I am off.'

Frain and Fabron automatically stood to come with me. Even Daymon Cein creaked stiffly to his feet. 'We will be riding, Grandfather,' I told him.

'Oh.' He creaked back down again. 'Your hospitality, Oorossy, until they return?'

'Of course.' Oorossy rubbed his hands in high spirits. He was clever, that Oorossy, sending us to interrupt Raz's looting. And of course he was looking forward to a jaunt of his own. 'Meanwhile, I will be mustering my men.'

Within a few hours Frain and Fabron and I took horse, well provisioned and well mounted, I on my old black with the black beast by my side, and my temper was as sour as the steed's. I felt ready in advance to hate Raz, I suspected

Oorossy of having gotten the better of me, and I darkly predicted that there would be Boda about. Actually, we met none. The journey went well. We found flat wooden bridges across the streams—too many for the Boda to guard or hold—and when we had to cross by fording the horses bore the brunt of it; I would not even look down. The beast would bugle its protest, then splash across at our heels. Presently we left the forest behind and rode across Eidden's rich river farmland. The sun beat down day after day, making the young crops hang limp. And they had been trampled; there was more devastation than drought could account for.

Oorossy had only a notion of where Raz might be, but we found him easily enough by following a trail of wailing villagers. Their lamentations set my teeth on edge. I could not afford to be touched by them or anyone. . . . Not that they came near us—I am sure they thought we were their nightmare embodied, with our swords and war steeds and the winged monster in our van. Even Frain could not comfort them. We had to ride by them, and he and Fabron would look straight ahead, as hard-faced as I. After several days of this we sighted Raz's campfires ahead in the dusk.

'Now what?' Fabron muttered. The old hound, he was worried about how to approach Raz; we had discussed it again and again. He was afraid of treachery, but we had been able to reach no decision because Frain held fast to that damned unnatural valour of his, and as for myself, I simply did not care. So we rode straight into Raz's camp and up to his royal self. I had not seen him for years, not since I was a child, but Oorossy had said we would have no trouble recognizing him, and indeed we did not. His tent looked more like a temple to avarice, all gaudy with gold thread and bits of gem, and he himself was a proper peacock of a man in a jewelled velvet cap and jewelled earrings; I was surprised he did not wear jewels in his nose. He sat at ease by his fire, picking at the capon a manservant offered to him and not bothering to rise as I, still mounted, towered over him.

'Yes?' he inquired blankly. He knew quite well who I was, curse his eyes! I could not bring myself to announce myself. Next he would have had me stating my business like a courier! I felt too angry to move, lest I slay him where he sat. The beast lunged out of the shadows and thundered toward him. Soldiers gasped and scattered, and the manservant dropped his platter of capon in the dirt.

'Ah,' Raz declared as if in sudden benign enlightenment. 'Tirell of Melior.' He got to his feet with oily grace, paying no attention to the beast that had stopped just short of his campfire. I dismounted to speak with him.

I could see why he preferred to remain seated. He was short, even shorter than Fabron; he came only to my shoulders. He did not have the advantage of Fabron's blacksmith's build, either. He dressed in layer on layer of sumptuous robes to hide his flab, and he strutted. I sighed and sent the beast away with a gesture and a hard stare. I had to deal with this man.

We sat around the fire. Raz snapped his multiringed fingers for slaves to take the horses, hit the manservant and sent him for more supper. 'How good-hearted of Oorossy to send you to visit me here,' he remarked.

'We are here on our own business,' I said levelly.

'Ah.' Incredible, the tones and overtones—irony, subtle mockery, cunning, and bland inquiry—that he managed to convey in that one simple exhalation.

Of course, he would not ask me my business, now that I wanted him to. And it should have waited until after we had eaten. Nevertheless, I blundered on. 'We have come to request your aid in the necessary overthrow of King Abas.'

'Ah.' Again. He stroked his pointed beard as I detailed my somewhat ill-formed plans. Wayte from Vaire, Sethym from Selt, Oorossy, and Raz, all of us to meet near Melior and make Abas dead, that was all. I wanted nothing more.

'And set you on the throne,' Raz prompted.

I shrugged, avoiding his eyes lest he see the flaring hatred in mine. He smelled of oil and musk. Supper came, but Raz sat back, letting it cool. 'Take hundreds of men, march to Melior, kill Abas, and crown his son,' he mused aloud. 'Now why would I want to do that?'

I met his eyes then. 'I am not sure why you do anything that you do,' I said.

He gave a squeak that must have been a laugh and regarded me with sudden interest. I had addressed the enigma, and he liked it.

'All of Vale is mad, and I alone am sane,' he proclaimed. 'Any noble in this accursed land would think I should leap at the opportunity to place on that throne yet another powerless King! Ruler of a parcel of land scarcely large enough to support his household, sustained only by tribute, offering not even good advice in return, of no function or use whatsoever except to be troublesome, to be flattered, to be killed for the goddess—'

'I do not intend to be killed for the goddess,' I said.

'A sensible intent,' he returned. Oh, the sneer even in that! 'But how, then, can you expect the throne? Thousands of sacks of wheat every year as tribute. Gold. Baubles and adulation—'

'I will have earned it,' I snapped, losing patience. 'Let the throne take care of itself. I ask only your aid in taking Abas. Name your reward.'

'By old Dahak,' he said smoothly, 'that will take some consideration! The proposal strikes me as troublesome, mightily expensive, a strain, a bore, and, worst of all, aimless. You, Fabron!' He turned suddenly on my silent companion. 'What possesses you to have thrown in your lot with this get of the madman? That idiot Sethym I can understand, and even Oorossy—he still holds to his silly ideals—but you! I thought you had sense, a streak of cleverness, even—'

Fabron flushed angrily. I spoke up before he could answer. 'I do not intend to give you my throne,' I told Raz. 'I do not care for it—sneer all you like, it is the truth—but it is mine, by Adalis, and I will sit on it. Take it from me if you like. Why have you not done so already? Or why have you not annexed Eidden, or Selt, or Vaire?' I followed the question with my stare and he stared back at me, a long, slow look from which all mockery was gone. He was thinking hard, though not, perhaps, of what I had asked him.

'Laziness,' he replied at last. 'Old habits are hard to break. I prefer to annex in the next generation. . . . I have one daughter left, Tirell of Melior.'

The way was clear. 'If we can come to terms,' I said promptly, 'I will marry her.'

'No!' It was Frain, the first word he had spoken; I had forgotten he was there. He jumped up, mightily distressed. 'Tirell, say no such thing!'

'Tirell has made the politic decision,' Fabron told his son tiredly. Fabron, taking my part in a quarrel with Frain? Was the whole world going insane? Frain ignored him.

'You will have years to regret it,' he said to me.

'Frain,' I warned, 'be silent!' I felt harried and hot—bad signs. Talking with Raz had depleted my small store of civility.

'Tirell, please listen.' Frain came over and knelt by me, entreating me. 'It is wrong to marry into a loveless union. You might as well marry a whore as marry without love.'

How could he say something so womanish in front of everyone? 'Frain,' I declared in barely controlled rage, 'you are an ass.'

'Would you *think*, Tirell!' he cried passionately. 'You have known what love is. You might yet know it again if you give yourself a chance—'

The reference to Mylitta, veiled though it was, undid me. I swung out blindly with my fist and knocked Frain over; I am lucky I did not knock him into the fire. I wanted to stand up and punish him for all I was worth. Only Raz's amused eyes on me prevented me. Fabron got up with a start, helped Frain up, and tried to lead him away.

'Let me alone!' He shook off Fabron's hand and turned to me for a parting shot.

'All right.' He rapped out the words. 'If you will not think of yourself, then think of the girl. Has anyone asked her opinion of you?'

He turned his back on me and strode off to the shadows where the black beast waited. Fabron sighed and sat down again by the fire. On the far side of it Raz lounged, comfortable and quite expressionless.

'All right,' I said to him. 'Terms.'

We agreed that he would bring a thousand men—and his daughter—to Melior. He would start back to Nisroch at once (I could hear Oorossy rejoicing), make his preparations, and march. He would send a messenger to Sethym. Meanwhile, I would backtrack to Qiturel and bring word to Oorossy.

We ate our supper, finally, amicably enough, and dozed around the fire. We did not see Frain. We did not see him the next morning, either, when we made our departure. His horse was gone. But the beast knew he was waiting half a mile away, so I was neither surprised nor gladdened to see him when he joined us. I sensed his disappointment, but I kept silence, and so did he. I did not apologize for my temper of the previous evening. I blamed it on Raz and on him, not on myself.

The quarrel made an uncomfortable ride, even for me. The few days seemed endless. But finally Qiturel greeted us, and Grandfather awaited us in his chamber there. 'So, you have found Raz,' he remarked as soon as he saw us. 'What is the fuss about?'

'Tirell has gone and got himself betrothed to Raz's daughter,' Frain answered bitterly, 'the one who was the cause of all this row to start with.'

'Why, lad, how can that be?' Daymon inquired innocently. 'The poor lass—Recilla is her name, is it not? She has never even met him.'

'You know what I mean.' Frain stomped across the room and sat with unnecessary force on the cot, sulking. 'All those vows of love. . . .' He knew better than to say more. I would have hit him again. Grandfather turned to me and gave me a long, seeing stare.

'So you have pledged your word,' he remarked.

'Of course I have,' I burst out—bellowed, really. 'We could not have stirred a foot without Raz.'

Grandfather smiled—an odd smile, the most baffled, whimsical and wondering of smiles. He turned back to my scowling brother. 'Tirell's reasons are all wrong, Frain. I grant you that,' he said.

'The whole thing is wrong, from start to finish,' Frain fumed. I clenched my fists.

'He has acted out of defiance, craft, and several varieties of rage,' Grandfather went on, ignoring both of us. 'Still, I feel

171

only good to come of his decision.'

'What?' Frain and I exclaimed in unison.

'Oh, it will make a sorry precedent, I grant you that,' Daymon sighed. 'Men and women should not be bound together by the cold agreements of power; all sense and instinct cry against it. That is the fate you will lay on your heirs, Tirell. But yet—and yet—and yet—I feel joy to come of his wedding.' The smile again, puzzled but full of hope. 'I make you no promise, lads, but that is the vision and comfort that come to me. Therefore it must somehow be right.'

Frain swallowed slowly, swallowing his wrath, looking at me askance. 'The hell you say,' he muttered. For my own part, I felt dazed and a little troubled.

'Now make peace, you two,' Grandfather ordered.

The oddest thing was that, though we set aside the quarrel, neither Frain nor I really believed Daymon, though we had believed him all our lives. I did not want joy. I wanted revenge and a life of noble sorrow. And Frain fought my decision all the way to Melior.

5

Oorossy was off raising troops in the hills. After a week he came back to Qiturel, but then there were more days of preparation before we could march. I fumed; I sometimes thought I could feel smoke curling out of my ears. Oorossy went about his affairs, whistling maddeningly. At last all was ready. I mounted my black charger, Frain and Fabron the horses Oorossy had given them. Grandfather was not coming with us, but he would not stay safe in Qiturel either, stubborn old man!

'I was roaming Vale before you were born, young my precious lord!' he argued perversely.

He would not have said that a few months before, I am sure. He intended to come along behind us at his own pace, and in spite of all my ire I knew he would be all right. The black beast stayed with him. I still remember looking back and seeing the pair of them ambling along side by side far behind us, he with his staff in one hand and the other on a black glossy back.

We took five hundred men to Melior—a laughable force, a pathetic force compared to Abas's thousands. But at least it was enough, as Frain said, to see us across the bridges. The dozen Boda who held the Terynon looked at us and galloped away. 'There goes news,' I said grimly, and we started across the rich lowlands of Tiela, making our way along the Chardri.

The march took some few weeks. We collected a couple hundred fortune-seeking youths as we dragged dustily along, and a plentiful supply of whores. I had noticed a few from the time we left Qiturel; where there is an army, there will be camp followers. But I believe that if Grandfather had been with us I might not have been such a brute with the whores and with Shamarra and Frain. To my shame.

I was all right until we reached Melior. Until the day, I think, that I looked across the river to the place where my love had lived and died. The holding was all deserted, in weeds, the cottage downtumbling, an abode of ill omen. For the first time in all my journey I sought Abas with my own mind, intent on cursing him, harrowing him with visions of my forthcoming vengeance. But I could not find him. I camped my army before the bridge that served Melior, blocking all access, able to do nothing more for the time. We had to wait for more men, for news or troops from Vaire or Selt or Tiela, for Abas to make a move. Really, I had no wish to touch one stone of my home or to spend one soldier's life; I only wanted Abas dead for what he had done. . . . I began to have a whore brought to me each night.

I made no secret of it; I would stand at my tent flap every evening and roar for my manservant to bring me a woman. The soldiers took to laying bets on my punctuality, Oorossy told me. Frain and Fabron said nothing to me about it at all. I obstinately rejoiced in their averted eyes. I felt taut inside, stretched to the breaking point, because I refused to admit the change looming within me. Even as I lusted to shed my father's blood I remembered—her, a warm, beating heart and soft lips, soft breast. . . . To spite the goddess, I expended my warm thoughts in the coldest way I knew. Then Shamarra came back, and all that was in me turned to a hard, heavy black sword. The cutting sword of double edge.

She rode in one day on her white mare. The whole camp, to a man, stood and gaped at her. I saw her coming and fled to my tent. As commanding officer it was my place to meet her, but, before all the gods, I could not do it. I would have struck her as soon as speak to her. Frain met her, the good fellow, greeted her as a friend, and I think she returned the greeting with better courtesy than she had ever shown him. Peering from my tent flap, I saw her lay her hand in his as she slipped down from her horse.

Later she came to me as I sat in council with my officers. With many a courtly flourish she presented to me a banner

174

patterned after my shield, the device being a winged black unicorn on a silver field. She gave me badges of office to match, and I was hard put to accept the things with even a scant show of courtesy. I could not look at her for rage. She had declared herself to be my lady with those gifts.

'Aftalun sends his greeting and his blessing to you, his rival and scion,' she proclaimed. 'He would join cause with you if he could, but it is unseemly for the dead or the immortal to meddle in the affairs of the living.'

'Are you no goddess, then, that you meddle?' I asked harshly. If she caused trouble with Raz—

She shrugged with a pretty air of pathos and a liquid look. 'I was immortal once. Perhaps I am not any more.'

I turned and strode away from her, out of the tent, all the angrier because she had routed me, made a fool of me in front of my men. That night I called for two whores and made sure the whole camp heard me.

The next week was a horror. From their ends of the stone spans over the Chardri the Boda watched us and watched us, never daring to move against us, the cowards. Their prying eyes enraged me. And there was no escaping the presence of Shamarra, her beauty or my men's awe of her aristocratic presence. Frain had told her I was betrothed, but she pretended she had not heard. What was I to do with her when Raz came? Within a few days I felt fit to be chained in a pit, though I still maintained an outward semblance of calm and control. Praise be to Eala, on the third day Sethym of Selt arrived with four hundred men after having ridden all the way from Gyotte blindfolded for fear of rabbits, white birds, and the like. He brought news: Abas had been seen with his army in Vaire. He had lifted that siege and was marching northward. Good news! Wayte would be able to muster his forces and come to our aid, and I would be able to engage my enemy at last. Abas was likely to find himself trapped between two armies. I had only to hold the bridges to prevent his obtaining help from Melior. I thirsted for battle now; my pent anger had heated me to battle fever. In a day or two we would march forth from camp and I would be freed of Shamarra for at least a battle's span. Damn the woman! Would nothing drive her away from me?

As it turned out, she herself offered me the way to be rid of her. When my man brought me my whore that evening, it was she. The poor fellow looked as if he wanted to hide. She had bullied him into it; I could see that in a moment. He scuttled away the instant the tent flap fell. Shamarra faced me in a queenly pose, her proud, pale face raised. 'Take me,' she said, perhaps thinking that she could shame me. But I barked out a laugh and seized her, ripped off her flimsy gown before she could gasp. The haughty slut, I wanted to make her scream! But she would not scream, not the whole long night through.

The longest of nights, but I will not dwell on it. I do not care to tell how I made the act of love into a ritual of hatred. I paid dearly for that night afterward. The memory of it poisoned my pleasure for years. But when Shamarra left me in the dark dawn, bruised and disheveled, I knew quite surely that she would not face me again. I shouted taunts after her, gleeful with victory and satisfied malice. I could have spit on her departing back! I was willing to pay any price to see her go. But I had not thought of losing my brother. I had not thought he could be so angry.

I slept for a few hours and awoke sometime after dawn to hear a couple of soldiers whispering near my tent. I suppose they thought I would be snoring for hours yet.

'Prince Frain will be off, I tell you!' one said. 'He'll not bear it, even from Tirell.'

'The lady went to him of her own will,' protested the other.

'I know it. She's as crazy as he. But Frain looks angry enough to weep blood. And it would have broken your heart, too, to see her go away with her head down and her hair falling over her face. She rode that white mare of hers at the slow walk all the way to Melior, and the Boda on the bridge made way for her without a word. She didn't even look at them. She went on as slowly as a swan, and Prince Frain stood watching after her every step of the steep way up to the castle.'

'What does she want in Melior?' the other asked.

'I don't know. Perhaps only that none of us can follow her there. But Frain has sworn he'll follow somehow, Boda or no Boda.'

I burst out of my tent, routing the soldiers, and hurried to

Frain's. He was not there. I ran to look for his horse; it was gone. I got my own and went blundering and swearing off to the north. But I met that fool, Sethym, and he did me a wise man's service. 'That way,' he said, and pointed me along the south road toward Melior.

Frain was standing just out of sight of camp, beyond a rise and nearly within bowshot of the Boda who held the Gerriew bridge. Fabron stood there with him. He started to move away when he saw me coming, but Frain motioned him to wait, unbuckled his sword, and gave it into Fabron's keeping. The gesture stunned me. As if he believed he might be tempted to draw it on me! I rode up and dismounted to face him, and I think I must have been ashamed even then, for I let him have the first words.

I cannot remember all that was said. I was dismayed by the force of his anger, passionate anger, and something more—pain? Despair? I did not know, I could not understand. His words scorched my soul, and I put up a cold, cold shield. Iron of hatred. After a while I stopped trying to answer him. I let my hard face be my shield.

I remember some. 'She has left defeated,' Frain said softly, with a softness that struck me to the core; I could have stood it better if he had abused me. 'She who is fit to fly with the flocks of Ascalonia and yet was snared by love of you, a mortal, and you defeated her love! You have dishonoured her in her own eyes and all eyes that judge her. Are you proud, Tirell, to have bent the head of a goddess?'

'She came to me of her own accord,' I answered sullenly.

'She came to lift you out of your morass of hatred, to shame you into sense. But you had to drag her down with you, into your filthy wallow! She wept on my shoulder when you were done with her.' His voice went husky, and I had to shift my gaze; I could not meet his eyes. 'She told me she had not believed you could take her lovelessly. As I have never believed you have lost all love for me. . . . But I begin to wonder now.'

'Why, if it will please you,' I retorted coldly, 'for the sake of your courtesy I will never bed a woman again.' I meant that as amends, in my twisted way, and as martyrdom. But

177

Frain allowed for no martyrdom.

'It does not please me,' he shot back. 'A woman who loves should be lovingly bedded. And even in her shame Shamarra loves and serves you better than you know. I would have followed her for pity, but she would not allow it. She rode through Melior to prevent it.'

'Why, you can follow her, for all of me,' I said coolly. 'I will give you the badge of an emissary to earn you safe conduct into Melior if you like.' What demon was in me! But I never really thought he would go. I trusted his brother-love for me even when I would not acknowledge it or endure its flame.

'Give me the emblem,' he said grimly, and I flung the black and silver thing at him as I mounted my horse. Fabron came running up.

'My lords, no!' he pleaded at both of us, and then to Frain: 'Dear Prince, you cannot leave him now! Not after all the miles—' He took Frain by the shoulders, and Frain stood like a red-hot poker in his grip. If I had found the courage or the sense to stay then, I think—but thinking is of no use. I spurred away. I risked a glance just before I crossed the rise. Frain had softened; Fabron held him in his arms.

Fabron would bring him back to me, I thought. I rode back to camp and slouched about for an hour, listless, waiting for Fabron and trying to pretend not to be waiting. Fabron came at last, with a look as if he could cheerfully skewer me.

'Frain has gone into Melior,' he said roughly, 'to see Shamarra and your mother, if he can. He says he will return.'

I ignored the look and the tone. 'Why, then he will return,' I murmured, fixing my mind on my brother's faithfulness.

'Small thanks to you if he does,' Fabron snapped. Men were watching; I thought I might have to fight him after all. But a soft voice spoke from behind both of us. There stood Grandfather with the black beast by his side.

'Put away anger,' he said. 'There is fear to be thought of. Abas is in Melior castle.'

'What!' I shouted with dismay that cracked my mask of a face; I felt it split. 'My report is that Abas is marching hither from Vaire, at the head of his army!'

'No, Grandson,' Daymon said quietly, 'he came back to

178

Melior just before you did, secretly, for your mother lay ill and likely to die—and she lies dead now. It is his fault, so he keeps the news to himself—and the knowledge does not improve his temper. I cannot think how he is likely to greet Frain.'

I turned to the king of Vaire, shaking and, for once in my life, earnest. 'Fabron,' I cried, 'if I had known this I would never have let him go, I swear it! I thought there was no one in that castle who would harm him.'

He didn't speak to me. Perhaps he couldn't speak. He stood looking away toward the blood-red towers of Melior, and the black beast went and nuzzled his hand.

'What is happening to Frain, Grandfather?' I demanded. 'Can you not see?'

Tears on his thin cheeks; his mind was with his daughter. 'They've taken him now,' he said. 'I can see nothing more.' He spoke gently. He has always been gentle with me when I find myself most clearly in the wrong.

I stared away at the glistening towers in my turn. 'Why, then,' I heard myself say, 'I will have to go in after him.'

6

Within the hour I rode over the Gerriew under flag of truce. I took with me a small retinue, for show, and I had dressed myself to the last detail in the best clothing I could muster—all black, of course. I carried my iron sword and iron shield, again for show. Fabron wanted to come with me, but I persuaded him to stay behind. I believed his presence would only enrage Abas, and the other kings agreed with me. They stayed in camp for the same reason, and so did Grandfather, and the beast with him. Grandfather saw me off without even a word of advice. All advice seemed futile when dealing with Abas.

I went to Melior with some harebrained notion of having Frain released by offering myself in his place. All very noble and impractical—if Abas had taken Frain prisoner, what was to prevent him from taking me as well? But I knew well enough, paint him as black as I liked, that he would not harm me unless I drove him to it. And I knew, chillingly, that he regarded Frain in quite a different way. He would not hesitate to harm Frain if the mood took him. And that made my errand imperative.

It was an eerie homecoming, or at least I felt it as such. I wondered how Frain had felt, passing those hostile, familiar gates. I left the horses standing in the courtyard with my men to guard them and I strode alone into the keep. No servant dared to speak to me, and I was too proud anyway to ask my way to the King—to beg for an audience, forsooth, with my own father! But I found him soon enough. He was sitting alone on the dais in the great, gloomy main hall, hunched over a cup of something, some liquor. He was probably drunk, though he did not show it; he never did. He stared at me sourly as I entered, seeming completely unsurprised.

'You've been taking your bloody time getting home!' he snapped.

I strode across to him in silence, walked up to him and looked down where he sat, unable to believe that he had no other reaction for me. I was expecting wrath, rage, love, sorrow, guilt—anything except his ill-tempered acceptance. I believe I could have moved back into my old room, pretended nothing had happened, and he would have fallen in with the farce. He did not seem to mind my standing and staring at him; he simply attended to his cup. He had aged since I had left, but the process had made him leaner and tougher than ever.

'Out nattering with an old man,' he grumbled after a while. 'Say hello to your mother, boy—she's dead.' With a casual movement he indicated something beyond the table. One of those awful carved coffins lay there with the pale, blind eyes staring up at the rafters. I winced at the sight of it, and for a moment I could not move. Then I walked over—I passed right behind my father's indifferent back—and I opened the casket lid. Mother faced me, already embalmed, looking very fair, even fairer than I had remembered. She had been dressed in rich, fine robes, laid on silk pillows, with no marks of any abuse on her that I could see. Her pale face seemed to float amid a ruff of ermine. Looking at her, I felt helplessness melt me down to a stump. I might as well have been a tiny boy again, no higher than her knee.

'She died to spite me,' Abas remarked sullenly, still turning his back. 'She died of spleen. I never touched her.'

Mother's cloak of ermine and purple was gathered with a pin I recognized, Frain's brooch. The dog, symbol of fidelity. . . . I unfastened it and held it up for Abas to see.

'My brother,' I said quietly. 'Where is he?'

'You're a fool if you think he is your brother.' Abas did not even look at me.

I circled the table to stand in front of him. 'Where is Frain?' I asked again.

'In a dungeon.' He met my eyes absently. 'Get to your chamber, boy.'

The arrogant—how could he think I would come back to him, after what he had done? And what mad whim had made him put Frain's pin in a coffin? Perhaps Frain was dead too. The thought made me forget resentment. 'I would like to see Frain,' I said, trying to steady my voice.

'Damn Frain,' he answered in dull anger. I had never heard such dead and heavy anger in him; it chilled me worse than any wind of his rage. 'I am tired of Frain. Suevi loves Frain, Tirell loves Frain, everyone loves Frain. Let him stay in his kennel for a while. The damn puppy, I believe he would even love me if I gave him the chance.' He spoke with loathing—of himself? Ai, how very much I was like him.

'Sire,' I said softly, trying not to threaten, 'you may have noticed that there is an army outside.'

He straightened and faced me, eyes glittering blue—poison blue. He did not speak a word, but I knew that I had gained his full and most dangerous attention.

'For a year and more I have planned revenge against you.' I kept my voice as dispassionate as possible; I had to be careful, very careful. 'But if it will see Frain freed, I offer to lay down my arms.'

'So it was the pup that drew you in here.' That same deathly tone. 'Well, let him keep you here. I'll put a lock on him and a leash on you.' The leash of love; the same power he had always held over me.

I considered, skirting his words. 'What are the conditions of Frain's release?' I asked.

'None. There will be no release.'

I could have gone to my room, waited my chance to steal a word with Frain, plotted our escape. And Abas could have kept me waiting, hoping and despairing, for months, even years. Suddenly I was no longer too proud to beg. Trembling, I offered him my most precious possessions—my selfhood, my dreams—never thinking that my dreams might be his nightmare. I did not think at all; I only felt. I unbuckled my long iron sword, placed it with the shield on my outstretched hands.

'Sire,' I began, 'for Frain's sake . . .' My voice quavered. I had probably never spoken to him so ardently, or not since I was six or thereabouts—but he did not hear me. His adder eyes caught on the shield and sword and he lunged up with a shout that sent the doves whistling off the turrets. He screamed like Morrghu, like blinding, screaming wind. I believe that until then he had scarcely noticed my gear, but he saw it now, by Eala! He stood pulled back like a strung bow, and spume started down from the corners of his mouth. I stood stunned, a bird before the snake.

All powers be thanked for what the dragons had taught me. Somehow I found strength to turn and flee. I could not have stayed alive in his presence more than a moment longer; I am sure of it. Looking at him I had looked into the face of death. Stupid, stupid of me to have showed him dark iron of Aftalun, the likeness of the beast! I heard him gibbering after me, something about rutting in the night. Striding away, I heard guards running toward me, and I carried my sword unsheathed to fend them off. But none of them dared to attack me. They were all in confusion, and Abas was too convulsed with fury and terror to speak. I reached the courtyard, swung onto my black, and cantered away with my men after me. They looked parchment white, and so did the Boda we passed. I believe Abas's cry must have been heard as far as the bridges.

Back in camp, I reported to Fabron as if he were my superior. He sat with Oorossy and the others in his tent, waiting.

'We had better attack at once if we are to find Frain alive,' he said shakily when he had heard my tale.

'With what?' Oorossy demanded. 'Where the hell is Raz?' He was right, of course; we did not have sufficient force to take the castle. But I only shrugged at him.

'Forthwith,' I promised Fabron. I ordered the necessary preparations.

Things could not have been much worse, or so I thought. But before we could move, scouts brought news that sent the outlook even deeper into dread. The King's forces from Vaire were approaching. That would have been all right if we could have fought them on our own terms, but we had to try to take Melior. Abas held the advantage for a certainty. Muttering curses, I ordered my army into action.

We had no plan and almost no hope.

We took the bridges. They were fortified, of course, and the few Boda who held them took many of my men away. But in the end they also left for the regions of Vieyra. I set troops of picked men to guarding the bloody spans against the enemy approaching from southward. Then I mounted my black charger, and with the black beast at my side I led the rest of my diminished force up the hill to assault Melior.

'We will be put to rout almost before they have had time to mock us,' Fabron said hollowly.

I knew that, but we had to try. I could not leave Frain without even a try. . . . Abas's defenders greeted us with jeers and a shower of arrows. No wonder they laughed. We had no proper equipment, no siege towers, no shelter of any kind, no sappers—only a tree trunk we had cut by way of a battering ram and a few scaling ladders, which were quickly knocked to bits. We swarmed and pounded at the gates and walls while they dropped things on us. If they had not been too amused to properly defend themselves, I doubt if any of us would have survived. And Fabron was right; within the hour I was forced to lift the assault and march to the aid of my men at the bridges. Abas's army had arrived. After a few more hours we had been pushed back beyond the summit of Melior to the valley between the paps. There we stuck, fighting for our lives.

'If we can hold out till Wayte comes—' Fabron panted beside me. I had kept my mount, but he had lost his. He fought afoot by my forequarter and I defended his back with my long iron sword. Wings sounded overhead, those ugly Luoni, flapping about and staring as they loved to do, waiting for my soul to stoop on. I ground my teeth in despair. The vicious things—

Then larger wings, brighter wings—the dragons! Down from the north they soared, half a dozen of them, with golden light flashing from their scales. My mouth hung speechless, but Fabron had the good sense to cheer, and my men took it up, glad to know that the apparitions were on their side. Over the ranks of the enemy the dragons raked, puffing flame—mostly at air, I must admit. They do not like to scorch living things. But the assault threw the men of Melior into a panic, and we surged forward.

'Courage,' said a quiet voice. The brown man of Eidden Lei

took his place by Fabron's side, swinging a great mace, and not a warrior in the field would face him.

'Now look who comes,' he added.

I rose on my steed to scan the distance. Flash of metal by Melior stone. . . . I knelt there quite silent while the battle shouted below me.

'What is it?' Fabron questioned eagerly. 'Wayte? Raz?'

'No,' I said. 'Abas.'

Chariot after chariot wheeled through the gates of the castle and down the hill. These were the great golden chariots of Melior with slashing knives on their hubs! Streams of footmen followed them under a glittering forest of lancetips. Abas drove his own chariot. I singled him out even at that distance and sat my black in a trance of admiration and—and hatred, of course; was it not hatred that I felt for him? Had I not come all this way to fight him? Odd. . . . He led the rest, set apart from them by his chalk-white lotus helm, the black and white fur that dripped from his blood-red tunic, the moon glow of his brooch. He stood at his full height and lashed his horses madly, sending them surging ahead of his warriors.

'He has been eating the red mushroom of Morrghu.' It was Sethym, speaking to me in a tight voice. The king of Selt had fought well and bravely, facing rabbits or whatever came his way, but he evidently did not like the look of those villainous chariots. Oorossy came up beside me as well.

'I have closed my line,' he told me, 'but those damned reaping machines will make mincemeat of us.'

Before I could reply, a nightmare blot appeared. A deathly, inky, goblin-grotesque thing bore down on Abas with a rattling shriek. I watched, feeling the rage, feeling that shriek rip my own throat; it was the beast. I waited, gloating, for Abas to cringe. I knew his terror and loathing of the beast, for I had felt it myself. But he must indeed have been eating the fungus that gave men mad valor in battle, as Sethym had said. He turned headlong to meet the rearing menace that towered over him, raised his sword, and stabbed as the beast crashed down on him and splintered his chariot to ruins. Black wings lay beating, fluttering amid the shards.

Like a storm wind rage tore out of me, hurtled me out of my

trance, found voice in a shout that must still echo somewhere, a madman's roar of sorrow. By blood, if he had slain
the beast now—Heedless of the army in my way, I spurred
toward vengeance, toward Abas the killer, he who had slain
my love, imprisoned my love, spurned my love! Men, mine
and his, scattered before me.

He crawled from the wreckage of his chariot and ran to
meet me, waving his dripping sword. I sprang down from my
horse, scorning to take any advantage. Let him have the run
on me! Come hither, Father, come to your death. . . . I held
the dark sword of Aftalun and waited for him, feeling years of
hatred rise to a peak. My time for revenge had come at last.

He bore down on me, panting and glaring like an animal,
without even a flicker of comprehension in his crazed blue
eyes. He would not even know that it was his son who killed
him, or why, or remember what he had done to earn it. He
had fed to satiety on Morrghu's food and his own poisonous
hatred; how I loathed him for what he had made me! And I
knew quite suddenly, as clearly as if his sword already
pierced my vitals, that I could not kill him. I hated him too
dearly. Slay my own beloved anger? I might as well slay a part
of myself. My mountain peak of rage crashed down all in a
moment and trapped me in the rubble. I could not move. I
had never felt so helpless, not by my dead mother's side, not
even when Mylitta fell. Abas faced me scarcely a yard away. I
watched without stirring as he raised his sword to strike.
Battle frenzy had turned his face to a pulsating flame. Fire and
blue, blue ice. . . . There could be no doubt of my death
beneath that blow.

I watched. And from beside me another sword flashed,
lifted, and struck Abas squarely in the throat. He gurgled and
fell, splattering me with his blood, shuddering and squirming
a moment before he lay still. In that moment I knew how
much I had loved him, how much and how hopelessly I had
wanted him to love me. I screamed a long, wailing shriek like
no sound I had ever known was in me, like the cry of harried
souls that ride the wind. All of life had betrayed me by the
hand of the one who stood, swaying and panting, by my side.
I turned on him in blind, maniacal fury and lunged at him,

186

still screaming; he had killed my father! My iron sword struck through flesh and crunched deep into bone. I tugged it free for another blow, and then skies and towers and all the ramparts of earth fell down upon me. It was Frain, my beloved brother, whom I had struck.

His eyes met mine with something more than pain—I could only call it love. He had not raised a hand against me. If there had been time I think I would have killed myself then and there. But there was no time; I had to catch him before he fell. Chariots and trampling horses and desperate men churned all around us.

I held him to my chest with one arm, felt his face resting against my own. I slashed my way out of the battle, struggling along, hating myself, swinging my sword and roaring and caterwauling while tears streamed down my face so that I could hardly tell friend from foe. Fabron joined me, hurrying along at my side, shouting anxious questions. I did not answer him. I carried Frain to the sacred grove. The goddess was good for something after all; no one would fight there if they could help it. The goddess preferred innocent blood of sacrifice, which was very nearly what I was bringing her.

I laid Frain down. He could not speak, but he touched my hand. Then he fainted. I ripped the tunic open and found the wound. It was his left shoulder I had struck, through flesh and bone, a terrible wound, a crippling wound, but it appeared no vitals were hurt—I tried to bind it up, but my hands shook, I could do nothing right. Fabron pushed me aside.

'Sit there,' he told me.

How could he speak to me, how could he not kill me? Surely he did not understand. 'I gave Frain that wound!' I shouted at him. 'I, the great Prince of Melior! Oh, Fabron, I am a wretched, hateful thing. . . .' My voice broke. I sobbed, and he reached over to pat me absently.

'I know,' he said, humouring me.

I wept—it seemed like hours that I wept. I hope no one ever has to weep like that again. I wept until I could scarcely breathe, until I thought I would die. Fabron tended to Frain, then put his arms around me; I shall always love him for that. But no one could help me much. Years of weeping were in me, for Mylitta, for Mother, for Abas whom I had loved, for Frain though he was still living, for myself. . . . I felt adrift in fate, floating in wells of sorrow, spun and eddied by a stream I could not direct, dark water—the world was dark; even the sky had gone dark while I wept. Great storm clouds had moved in from the Perin Tyr, and the battle clanged beneath them.

And Frain moaned and stirred by my side. And the brown man walked toward me. He came slowly into the grove with the beast following him as he led and urged and encouraged it toward me. It left a trail of red all the way, red running down from slashes on its shoulders; its wings hung limp and tattered and one leg dragged the ground, nearly severed. It fell at my feet and lay in silent agony. The brown man stood watching me weep.

'Accursed, the whole line of Melior is accursed,' Frain cried aloud. 'I might as well be dead.'

They would die, they would all die and leave me living and in such misery—

'Hush,' Fabron soothed him.

'Accursed!' Frain insisted. He spoke thickly, half delirious with pain. 'I might as well go mad. The Luoni will come for me. I am a parricide.'

'You are not,' Fabron told him quite levelly.

'I *killed*—'

'You slew a madman. You have not killed your father. I am your father.'

I turned to them, my tears suddenly abated, my tangle of emotions in abeyance. All of the world seemed caught in calm that moment in spite of the battle uproar out beyond the grove. Frain lay gazing up at Fabron suddenly quite lucid, though pain pulled at his face. 'What?' he whispered.

'I am your father. I sold you, in my greed and to my shame.'

'But—how—' Frain lay stunned, uncomprehending. Fabron caressed his forehead with a trembling hand.

'Never mind. You are my son whom I love,' he said, though he could scarcely speak. 'Let suffering go awhile.'

And suddenly Frain moved as if to get up. The colour came back into his cheeks. 'The pain,' he said, amazed. 'It's gone.'

One step took me to his side, hoping—no. The wound was still there; my guilt would not so easily disappear. Frain looked up at his father in wonder, then at me. I pillowed his head on my lap.

'The healer has come out of shame into truth at last!' It was the brown man, his deep voice booming. 'The beast, Fabron, help the beast! Come over here. Bring that great sword.'

None of us would have dreamed of questioning his command. Fabron picked up my heavy iron sword and walked to where the beast lay, walked as if in a trance. The creature still breathed, but barely. Fabron knelt between its sprawling legs and laid the sword of Aftalun full length down the prone, heaving ribs. On it he placed his muscular hands. And slowly, softly, he recited the healer's chant. I had heard it many times as a child, but only this time did I comprehend it. The words echoed and magnified in my mind, and I waited, holding on to my brother as if he were the only solid thing in my world.

> *Black and white,*
> *Day and night,*
> *Darkness and light*
> *Can be one.*
> *Moon and sun*
> *Meet in the halls*
> *Of Aftalun.*

A shock of blinding bright power, a huge splinter of sunlight, burst through Fabron and into the still form beneath his hands. I should have known better than to think that a gentle healing could come to the beast! Fabron fell back with a cry of pain and the beast leaped up with a cry, I think, of exultation. Aftalun's sword lay melted and shriveled on the ground, and the beast took wing. The beast took wing!

We all watched, stunned, breathless at Fabron who had been hurled to the ground. The brown man went to him and held him half sitting so he could watch the beast fly. The beast took flight! Straight up through the trees it burst, its broad wings rattling the branches, and out it shot into sunset light, riding the rising wind beneath the rain clouds, thunder god. . . . Three times it circled above us with soaring joy in every curve of its wings and high-flung head. It shone like a black jewel—lovely. And oh, the light on its wings, and on the dragon wings, and on the clouds. . . . It gave tongue, a deep, belling call I can hear even now, and an answering call tore from me.

'Tyr!' I cried. I scrambled up and ran out of the grove. The world was caught up in waiting. Even the battle seemed to have quieted, and instead of battle noise there sounded other noise now, thunder noise.

'Tyr!'

He came down at once, landed lightly on deft black hooves, folded his sleek wings and stood at a little distance, meeting my gaze. 'Tyr,' I whispered. He was a person to me now, an ancestor, an other, and he looked to me for what only I could grant him. I swallowed and shook my head, closed my eyes against prickling tears. All around me rang a profound, waiting silence. How could he wish to leave me, after all the miles? Yet how could I deny him? He had served the line of Melior long enough.

'All right,' I said. 'Go. Be at peace.'

He sprang up, bugled, and shot off westward, where orange light blazed between dark rain clouds and dark mountains and where the altar loomed, the White Rock of Eala. The sun had become a pulsing blood-red ball that rested on it and sent its shadow edging toward me. . . . Over the Rock the beast skimmed, let out his harsh cry, then spiraled, closing and closing, higher and higher, until he disappeared into the black clouds above.

And a roar of thunder came that shook the ground, and a mighty flare of lightning. And with a crack like the thunder the altar split and toppled in upon itself and stood there broken, and the sun hung free.

Then silence, utter calm except for the voices of frightened men. Tyr drifted out of the clouds, dipped in a sort of salute—to whom?—and flew away, over the mountains of Acheron and into the arms of his father Aftalun—into sunset glory. I watched until that glow embraced him, and I never saw him again. I stood staring after him with quiet, easy tears dropping down my face. Then the rain began, rustling like a living thing, sending up little spurts of dust from the dry earth as it fell. I stood in it, letting it wash me, understanding vaguely that something vast had changed.

'It's the doom of Melior!' someone cried.

'Deliverance!' came a deeper voice.

I had forgotten about the brown man until he hugged me. Instinctively I returned the embrace, laying my head for a moment against the flat, coarse hair of his neck and shoulders, feeling warmth and strength creep through me. Afraid? Why should I be? I had been a beast, too, or I had loved one. . . .

'Doom and deliverance,' he averred. 'Tirell, can you see what marvel you have done? The beast is gone, freed and vanquished by your love. Altar, beast, blood bird, and madness—gone for all time! Melior as men have known it will never return!' His voice trembled with feeling, and he brushed my face with his mouth in a gesture I did not at first realize was a kiss. I stood dazed.

Then Oorossy and Sethym were kneeling before me. 'King of Melior,' they said, 'claim your throne.'

The throne! A pox on the throne! Frain was wounded, my father dead, the beast gone, and the altar destroyed; the whole world had turned upside down and now they wanted me to take a throne! 'Why?' I challenged them.

'Abas's captains have surrendered,' Oorossy explained patiently. 'Their King is dead—'

'That is the least of it!' Sethym bleated. 'The true King stands here! Look, the whole sky hails him!' The rain softly fell.

'Frain will do better in the castle,' Fabron said wearily from behind me, and then I moved. Fabron looked none too hearty himself. I signaled the captains, Abas's and mine. The dragons soared off northward, and we all packed up our wounded and went home to Melior. I put Fabron on my black steed and carried Frain myself; he had settled into a deep swoon and the jarring did not trouble him. The brown man walked by my side, and the rain poured down, cleansing the dead and the living, enriching the earth. All along the way to

191

the castle people stood cheering and dancing in the rain. Sethym tried to give me his horse. He would have it that they cheered for me, for a victory. I thought he was mad. I continued afoot, cradling my brother.

We toiled up the hill to my home, and there at the gate stood Daymon Cein. 'All powers be praised, lad, you have done it!' he exclaimed, embracing me. I could not understand his happiness.

'Frain is wounded,' I told him.

'I can see that,' he snapped, but he sobered just the same. 'How badly?'

'I think he will be crippled.' There was a catch in my voice, and Grandfather peered at me.

'And you did it.' He spoke gently, very gently; I had never heard such gentle forgiveness even from him. 'Men will come to love you for it. Tirell, the King who did wrong. Life is an aching, comical, marvellous thing. Can you feel the wonder of it?'

I felt only the ache just then. 'Help Fabron,' I said. 'Help me get them in bed.'

The brown man helped, too. We took them to the very chamber Frain and I had once shared as boys. The old wooden bedstead, scarred and carved by boys now as dead, in their way, as Mylitta. . . . How odd, that nothing had been disturbed. Fabron fell asleep at once, and Frain lay quietly, so I walked to a little balcony nearby and stood once again in the gentle, steady rain. I could hear people singing somewhere below, and glad shouts. Grandfather came and stood beside me, reached out and caught the rain on his parched old fingers.

'The tears of the King,' he said, and then I began to understand.

192

7

It rained, softly and steadily, for three days.

I sent my parents away to rest in that rain, on the Chardri. I found I was no longer afraid of the living water—everything else had changed, why not that? So Guron and I—he was my captain now—and some other household officials made our way down to the river with the heavy ironwood casques riding on staves between us. In mine, I knew, lay Abas in his ermine and his torque and his great royal brooch. I would never wear it, the twenty-headed thing! And in the other lay Suevi. . . . Grandfather walked along with us to bid his daughter farewell. We laid the caskets in the water with their solemn, painted eyes staring skyward. I did not know what Chardri would do—I had not had many dealings with Chardri—but he took them graciously, eddying them out into midstream and carrying them away with a low, musical sound. I shall always hear in the lapping of water the peace of that moment when we stood by the river in the soft rain. Souls and swans float the watery ways. . . . I appointed a retinue of trusty men to ride along the river and see the dead safely to Coire Adalis.

I received my bride also in the rain. Raz arrived at last, with his army of two thousand, just in time to be of no use, and with great pomp he brought the girl across the Balliew—Recilla. Never again would she be just the girl to me, the ceremonial bride. I had one look at her, dark eyes scared and defiant in her flower of a face, and I knew that I would love her, that I would court her to love me. Joy awaited me, as the old man had said. What a fool I had been! All the way around the Vale, to wed the lass my father had chosen for me in the first place! I wanted to shout, to laugh. I wanted to tell Frain. Frain, my brother and friend. . . . He still lay in the stupor of his wound.

By the time he awoke, four days after the battle, the rain had stopped and a gentle sun shone. Already the land was sending forth fresh blades of green. I wore a crown and a crimson robe, I was King of Melior, and I had taken Recilla to wife and planted the seed of love in her. The canton kings had taken their armies and gone on home, all except Fabron. Everything had changed. Frain looked up at me in bewilderment.

'You are all right,' he murmured.

I hardly knew what to say. Within the span of a few days I had become a stranger to him. I sat by his bedside and took his hand, held it between both of mine, met his clear eyes. That was hard, but I had to give him what I could; I had hurt him.

'Really all right!' he marvelled. 'I would have given more than an arm for that, Tirell.' Joy lit his pale face. How his love unmanned me—I had to look away.

'Frain, I am so sorry—' I, who had never needed to say I was sorry.

'Let it pass,' he told me.

'I will let it pass, but some things have to be said. I have been a brute to you these many months.'

He smiled—he almost laughed, but pain stopped him. 'I can take a few rough words,' he protested. 'You were sore of heart, brother. Let it pass, I say!'

'Words were the least of it. I sent you off to Melior, into a den of death—'

'My home, a den of death?' Frain teased.

'And Shamarra.' I could not go on. Suddenly Shamarra seemed very fragile and fair to me, and my crime iniquitous.

And Frain did not answer. He looked away in his turn, and with a shock I sensed the bitterness beneath his forgiveness. But we could not admit that we would part—not yet.

'You accepted me,' he whispered.

'What?' I did not understand.

'You knew, did you not, before Fabron told me? You seemed none too surprised.'

That he was Fabron's son. I had to smile. 'I saw them bring

194

you,' I admitted, 'the night you were born—well, the night you came.'

'And you accepted me, all those years. . . .'

He seemed touched. I could not believe what he was saying. 'The debt was all mine!' I tried to explain. 'You—you were here with me, always by me—'

Without him I would have been only another mad King of Melior, another Abas.

'Some good fate sent you to me,' I told him. 'Some blessing is on me. Frain, the altar is gone.'

'What?' he exclaimed.

'You don't remember?'

'I remember—Guron set me free, and I ran and ran to find you—then Abas—and Fabron healing the beast, and—tears on your face.'

We talked for a long time, until he was tired. By the time we were done, fight it though I might, I knew things would never again be the same between us. I had everything now, all happiness, and Frain had—even less than I imagined. There was the wound, and there was a need I did not want to see.

'Shamarra,' he said. 'Where is she, do you know? She did not come here.'

'Folk say she has gone back to Acheron.' All of Melior had noted that swanlike passing. I did not care to speak of Shamarra.

'Fabron is hoping, expecting, that you will return with him to Vaire and be his heir,' I said. 'I promised you to him once—but we have no quarrel, we both know I was an ass then. Really, the choice must be yours. Melior has always been your home, and you are welcome to stay here as long as you live.' Then Fabron came in, his smile all for his son, and I left them together.

Days went by while Frain's body slowly mended. He began to walk about with his arm in a sling, but some inner wound failed to heal; he went silent, his russet hair eerily bright above his pale face. The brown man laid warm hands on him for comfort, then went back to his northern home. Fabron laid hands and iron on him to no effect at all—the power had left him again for good. He watched his son with anxious eyes. Daymon Cein settled serenely into a chamber near the kitchen and seemed to be paying no attention to any of us. He let the servants wait on him; he had become very frail. I kept an eye on everyone, but I spent my days mostly with Recilla, laughing, talking, guilty in my own happiness, watching her blossom into love of me. Frain smiled at us sometimes, but he seldom joined us or spoke.

I lay warm in my bed those days. I slept peacefully, but Guron told me that Frain had taken to wandering the night as I had once done. So I went to him a few times in the midnight chill, tried to talk to him, but there was nothing to say and all too much to say, and all I could do was be by his side. He would not look at me. He stood and watched the western stars.

'Will you help me take off this torque?' he requested once. 'I am no prince.'

We undid the golden thing. It left a mark like a whip weal on his neck. I should have known then that he would not remain in Melior, but like a fool I continued to hope. Even if he went to Vaire, I told myself, I might see him often; it was not so very far. . . . In my heart I knew I was losing him forever. Still, I did not expect to lose him in the way I did. Not to the shadowed path.

He made his choice on the day the sling came off for good. His arm hung twisted and useless, like an arm of warm wax pulled awry. He stood aimlessly, and Fabron and I sat in silent despair, and I forced myself to look up, to meet my brother's eyes. The hatred in them stunned me, the hatred locked and warring with the love. Eala, what was to become of him? If only he could have shouted at me, struck me, killed me—but I was his beloved brother, and neither of us could give that up.

'I am helpless,' Frain said woodenly. 'I am a cripple.' I flinched at the word, and he touched me as if to ask my pardon—I, who had done this to him.

'I don't mean the arm,' he said.

Puzzled, I looked up at him again. Weary and utterly calm, he met my gaze.

'I hate what I have become,' he said. 'I am adrift in my life,

lost, full of bitterness—Tirell, I cannot stand another day of
this. I am going.'

'To Vaire?' I asked, staring at him stupidly.

'No. Torn between you two—no. To Acheron.'

'What?' I cried out, Fabron cried out, we both jumped up,
and I took a hold of my brother, seized his sagging shoulders,
and Fabron pleaded with him.

'My son, don't say that! You know I—we love you, a throne
awaits you—'

'I cannot help it, Father. I am doomed, drawn, caught,
ensnared. Do not think I shall return.' Frain's calm was the
most frightening thing about him, really—his calm and those
locked eyes. 'Make Wayte your heir. He has served you well.'

'But—to Acheron. . . .' Fabron faltered to a stop, choking
on the name of Acheron, and he turned on me angrily.

'This is all your fault, Tirell,' he accused. 'If you had not
driven her away—'

'Stop it,' Frain ordered with something of his former fire.
He stepped back, breaking free of the two of us. I sat down in
astonishment.

'Is it Shamarra you go to seek?' I asked Frain.

'Yes. Lady Death.'

His resolve seemed inexplicable to me. I glared at him in
exasperation. 'But Frain, why? You owe her nothing. The
fault is all mine.'

'You dolt,' he said, 'I love her.'

I felt walls and defences crumble around me, my face
crumble. For a moment I could not see, but I heard a small
sound from Frain. He flung himself down beside me as if he
had hurt me, laid his head against my side.

It had never occurred to me that he loved Shamarra.

It seems incredible now that I was so blind. That was what
my shield of insanity had done to me. I had been blind to
everything except my own visions of rage, numb to all needs
except my own, and I had not understood that he could love
where I so heartily hated. I had thought it was his unfailing
courtesy that had made him lend her his horse, sit by her
side, walk the halls of Gyotte in concern for her safety, rail at
me when I had dishonoured her. What an ass I had been! I

197

had thought he was still all mine, the child that had followed me since he was old enough to walk. And it had seemed to me not at all odd that he always slept alone; he was old enough to fight for me, after all, but far too young for women. What a bloody-minded braying idiot I had been!

'And I did that to her,' I whispered. 'Frain, I have hurt you in every way.'

'Never mind,' he mumbled into the fair silk of my shirt.

'How can you abide me? How can you not kill me?'

'No more of that,' he said sharply, and Fabron broke in, bending over him urgently.

'Frain,' he begged, 'come back to Vaire with me. Things may not always seem the same, so hopeless. If you are not better by spring—'

'No.' Frain stood and faced him. 'My father, I wish I could stay, I wish I could always be with you. But I must go, and now, within the hour. Even though the day is half spent.' His words were firm, but a wild desperation was growing in his eyes.

'Only wait a day or two,' Fabron pleaded, 'an hour, even, until I have thought of what to say to you—'

'He should not have to bear it even another hour.' It was my own voice, coming out of me as I listened in vague surprise. 'I know that tug. By Adalis, by the ancient Five . . .' I trailed to a stop, feeling the invisible eyes in the room, feeling fate brooding like a dark bird in the rafters. Such a cruel fate, such a lonely fate. There would be no king for him to kill.

'Go see Grandfather,' I told Frain. 'I will make ready your horse and provisions.'

He kissed his father, and then we went out, leaving Fabron standing like a stone. He stood there a day and then took horse toward Vaire without a word to me. He could not face Frain again; he could not face Acheron.

Within the hour Frain left Daymon Cein and came to me, dreamwalking, where I awaited him in the stable. 'Grandfather knew already,' he told me.

'Of course. He would.' That sly old man.

'He said there would be no place for me, no rest, even in Acheron. He said I must find healing and dwelling within myself.'

'But you are still to go?' I could not help asking.

'Of course. I have no choice. It is only for—for love of you that I have waited this long. You are strong now. You will be able to manage without me.'

It was true. I briefly considered belying the truth, making a weakling of myself, but I had felt the wing of fate. 'I will ride with you as far as the Wall,' I said.

'All right.' He mounted, took the reins with his one good hand.

We rode out at walk and gentle trot, all the way to the Hill of Vision with scarcely a word between us. A few years before we would have raced the distance, whooping, in half the time. But we felt no desire to speed our way that day. . . . How the wheel had turned. Fate rode above us on the wind; I could almost see it. Ever since my brother had set foot in that dark mountain lake he had been changed in some subtle way—what strange force was tearing him from me?

'It is not your fault, any of it,' Frain hurled the words defensively into the silence.

'Oh, it's not, is it?' I glanced over at him, baiting, amused in spite of myself. But he faced stoically forward.

'No. None of it,' he said flatly. 'You were not well.'

'And you're a prig,' I flared, suddenly annoyed. 'Must you always be perfect, Frain?' Why would he not shout? But he did not have the strength for anger.

'Perfect?' he murmured in honest disbelief. 'I have always been a shadow next to you.'

I snapped my head around to look at him, then rode on a while silenced by insight. 'So you truly must go alone,' I said at last, hesitantly, hating to admit it. 'I—it hurts me that you have to brave it alone. You were always there for me.'

'Great Morrghu,' Frain whispered, reining back his horse as if he had sighted a panther. Sudden sweat of fear ran down his face.

We had arrived. Just beyond the shattered Wall the twisted trees stood, idly whistling and twittering and popping the joints of their twiggy fingers, much as they had ever done. 'Great Morrghu,' Frain breathed again. 'What has happened?'

'I told you.' I thought I had. 'Did I forget to tell you? On that

199

same battle day, just as I was learning the true meaning of despair, they suddenly rushed down. The trees, I mean—they moved. The Boda who held this Wall fled, scattered, but the trees stopped where they stand as suddenly as they had come. Grandfather says to let them be and let the Wall lie, too, for it is no use trying to shut out Acheron. That is where Abas made his mistake.'

Frain stared in terror. I felt no concern for the haggish trees, only for him. He sat stiff with fear on his mount.

'I know they've moved, but I—they've changed. They're leering, contemptuous, they're—they're naked.'

'They always looked obscene to me.' I eyed him with pity and a foolish hope. 'Brother mine, it is still not too late to turn back.'

'No, thank you. I am in thrall. I might as well be dead as disobedient.' He took a deep breath, trying to steady himself. 'This is going to be harder than I thought, that is all. Tirell, go on back.'

I looked down at my horse's mane and shook my head. Frain sat bolt upright in surprise. He had not thought I would refuse him so simple a request.

'Go on back,' he repeated. 'I don't want you to see me shaking.'

'I have to watch,' I told him, trying to discipline my voice, 'or I am likely to dream against all reason that I will see you again, that you have turned aside to wander Vaire or the Lorc Dahak, that some wind of chance will bring you back to me.' The words broke the taut control I had managed to maintain for his sake. Tears fell down from my eyes and onto my hands that plaited the horse's mane.

'All right,' Frain acceded softly. 'All right, my brother.' He reached over to me and we embraced; I remember yet the warmth of that embrace. Then he turned and, not even shaking—but with eyes shut tight—he spurred his horse into Acheron.

I lingered awhile. Then I rode slowly back to my bride with the words of an old song, a lament, hazily forming in my mind.

Like a swan on the still willow rivers,
Like a swan on the streams of Ogygia,
My sorrow floats the winding ways,
The shadowshining ways of mind.
Like a serpent out of a mountain cavern,
A serpent of wind, my sorrow stings.
My love, oh when will I see you again?
My love, oh my little child?

It seemed so unfair, what he had to face. He was only seventeen.

Epilogue

I had become a foolish old man in many ways—I, Daymon Cein, the great seer! And I felt sure my time must soon come. I no longer took any particular notice of anything. I lay in my warm chamber and let my mind stray; sometimes it happened on truth and more often on shadows, mice scurrying through forgotten garrets. . . . But when Frain left, vision swept me up one last time on wings the strongest I had ever known, vision like none I had experienced since that first searing night under the White Rock of Eala. But I was young then and hung back for fear of annihilation, and this time I was old and no longer afraid. I was no longer . . . I was not. I was with Frain. I was at one with Frain.

I rode with him, I feared with him, I plunged with him into the forest. I fared with him for days. To be sure, my body lay in its chamber in Melior. It moved, ate a little, even spoke. Tirell prowled around it, came and went and pestered. There was no need for me to concern myself with him; he had Recilla to look after him.

'Is Frain all right?' he demanded.

'He travels through Acheron.' The strange black lotus of Acheron drifted through my dreams and his, the stooping trees whispered over us both, the moss brushed my face. The terms of that land were not the terms of Vale. Tirell's question seemed meaningless there. Frain was no longer unhappy, any more than a floating leaf is unhappy.

'But is he any better?' Tirell insisted.

'He is himself, as he has always been.'

'Contrary old man,' Tirell muttered, and stalked off. But he came back the next day and sat beside me for hours.

'Frain has come to the lake,' I told him on toward evening.

'What!' he exclaimed. 'What does he find there?'

'Your beast, lying by the verge. Only it is no longer black, but white. The reflection is black.'

The beast inclined its head at Frain's approach. He walked over to greet it, stroking the curve of its neck, then knelt by it and looked into the water of the lake. He gasped and nearly toppled in, almost as if some bodiless thing had caught at him. But he held onto the beast for support, turned his face away and hid it against a white, silken flank, quivering. I saw nothing in the lake, not even myself; what could he have seen? I said nothing to Tirell, having no answer.

'There is his mother,' I said after a while. She must have been there the whole time. She sat on a grassy bank beneath a willow tree, clad in moss green, quiet as the lake.

'What! Fabron's wife?' Tirell could not remember her name.

'Mela, yes.' I paused, caught up by the Sight. 'What is the matter with the swan? It has gone black, and the wing trails crookedly through a pale shadow in the water.'

'What about Mela?' Tirell asked impatiently.

'He is walking over to her now.' She was a regal, red-haired presence, not the Mela he had known, and he did not recognize the goddess as the wan queen, tangled in bitterness, whom he had tried to save. Nor, in any mortal sense, did she know him—I think. It was Acheron, after all. But she addressed him with a mother's tender mockery, for she was at one with the All-Mother now.

'I have come to speak with Shamarra,' Frain told her.

'Fool,' she chided. 'You poor fool. What ever gave you the notion that you could woo a goddess? Only princes of the line of Melior possess that dangerous privilege.'

'I thought I was such a prince when I began. And now—'

'You are trapped like a fly in a casement. Poor fool, can you not see that you would have loved her anyway? You are what you are.'

Frain shrugged, standing restively before her. 'Where is Shamarra?' he asked in a tone just short of demand.

'Well, let me tell you.' She gestured amiably, forgiving his impatience in her eagerness to talk to someone, for very few folk came there. 'Sit, child, and let me tell you the tale. Shamarra was very angry at your so-called brother Prince Tirell. Yes, very angry indeed.'

'I can well believe it,' Frain muttered, seating himself resignedly on the grey-green slope.

'So she sent the trees to destroy him while he was exposed in battle,' Mela went on in a kind of awed delight. 'An act of interference far exceeding her authority. She had already pressed her limits by leaving her lake unattended and following a mere man with such unbecoming devotion—and getting herself humiliated after all—'

'I don't care about that,' Frain burst out. 'Where is she?'

'I am telling you,' Mela reproved. 'She sent her minions toward Melior, and the All-Mother herself had to trouble herself to stop them. Adalis was mightily in wrath.' Mela shivered. 'Shamarra should never have come back here at all. She had forfeited her position by leaving.'

Frain did not say a word. He got up stiffly, licking his dry lips, waiting.

'So Adalis laid a punishment on Shamarra. She stripped her of her personhood and gave her to the wind.'

'What? She is dead?' Frain whispered in shock. Mela shook her head ruefully at his innocence.

'No, not dead! Immortals do not die so easily. She wanders with the wind. She is a bird.'

'What is happening?' Tirell demanded.

'Shamarra is gone.'

Dusk was coming on. Frain turned without a sound and walked to the verge of the darkening lake, where he stood staring at the black and crippled swan.

'Not that one,' Mela called on him. 'Nothing so favoured. Shamarra is not to fly with the flocks of Ascalonia. She is a night bird.'

How appropriate. She still ruled death, then. I wondered if Frain knew that he wooed Vieyra.

He looked at his hands. 'Where? Lorc Tutosel?' he asked softly.

'Adalis knows.'

Frain sat by the lake as dusk deepened into night. He refused the food Mela offered him, and she left him there alone. I knew he could not feel anything quite so unreasonably as he formerly might have, not in that place of shifting shadows, of dreams and reflections. Still, I felt a nudge of fear. Mela also must have felt some small tug of anxiety, because sometime in the starless nadir of night she came out to him, walking easily without a lamp.

'Do not go into that lake unless you are fully prepared to die,' she warned. 'A strange fate lies on the mortal who enters it and lives.'

She could not see his face, and neither could I, but I felt the lurch of his heart. 'And what is that fate?' he asked evenly.

'Well, he would have to be a special one. . . .' She hesitated. 'He would have to be very pure to survive. But supposing one came whose own darkness did not drag him down, he would become immortal, yet enslaved.'

'To what?' Frain no longer hid his agitation.

'To whatever passions ruled him at the time. A more cruel fate than you might be able to imagine.'

But he comprehended all too well. 'Then there is to be no end of this?' he whispered.

She did not hear or understand, but perhaps she understood his mood. She sat by his side and spoke to him in motherly tones. 'Frain, you seem to be a nice young man. I just want you to know that if you go in that lake there is no hope and no turning back. So think well.'

'Go away,' Frain said. 'I wish I were dead.'

She shrugged and returned to her pavilion. Frain sat by the lakeside through the night, his feet nearly in the water. Immortals do not weaken and die, but they can be killed. . . . I sat with him in terror, though my body lay on the couch at Melior. But he did not move until owl light turned to dawn and into early sunrise. Then he glanced at the brightening mountain peaks behind him. And he rose and stood entranced, his back to the lake.

'I should have known,' I sighed.

The heights had called him from his earliest days. And what now could hold him back from them? He stripped his

205

horse of its gear and turned the animal loose to crop the lakeside grass. He nodded at the white beast, shouldered a pack of provisions, and started away westward.

'Wherever are you going?' Mela called to him from her doorflap. Nothing lay that way except vast ranges of mountain peaks, scaling ever higher.

'To seek death,' he called back, smiling sourly.

'Death?' She frowned, perplexed. 'There is death everywhere, and nowhere more than here.'

'Ah, but I am very particular. Her name is Shamarra.' So he knew. The immortal in search of his doom. 'And I will find her if I have to go as far as Ogygia to do it. If I have to beard Adalis herself.' He walked on as he talked.

'Swans and serpents! But youngster, why?' Mela cried in exasperation. 'She no longer has a very winsome face.'

Frain paused long enough to turn and cast her a glance of astonished scorn. 'Because of what I am,' he said finally. 'Goodbye, Lady.'

'Frain, listen to me.' She took a few steps after him. 'You can no more reach Ogygia than yonder crippled swan. Even if you could find it, what makes you think Adalis would speak to you? The penalties are severe for impertinence. And what makes you think Ogygia lies west?'

'A vision.' My vision of long ago, forsooth! He had listened well. He smiled at his mother—she had come close enough for a smile. 'Good-bye, old woman,' he told her almost gaily, and turned to the path.

'He's on his way,' I whispered to the King who sat by my bedside. Tirell heard and asked me, 'Where?' But I never answered. I was with Frain.

It took him days to climb those awful cliffs. All those days I lay uneating, unresting, unwaking, suspended in the magic and terror of his journey. Sheer rocks and tiny, clinging plants, spiraling winds and ever more limpid sky. . . . It was all sky at the end. He found the dim trail at last, made the top of the last divide, and looked beyond. I could see his smile, nothing more—a marvellous, ardent, lovestruck smile. Something utterly beautiful lay there. He took breath, gazing like a stag that scents the wind, with quivering attention. Then he stepped out of sight.

I never told Tirell. I spoke no word to any living person concerning any of this. For at the moment Frain traversed that tall divide, I, too, passed a barrier. The dead go through many changes; they fly in form of moth or hawk; they swim the flood beneath. But it is a voice from the nameless beyond that speaks to you now.

THE END

A SELECTION OF SCIENCE FICTION AND FANTASY TITLES AVAILABLE FROM CORGI

While every effort is made to keep prices low, it is sometimes necessary to increase prices at short notice. Corgi Books reserve the right to show new retail prices on covers which may differ from those previously advertised in the text or elsewhere.

The prices shown below were correct at the time of going to press.

☐	12284 X	BOOK ONE OF THE BELGARIAD: PAWN OF PROPHECY	David Eddings	£1.95
☐	12348 X	BOOK TWO OF THE BELGARIAD: QUEEN OF SORCERY	David Eddings	£1.95
☐	12382 X	BOOK THREE OF THE BELGARIAD: MAGICIAN'S GAMBIT	David Eddings	£1.95
☐	12435 4	BOOK FOUR OF THE BELGARIAD: CASTLE OF WIZARDRY	David Eddings	£1.95
☐	12447 8	BOOK FIVE OF THE BELGARIAD: ENCHANTERS' END GAME	David Eddings	£1.95
☐	12688 8	STARMAN	Alan Dean Foster	£1.95
☐	12278 5	KRULL	Alan Dean Foster	£1.50
☐	17154 2	DAMIANO	R.A. MacAvoy	£1.95
☐	08453 0	DRAGONFLIGHT	Anne McCaffrey	£1.75
☐	11635 1	DRAGONQUEST	Anne McCaffrey	£1.95
☐	11313 1	THE WHITE DRAGON	Anne McCaffrey	£2.50
☐	12499 0	MORETA: DRAGONLADY OF PERN	Anne McCaffrey	£1.95
☐	10661 5	DRAGONSONG	Anne McCaffrey	£1.75
☐	10881 2	DRAGONSINGER: HARPER OF PERN	Anne McCaffrey	£1.75
☐	11804 4	DRAGONDRUMS	Anne McCaffrey	£1.75
☐	10965 7	GET OFF THE UNICORN	Anne McCaffrey	£1.95
☐	09115 4	THE SHIP WHO SANG	Anne McCaffrey	£1.75
☐	08661 4	DECISION AT DOONA	Anne McCaffrey	£1.75
☐	08344 5	RESTOREE	Anne McCaffrey	£1.75
☐	12097 9	THE CRYSTAL SINGER	Anne McCaffrey	£1.95
☐	12475 3	THE COLOUR OF MAGIC	Terry Pratchett	£1.75
☐	12426 5	THE SILVER SUN	Nancy Springer	£1.75
☐	12403 6	THE WHITE HART	Nancy Springer	£1.75

ORDER FORM

All these books are available at your book shop or newsagent, or can be ordered direct from the publisher. Just tick the titles you want and fill in the form below.

CORGI BOOKS, Cash Sales Department, P.O. Box 11, Falmouth, Cornwall.

Please send cheque or postal order, no currency.

Please allow cost of book(s) plus the following for postage and packing:

U.K. Customers—Allow 55p for the first book, 22p for the second book and 14p for each additional book ordered, to a maximum charge of £1.75.

B.F.P.O. and Eire—Allow 55p for the first book, 22p for the second book plus 14p per copy for the next seven books, thereafter 8p per book.

Overseas Customers—Allow £1.00 for the first book and 25p per copy for each additional book.

NAME (Block Letters) ....

ADDRESS ....

....